Hannah

"... the love of the dead is strong."

Praise for *Meant to Be*

"Rita Coburn Whack's considerable narrative ability and the color and vigor of her prose add up to a highly readable tale."
—*Publishers Weekly*

"The call of the big city is at the center of this strong autobiographical first novel, and the vibrant Chicago setting—from the jazz clubs and the glamorous lakefront to the black working-class suburbs—roots the story across generations. . . . It's the trouble and the aching family discoveries that will speak to many readers."
—*Booklist*

"*Meant to Be* convincingly charts the spiritual awakening of Patience Jan Campbell, who struggles to come to terms with her blue-collar past."
—*Essence*

"A lovely debut full of wit, wisdom and spiritual food for the journey."
—DAWN TURNER TRICE, author of *An Eighth of August* and *Only Twice I've Wished for Heaven*

"Buy two—'cause this is one to read and talk about with a good friend."
—BERTRICE BERRY, Ph.D., author of *Redemption Song* and *The Haunting of Hip Hop*

"*Meant to Be* is bursting with history, down-home vernacular and spiritual wisdom. The author, an award-winning TV and radio producer, has an obvious love for black history and culture and takes every opportunity to incorporate it into the story. Her narrative often goes out on a limb, using different literary genres to blend several stories in the earthly and spiritual realms."
—*Chicago Tribune*

Meant To Be

A Novel

RITA COBURN WHACK

ONE WORLD
BALLANTINE BOOKS • NEW YORK

2008 One World Books Mass Market Edition

Published in the United States by One World Books, an imprint of The Random House Publishing Group, a division of Random House, Inc., New York.

ONE WORLD is a registered trademark and the One World colophon is a trademark of Random House, Inc.

Originally published in trade paperback in the United States by Strivers Row, an imprint of Villard Books, a division of Random House, Inc. in 2002.

ISBN 978-0-345-50646-7

www.oneworldbooks.net

OPM 9 8 7 6 5 4 3 2 1

*Now faith is the substance of things hoped for,
the evidence of things not yet seen.*
HEBREWS 11:1

Patience Jan Campbell

". . . that's P.J. to you."

Beginnings

"*J*esus!"

Turning around, I was just in time to see old Mother Brock hike her long white skirt above her knees and climb onto the pew.

"He ain't nothing but a honey!" A white handkerchief held high in one hand waved surrender toward heaven and the joyous shout signaled all of us in the old woman's path to clear the way. Scooting sideways, I watched her legs, stockings knotted just above the knee, rise above one pew and thump down on the next. The Spirit had "gotten a holt" to Mother Brock and she was pew-stepping, bench-hopping happy, going at it from row to row.

"Walk that bench, Ma Brock," Essie Tolbert encouraged. "Walk it now!"

Elder Yancy stood. Tall enough to reach the ceiling fans and as dark as the sin he rocked back and forth against, he closed his eyes. His arms, reaching out, trembled over the heads beneath them as he moved in the rhythm of his tambourine.

With a "Hallelujah! Praise His name!" Sister Hattie Jones sailed from the choir stand. Her robe flared, then billowed like a large puff of cotton. Descending, it settled close to her waist, held tight by two balled fists. She swished the robe around her body and headed for the side aisle.

Combing each aisle like a lost traveler, Sister Jones

asked folks for directions most Sundays. Eyeballing whomever she felt called, she'd stick her pointed face in theirs: "Will you praise Him? Can you rebuke the Devil? Won't you give all glory to God?"

I rubbed the piece of paper in my Bible as if it would help me. My aunt Ada always said the church was "the best ground for spiritual warfare," but I hadn't prepared to deliver my speech during one of its battles. I'd written my words while Sarah Vaughan's voice rang clear above the bass, saxophone, and piano on my record player. Then I'd called Mama Ada, whom I'd never witnessed saying more than a quiet amen in the middle of a church service. We went over what I was to say. It had all been calm. Well, that was then, and this was now.

Reverend Tyler stood and the pianist, Mr. Fulton, tried to strike a few solemn chords. But unlike Reverend Tyler, Mr. Fulton was still enchanted. His feet pumped the pedals as his hands played another chorus of "When I Get to Heaven Gonna Shout." On the risers behind him, choir members cried and swayed; some held each other or fanned those seated.

Reverend Tyler cleared his throat. I swallowed hard against the lump in mine and made my way across the pew, saying "excuse me, ma'am" and "pardon me, sir" as proper as I could in the middle of a holy war. At the back of the church, I was careful to cross over the center aisle since, unlike Mother Brock, I didn't have a big position in the church and lacked permission to walk down the scarlet carpet that led to the altar.

Behind the glass window of the nursery, a mother seemed not to notice that the diaper covering her breast had fallen. The infant on her hip, a trickle of milk sliding from the corner of his mouth toward his chin, looked at me from the biggest tit I'd ever seen. The breast, so swollen it stretched the black dots around the nipple until I thought of buttons, pointed at me. I looked away.

Ahead, Hester Cochren, as if sin could seep right through his toothy mouth, eyed the dresses in front of him from the waist down. I thought of the "Jelly, jelly, jelly" song. The pianist hit a few slow chords and seemed like he was praying for calm.

Reverend Tyler, not one to join in these celebrations, held up both hands and said, "All glory be to God."

As I made my way to the front of the church I met the half smile on Sheila Flowers' face and thought it was a good thing I wasn't God. In the middle of all the hoopla I could have made the neighborhood bully disappear, and I knew for sure the entire eighth grade would have less worry and misery.

At the altar, Mother Brock was whispering to herself and taking the privileged center aisle back to her seat. Reverend Tyler's voice continued to quiet the storm inside the Second Baptist Church of Moleen. I stepped forward and waited for his acknowledgment.

"Let's welcome Miss Patience Jan Campbell." The sound of my full name was an embarrassment. "P.J." would have been just fine. I could just hear Sheila calling me "Patience" in front of a crowd. Reverend Tyler kept going. "Miss Campbell just turned thirteen, and as is our custom, she's going to come forth and share her favorite verse, with a self-interpretation."

"Out of the mouths of babes," exclaimed Elder Yancy's wife.

"Mercy, mercy," I heard a woman say as I walked up the side steps and over to the podium. I wished my mama had stopped preparing Sunday's dinner long enough to come. Placing my Bible on the podium, I opened it and read from Ephesians: "And, ye fathers, provoke not your children to wrath: but bring them up in the nurture and admonition of the Lord." Then I looked into the congregation and spoke.

After my first words, "I think this scripture means

that children know every shut eye ain't sleep and every head bowed ain't praying, so grown-ups ain't fooling us or God," it seemed like a pall fell over the church. Satisfied I had everybody's attention, I kept going and don't rightly know what I said, but I finished up with "So nobody should hold a child back from God just 'cause they may be having trouble finding Him." The air changed again, hot around my face, dry and even more still. It stayed that way, and later when I left the church, I didn't have to weave around pools of chitchatters. My path was more than cleared. A group of women gathered in the parking lot, shifting hips, straining necks, rolling their eyes to meet the brims of wax flower–burdened hats. One snipped, "You know what the Good Book says, 'Pride comes before a fall.' "

A chorus of "uh-huhs" rose until another soloist stuck her neck down toward me. "Well, somebody better get ready to catch that one 'cause she's bound to tumble, as big as that chip is on her shoulder." I forced my head up and was careful not to go any faster than I needed, thinking they should have each taken a hand fan—with perfect family portraits of gussied-up mother, father, sister, and brother on one side and the name of the nearest funeral home on the other—and cooled themselves off. Especially since I knew what they did not. If they craned their necks down a little lower or accidentally touched me, taking that "every child that's a child of God is my child" idea far enough to lay a hand on me that wasn't trying to put the blessing of the holies in my bones, Charlie Guss Campbell would walk the streets of old and new Moleen until he found them. Then he'd put his "size 13 triple E's so far up where the sun don't shine" they would truly be pleading the blood of Jesus. Humph! I strutted past them biddies looking as high up as they were looking down.

Children of Discontent

By the time I turned the corner, my daddy was done doing what he did most Sunday mornings, fixing on dilapidated old cars that sounded like motorcycles and would be headed to the junkyard by the year's end anyway. He was sitting in his favorite spot on the porch, so I sat next to him and rubbed my face, fighting the urge to scratch the acne that almost covered it.

"Hot as Mississippi," he greeted me and I watched him caress the sky with homesick eyes.

"Yep." It did seem like heat was pouring down from the sky in waves. But I was only agreeing to the heat; I'd never been anywhere near Mississippi and probably wouldn't choose a South filled with the stories I'd heard. "North Mississippi," which is what grown folks called Chicago since so many people from Mississippi had settled there, was just fine with me. In fact, Chicago and not the West Side, but as close to downtown as I could get, was my next stop. After reading books and watching TV I'd decided Chicago was close enough not to be confused with a fairy tale you couldn't get to, and the best place for a girl like myself.

"Well, Sister P.J., how was church?" my daddy asked, teasing and looking at my Bible and fancy dress. It was down past my knees, lemon yellow with a big bow in the back. I stuck my Vaseline-shined legs out and crossed them at the ankle, making sure the ruffles touched and leaning them to the side like Ada taught me, even if I was just sitting on the porch. I knew my daddy thought of Ada when he saw me going to and coming from church. I wondered if he knew she called herself "my brother's keeper" when she took care of me. They always talked about each other as if they were sad and happy at the same time. I hugged my shoulders to keep from scratching my face and told the truth.

"The kids were okay, I guess, didn't pay them no mind. The sermon was good, I got to speak. Ma Brock walked the bench and it all got out of control. Them old church biddies know how to dress better than they know how to act and it went on too long." I started to say I was glad I'd had some gum and an extra Nut Chew to tide me over, but remembered I wasn't supposed to go to the corner store, so I swallowed my bubble gum and looked at my daddy to see if he could tell I'd been to the store.

"I reckon you 'bout summed it up. Hot as Mississippi," he repeated.

"Tell me about a hot day, Daddy, the hottest day you can remember in M-i-s, s-i-s, s-i-p-p-i." I spelled the letters out like we did when we played double Dutch and asked for the story to make up for my stopping by the corner store.

"Well, let's see."

My mama always said my daddy enjoyed telling a story. So I knew any stalling he was doing was just trying to figure out which one he hadn't told in a long time or seeing if he could conjure up a new one, but he began each one the same.

"We didn't have enough money to buy a gnat a wrestling jacket, a pot to piss in, or a nearby window to throw it out." Now he was ready to begin. "So every day was hot. Heat is what po' folks got to deal with every day, all manner of heat."

This time, I watched his hair and it looked like dried grass, higher than any other grown man I'd seen wear their hair, and darker. It was the pitch black of dreams when they cannot be reached, darker than night and hard to remember. His skin was not much lighter than his hair, and his eyes, a dimming white with coal black pupils, looked out onto the street.

I imagine my daddy had always been large, never very tall, but more than sturdy. This was the summer of 1967, he was forty-eight, and what my mama referred to as a "sturdy build" was called fat by most people.

"We had an ol' red plank house, roof was tattered till air coming in could've been air-conditioning. But it was hot too, and my mama was always standing in the yard." I imagined Hannah, my grandmother, her long thick black hair in waves down her back, shining without oil. She was a Black Indian, mixed Cherokee, and my daddy always said the redness of her skin was only the beginning of that color in her. I never knew her, she died before my daddy was grown, but her spirit still visited Ada and both my daddy and Ada talked about Hannah enough for me to see her when they did.

"Before I was old enough to go to school, my mama stood me up on a high table in the kitchen, hugged me, then sat on the floor. 'Jump!' she shouted, stretching her arms out. 'I'll catch you.'

"I'd put on a hesitation at first, knowing I shouldn't be standing on the table, but it was my mama who'd turned the place of meals into a space to play.

" 'Jump!' she told me again.

"Shoot, I jumped, laughing, into her arms. Hugged in the sweat of her bosom on a day when bread would be made. A 'heated hot day,' my sisters had called it, 'hot enough for bread to rise in half the time.'

" 'Jump!' My mother kept at me and I took her up on it every time. Wasn't every day you got to break a rule without a punishment." My father's face looked like there was something delicious about breaking a rule then and now.

"One time"—he paused and I could see Hannah's white teeth flashing and her black hair swinging—"she didn't catch me."

His face went back to that day and got stuck, until time spread over it and I could see now that a little piece of that look was always with him.

"It didn't mean much to my sisters. They just teased me, saying I cried 'for almost ever.' Even now, Ada laughs about the way I flinched when Mama tried to pick me up after that.

"Hell, I wasn't no fool, ready to hug and all. My mama had just dropped me on the floor."

I knew then that this was the day his heart stopped working one way and started working another. That's the way things go. You find out something and it changes everything until it won't change back. Still, I wondered if Hannah was sorry.

"Did you cry, Daddy?" I asked him.

"Yep. Yes sirree Bob, wailed like my mama'd killed me."

I suspected a part of him did die and I imagined Hannah trying to pull him close, his pudgy self scuffling to get away. I wondered if she cried too, like Ada did the one time she had to "reprimand" me and give me a tanning for something I can't even remember. Her cryin' was worse than the whippin'. I wondered about Hannah though, everybody said she was tough and even harder than my daddy. But she'd dropped him and he cried and she should have at least squeezed out a tear, one of her own to mix with his many.

"'Never trust anyone. No one, you hear. Not even your mama, Charles.' That's what my mama whispered. 'Never trust anyone. Don't ever forget.' I remember her saying that, but I don't remember her crying. Nah, don't 'member her getting glassy 'bout the eye at all."

I guess that was a hot day, hot enough to boil his tears, especially if he cried alone. We sat a while listening to tires rolling over the asphalt. When a car appeared we both waved, and I wondered out loud, "Did you learn the lesson, Daddy?"

"The lesson?" he asked me.

"Do you still trust people?"

He didn't answer and I waited long enough to forget about not scratching and gave my itching face a good going over.

"P.J.!" My father's voice made me think of his shoe size. "I told you what to do for that rash." I knew what was coming, more about how he'd watched his mama wipe the faces of babies with their wet diapers.

"Daddy!" I had to stop him. Did he really think I was going to do that pee thing? Why would anybody want pee on their face? How would anybody get pee on their face, anyway? Ugh!

I just knew I was adopted. Nobody would tell their own child to put pee on their own face. My face is long and thin, without any dimples. His is boxy with a dimple so deep in his forehead you'd think he fell on something. My skin is so light, last year, Sheila Flowers led the whole seventh grade in calling me Banana, Albino, and anything else yellow. My hair is so nappy, the kitchen—naps on the back of my neck—looks like an army with each man marching on his own. With Brylcreme, my daddy's high grass bush hair would lie down faster than Hester Cochren. Our lips might look alike, but that don't count since that's why I get called Sausage Lips, Bubbles, and all that.

Adopted! And now my daddy wanted me to pee and smear it on myself. I'd had enough. Those women at church still had me hot as the day and twice as bothered.

I had a mind to tell on 'em right then. That jumping off the table story had me ticked at Hannah and here he was bringing her up again. He was mad at her too, and still quoting her like she was scripture. I stood and walked into the house.

Inside, the wood floors squeaked as I began to cross the living room. It's a big rectangular room without knick-knacks like Ada's. The sofa needs to be reupholstered, neither one of the chairs matches, the end table has a rickety leg, and the television in the cabinet is broken. But the record player works. The albums of all the great jazz kings and queens are there. Besides playing records in my room, when no one is home I spread the albums out across the floor and play different selections from one to another. On some songs I dance like the grown-ups do when they have a party in the basement, selling ham and cheese sandwiches stuffed with lettuce and tomatoes on the table in the back and using yellow light-bulbs. I have slow dances with myself, memorizing the words of Ella, Sarah, Billie, Dinah, Bessie, and all the girls that I would tell, "Just call me P.J.," if we met up.

I walked over to the round drum table in front of the picture window. A doily lopped over its sides, protecting the table from a tall lamp with icicles hanging down in crystal. Its lacy shade had shingles hanging down all around it, and I looked out the window to see if my daddy's face had an angry look for me. I couldn't tell, so I grabbed hold of one of the icicles, then remembered myself and let it go very carefully. When it hit the icicle next to it, each tapped the other, all swayed slowly and the sunlight helped them make a rainbow of colors.

Just then I saw my daddy get up and I made quick-like to the kitchen. I could hear the sound of the crystal, see the sunbeams coming in through the door, and smell the chicken my mama was frying for an early dinner.

"Hey, Mama," I said. She was in her usual position—hunched over frying skillets and boiling pots.

"Hungry, Jan?" she asked me. She never wanted to call me P.J. Truth was, she wanted to call me Patience, but knew I'd knot up on the inside, so Jan was our way of meeting in the middle.

"Yep. Smells good, Mama," I said, but didn't stop since my daddy was going to be on my heels soon. I went on to the bathroom where I could hear what they'd be talking about. Even if they talked low, I could put my ear to the vent and every word would be so clear, it was like being on the telephone.

"The woman is stirring in that chil', Jessie."

"Humph."

"Spending too much time in her room listening to music twice as old as she is, putting this blouse with that skirt. I know she been after a relaxer for her hair and that ain't nothing but a conk!" He waited and when my mama didn't say nothing, my father got louder. "Girl tipping around in them church dresses, acting like her shoes hurt and always begging money for something new to treat that rash when I done told her what to do!"

"Humph." Now Mama was mumbling under her breath.

"You got something to say? Say it." My daddy was angry now, but I knew that anger in his voice would be the end of it. Once I heard my mama talking to Mrs. Mont T and Mrs. Ester about how when my mama and daddy were first married and she was skinny, he had knocked her backward on the bed for staying up all night reading piles of books, "just 'cause he couldn't read." She'd tucked her knees into her chest, bounced off the bed, and knocked him into the wall, then "grabbed the lamp and threw *Oedipus the King, The Iliad, The Odyssey,* and *A Simple Heart* against his brains" until he ran out. She might grunt and he might raise his voice, but I wasn't worried that it would go further, so I lay down and got comfortable next to the vent.

"As soon as I can rub two nickels together, I'm gonna put a relaxer in them naps and ease my burden, so help me!"

Hallelujah! I wanted to dance. *I'm gonna get a relaxer, look just like the girls in the magazines. I might even be a model. Hallelujah.*

"Ah, shit! Both a y'all crazy. Trouble sittin' right down on the front porch with me and you can't see it. The face is a woman's calling card, it ain't got nothing to do with being a girl. Chil' growing up too fast and you can't see it. Just gonna add to it like a fool."

"I know you didn't call me a fool. I bet you one thing. A fool know where his bed is made and know how to lay down in it. Even a fool don't open the wrong door and spend his time at the wrong house and then try to take care of his own, too late. Who the fool?"

I smelled the chicken burning, saw Hester Cochren in my daddy and my stomach didn't feel good and my mind felt worse. I was getting my dress dirty on the floor, and I wasn't a girl anymore, anyway. I was a lady and I was gonna have long straight hair, even if people called it "nigger blond," and I was gonna have a smooth face.

I got up, ran some hot water in the sink, pressed hot towels on my forehead, then let the water out. My face was red as a geranium. I looked in the cabinet. Noxzema, calamine lotion, peroxide, iodine. It's true, I'd tried them all at least twice. I remembered the photographs of my cousins who lived in the South. Not one of them had acne. Hannah may have been mean, even double evil, but that didn't stop her from being right. I locked the door, stopped the sink, pulled my dress up, my panties down, hopped on top of the face bowl, and peed.

In my room, I could watch the leaves of the willow tree. I thought about my mama. She'd told me that chains held swinging tires onto a mulberry tree lit by the valley sun where she grew up. It was called Crawfordsville, Georgia. Everybody knew that anywhere in Georgia was better than everywhere in Mississippi, so I knew my mama had better things than my daddy did when they were coming up. She talked about a long wooden table between two white oak trees, being filled with food, most of it prepared then fished out of a black wash kettle by her daddy, the town cook. They called my grandfather Professor Jack and he had married three times, outlived all his wives, but he still died before my mama was eighteen. Most people used black kettles for the wash, but he used it for beef simmered with corn cut fresh from the cob, garden tomatoes, lima and string beans seasoned with diced livers, neck bone meat, sherlock onions, and peppers. The whole town came to fill their pots and traded with everything from plates to dresses, all for some of Professor Jack's stew.

These were some of the stories my mama told me when she was tired of not talking to my daddy. Others I heard from my place at the table when the women came to shell peas, pick the corns off their toes, fry their hair with pressing irons, or "borrow a dollar and some talk." Some stories I heard from my secret place in the bathroom. Still, I liked it best when my mama just told me things straight for me, but we weren't talking much lately. And I think I knew why. My daddy was treating her bad. I looked out the window and thought I saw a haint, a bad spirit, not a good one. Maybe I could see the spirits now, just like Ada. It was in the way the willow trembled and the air was so still there could no ways be a wind. The willow shuddered like it was cold and a storm was on the way. I got up and went closer. Tomatoes pulled down the vine but the leaves didn't move.

Beans climbed the fence, spinach wilted in the sun.
Nothing moved but that willow. It shook like Betty
Lou's grandmother, who had the palsies.

The rows of bloodred geraniums; a rainbow of petunias; red, white, and yellow roses; and the woman in the
kitchen and the man on the porch; didn't go together.
That was why the willow shook. They were hurting
each other more than the arguing. There was something
in the sounds that was deeper than words and God did
not like ugly. The thing shaking the willow tree was ugly
awful, a spirit, and I could tell. I started to go to the
phone and call Ada, then I remembered she'd told me
what to do. "When you come close to evil, say a prayer.
Tell God you adore Him because He made you and
everything else, repent for any wrong you can remember, say thank you because you will be forgiven, then
make your supplications known." The last thing just
meant ask for what you want, but Ada knew big words
and would not make them little just because you didn't
understand them, even for Uncle Albert who didn't talk
the same way as Ada. She said old was old and new was
new, I was part of the new and she talked up, not down.

I followed her instructions.

*I adore You for letting me speak at church today and
get safely past the biddies to come home and for letting
me see Hannah through Daddy and for taking the pimples from my face. I'm sorry I may have caused an argument because my hair is so nappy, but I'm glad I'm
going to get a relaxer. I'm sorry if I have anything to do
with why my mama and daddy don't love each other.
Sorry I got angry at the dead. Hannah must have had a
reason for dropping my daddy and trying to get him not
to trust people. I'm sorry for wanting to make Sheila
Flowers disappear. I know You can take care of Your
own people. I just hope You didn't make too many. I'm
thankful You made me and I am going to try to do bet-*

ter. Sorry about the Nut Chews and all. Thank You for
the good food and sweets and chicken frying 'cause I
know some people in Old Moleen don't have that. Far
as my supplications, I would like to be able to talk intelligent like Ada, get an education and move to the city,
find a man to marry that won't try to cheat or fight me,
and have some children, too. If a chip on my shoulder
would help me, please send one. I'd like to know what
Your book says without having to make up the parts I
don't understand. And a smooth face and nice hair. In
Jesus' name, amen.

When I looked up, the willow was still and I blew on
my fist and rubbed it on my chest. I knew how to pray
away a bad spirit.

"Mama." I walked into the kitchen.

My mama closed the drawer real quick and I saw the
towel sticking out. She acted like I didn't know she kept
Salerno butter cookies in the drawer next to the silverware, covered with a towel. She could pick the cookies
up by twos until a row of them would be gone in no
time. She pulled the towel out of the drawer, wiped her
hands, which were puffy, each finger wrinkled with fat,
and began to peel scorched skin from the chicken.

"What is it, Jan?" She turned her back to me, working
on the chicken and trying to keep me from seeing her
face.

"Can I call Mama Ada?"

"Uh-huh," she said, then looked over her shoulder
like she wished I would talk to her instead, but before I
could think of something to say she turned around
again. I looked out the front door onto the porch. My
daddy was sitting there, I could see his back and the sky.
It was blue beautiful and didn't have any bit of a cloud.
Under that kind of a sky there had to be a better place. I
could feel all of us sharing that feeling. My daddy
rocked it, my mama remembered it, and I aimed to find

it. The sun warmed it and for a while silence lived from the front of the house to the back until I picked up the telephone. I knew Rockwell four, three four one eight by heart; the hardest part was waiting the three rings it took for my aunt to answer.

"Mama Ada, did I interrupt you?"

"You know better. A call from you is the best part of my day. I'm always ready to talk to my favorite girl."

"What did you read about today?" I asked, since I knew she was sitting at the dining room table. It was dark wood and shiny, with a china cabinet behind her full of dishes trimmed in flowers. There was always a white linen cloth on the table and her Bible, black leather, old and cracked, with pages that were thin and smudged.

"Abel and Cain."

"What's the memory verse?"

" 'If you do well, will not your countenance be lifted up? And if you do not do well, sin is crouching at the door; and its desire is for you, but you must master it.' "

"What's a countenance?"

"Your face. Keep your face lifted up, your spirits high, looking to God."

"Hmmm." Countenance. I bet if I used that word at school some of the teachers wouldn't know what it meant. I'd top Geraldine Kelly and Sheila Flowers would call me a show-off for sure, but I was going to use it.

"What's crouching at the door and all that stuff?" As soon as I'd said *stuff* I hurried to find another word. "Would you explain the verse, please?" That ought to do it. I guess practice could make perfect, using manners, good speech, and all.

"Well Jan, evil is always around, waiting to assist you in making the wrong choice, but the best words in that verse are *if* and *master. If* means it's up to you and *mas-*

ter means God always makes a way for you to get the upper hand on evil."

"I did it, I did it. Did it!"

Ada didn't say anything. She was waiting on me and I gave her an earful, from my speech to the church biddies, the willow tree, and my prayer. She listened and I went on and on. Now, I added a little bit here and there. I made one of the biddies' hats fall off, but I stopped myself before I had Ma Brock slip on a pew.

When my mama called out, "Dinner!" I wanted to keep talking with Ada, get her side to my story, but I could tell this was not a day to be late. When I got to the kitchen my mama was pushing some newspapers to the back of the table with one hand. With the other hand she sat a plate of hard fried chicken on the table. On some pieces, the cream tones peeked through crisp brown skin with a ring of black around it.

"Charles! Come get your dinner!"

Now, some people might call it dinner, but I knew we were going to sit around the table, chew for a while, then swallow.

Fall's Cold Song

By the time school started, we'd eaten the last fresh tomato and had filled mason jars on all the pantry shelves. Peas were in the freezer, along with string beans full of milky juice and fatback. The collards were waiting for the first frost, but it was already cold inside our house. Doors slammed more often and my mama talked to everybody less. She looked right through my daddy and me too, most days. Her friends didn't come over as much. Mrs. Mont T would come, but they kept me waiting up to a half hour with my ear to the vent before they said anything worth me lying there. And some mornings my daddy did not sing his work song.

> *Rain or shine*
> *Sleet or snow*
> *Charlie Campbell got to go*
> *One foot in my underwear*
> *The other out the door*
> *Charlie Campbell got to go*

From the day I cried 'cause I didn't want to go to school, my daddy made up that song. He said nobody in first grade knew how to read or write and that was why I was going. And he said nobody would put a roof over our heads if he didn't go to work. So we made a deal. If he went to work, then I would go to school. He made up the song to remind me that I'd made a promise and when I heard it, I got out of bed and waved him off to work, then got ready for school. I'd been outgrowing that song for years and had said so, but that never stopped his big baritone voice drifting from the kitchen all the way back to my room, and it never woke my mama up. My mama would stay asleep. It was part of their arrangement.

She cooked at a factory from three to eleven, got home after midnight and listened to her albums, read books, or looked at something on the television, when it worked, then went to bed. My daddy got up early for the seven to three shift at the steel mill and made his breakfast. He didn't have to sing, because I could smell. He could cook better than mama, even if her daddy had been the town cook and she had a job preparing food, which was really just warming up frozen food and putting it under hot lamps. If my daddy was in the mood, which was most mornings, he'd cook, eat, and leave some combination of crackling bread, hot water bread, hot cakes, home fries, grits, eggs with cheese, pan-fried Polish sausage, bacon, sausage patties, or fried bologna on the stove. But he always left with our song. At first, when the song stopped I was late for school and had to rush out so quick I didn't notice anything else.

Now, most mornings, there was nothing on the stove. When my mama started getting up to make breakfast, I figured things out. My daddy didn't stop singing because I was in eighth grade and too old for tricks that had worked years ago. He stopped singing because he didn't come home every night. He wasn't in my mama's room either.

In his room, the brown blanket was pulled across the full-size bed and his pillow didn't have a dent in it. It smelled like Old Spice, but not like aftershave splashed fresh that day. The scent was days old and barely there.

His clothes were still in his closet and the Old Grand-Dad 100 proof was still inside his winter boots. He was coming home, just not every night. After a while, some mornings, he would be on the floor in the hallway, smelling like a fifth instead of a pint of Old Grand-Dad. My mama would step right over him. I would put his blanket over him or walk around him quiet.

On other mornings, we would be alone and my mama would warm up some of the food she'd brought home from the factory. I like fish sticks all right, but it sure ain't breakfast food. I was thinking about telling her that I didn't mind cold cereal one morning when she sat down at the table with me. She was twisting the towel on the table so bad, I started to go get her cookies.

"Jan?"

I put down the packet of ketchup and settled in. We were due for a talk and I wanted to try some of my new words out on her. Unlike my daddy, she'd finished high school and almost went to college. But before I could figure out one of the long sentences I had been practicing, she interrupted.

"I bought you an alarm clock, so you can use it to wake yourself up in the morning."

"Thank you." I started to tell her daddy could get me up okay, but her eyes were sad and we both knew the truth.

I just said thank you again and finished my fish sticks so she could stop playing with her coffee cup and go get some cookies.

Our house had always been more empty than I thought it should be. Not enough furniture for comfort, just enough to live by. When things got broken, nobody would fix them. I tried. When the knob on the bathroom door came off, I tied an orange and blue scarf in the hole where the doorknob used to be and made a knot so you could pull it shut. A lot of things didn't seem to work anymore.

I kept going to church, but people were still treating me like I'd done something wrong that Sunday in summer. Even if I did, which I did not, I thought I would've been forgiven by now and if I wasn't by them, I would have been by Jesus. According to me, and I assumed Him, the Second Baptist Church of Moleen was falling short. Some Sundays I just went walking and spent my whole offering at the corner store.

Eighth grade was not bad. What I didn't have in friends I made up for with good grades. I won the spelling bee on the word *pernicious* and Mrs. Pearson gave me a calendar with a new word and its definition for each day. After our class studied poetry, she said she liked the way my "speech, intonations, and articulations" had "improved" and gave me two books of poems from what she called her "private collection." One was by Elizabeth Barrett Browning and the other by John Donne. Everybody kept quoting *How do I love thee let me count the ways,* but my favorite poem was the one where she wrote *Colors seen by candlelight will not look the same by day.* I didn't like John Donne. Even I could figure out he was married and seeing a woman, which they called a mistress back then. Her name was Stella and at the end of every poem he wrote something like *I from Stella am not removed* and *I do Stella love.* I guess people have been lying to themselves and cheating on other folks from one century to the next.

In October, it was already cold and my house seemed empty all the time. After I studied, I filled it with Billie, Ella, Sarah, Dinah, Carmen, Nancy, and even a little Joe Williams, Billy Eckstine, and Cab Calloway. They were all good, but the truth was I preferred to hear the women and wanted to learn more about them. I called Ada 'cause her jazz was almost as good as her scripture.

". . . When I came to Chicago we worked hard during the day. Some people had day work, cleaning folks' houses. Some did that early in the morning and another job at a factory, a sweatshop, sewing, or something like that until the sun went down. But at night, we dressed in waist-fitting short jackets and skirts that hugged our hip line and went to the mecca of jazz."

"What's a mecca?" I hadn't heard that word and wondered how it was spelled, but didn't want to ask too many questions.

"It can be a religious place, like when Malcolm X went to Medina in Saudi Arabia. He considered it a pilgrimage, going back to the beginnings of his Muslim faith. For us, Jerusalem might be considered the mecca, but Chicago was and is the mecca of jazz."

"Jazz began here?" I thought jazz had been around since Hannah was born but Ada said that wasn't so and that God made music, gave some of it to people, and Negroes came up with blues and jazz.

"Forty-seventh Street was the mecca, child. There were Monday morning breakfast dances for folks who had been out all night Sunday until the morning had to catch up with their jitterbug. And after a hot meal, a slow dance, and the Charleston, you'd go on to work."

"You went to those clubs?" I was having trouble trying to see Ada dancing at all. Dancing all night and then going to work sounded like something a rapscallion would do. Besides, Ada had been old ever since I was born.

"On some Sundays, I went to church in the morning, had dinner and a nap, then Albert and I danced until Monday morning and went straight to work. There's a time for everything under the sun, Jan. Don't forget that. I couldn't do it now, these bones are tired, but I'm glad I did it then."

I thought of Ada's long hair, which I loved to brush. It

was probably black like Daddy's then, even if it was streaked with so much silver now. She probably pulled it back or made a French roll. I would have let it hang so that it would move when I danced. Her clothes were always the best. She said you should buy two classic outfits at the end of each season and you would always have a proper wardrobe. When I got old enough to have my own money, I was gonna find out when the seasons were, wait till they ended, and buy like hotcakes. Now, I knew Ada had put on weight, but she still had a waist much smaller than her hips and I thought a short jacket would've looked good on her, so that's what I imagined her wearing.

"Jan, I saw everybody you're listening to now. Everybody and then some." I pressed the phone tighter to my ear.

"You saw the kings and queens, Mama Ada?"

"Princes, knights, jacks, and jesters. Bessie Smith was a regular when she was in town from Harlem and when Dinah Washington would sing 'A Man Only Does What a Woman Makes Him Do,' men and women would get to arguing right there in Club DeLisa. But, it was all in fun. We would go to the Regal and see Dizzy Gillespie, Charlie Parker, and Nancy Wilson, two movies, and get a dime back from a dollar."

I was still stuck on Dinah Washington and her song. I planned to memorize it, play it enough until I could tell whether or not it was true.

"How did all those women get started?" I knew if women back then could be someone special I could. I studied hard, but it seemed like you needed something more.

"Before they got to Club DeLisa, Dinah and them practiced all the time. Dinah lived right over here on the West Side. They had folks drifting into garages and backyards to hear them. Sometimes they'd charge a quarter or send a plate around. Before long, they was playing in dives, li'l joints half the size of somebody's back room. They dug down deep into themselves, Jan. Stood on all the strength they had and developed a faith in the voice God gave them.

"Everybody can't sing. If you got a voice, you supposed to make the most of it, sing to the Lord and sing to the people if you feel called. But you got to sing it true. They struggled and lived a lot of their songs. They weren't angels, Jan. Billie died from a drug overdose. Bessie drank enough gin to empty a bottle of vermouth and was proud, known to drag her fur on the floor and had enough gall to knock a white woman down. Folks say a white woman in New York had thrown a party for her and ran up to hug Bessie and Bessie didn't know her and leveled her to the ground." A laugh slipped out of Ada. "Billy Eckstine, as sophisticated as he sang, would pull a knife out in a heartbeat to defend himself, and he needed to since he was always taking up with another man's wife. Then Sarah Vaughan would defend him until people thought they were an item, but when you got up close everybody knew they were just friends."

Ada went on and I got comfortable with the way her voice went up and down in my ears. I dozed a little, but came back with a question every once in a while, to keep her going. I couldn't remember everything, but the next time I played some of those albums, I was going to listen for the stories in the music and try to put together the parts even Ada didn't know. This was front-page, on-the-television news.

"Most of them forgot to just play the clubs, they lived the club life—drinking, taking drugs, and spending time where they didn't have no business. But that's because evil follows good. Every last one of their voices was a gift, a chance at a life few Negroes would ever see, and they had choices."

I thought about that Bible story with Abel and Cain. Especially that verse about sin crouching at the door and its challenge, "If you master it."

"Ada?"

"Yes, baby."

"I love the music so much, but I can't sing."

"Then pray. Maybe God will give you something else to do with music. You'll be fine. He loves what you love, just know what you love."

When I finished talking to Ada, I felt better, until my daddy didn't come home for three days. My mama didn't do anything but work and I played my songs and waited. I tried to be the best student in school, but Geraldine Kelly beat me out most times. When I left school some days, her twin brother, Herbert, would follow me home.

"P.J. You after ol' Geraldine, ain't you?"

"No, I am not." I showed him. I didn't use *ain't* except when no one was around. Even if all the jazz women said "ain't" just like it was proper English, especially Billie Holiday, who only half counts since Ada said Lady Day was always telling people she sang blues even though it sounded like jazz to me. Still, I watched my language. I didn't want Herbert Kelly going home telling his sister I was country.

"Want me to carry your books?"

"No." I was not interested in Herbert Kelly following me home. I wasn't interested in anyone following me home. I never knew when my daddy was going to show up, our house was not properly furnished, and I'd stopped having the little company I used to have months ago. I was through playing Monopoly, you could hardly find anybody that liked Scrabble, and no one I knew wanted to listen to my music. They mostly listened to the Beatles, Archie Bell and the Drells, and the Jackson

Five. It was true, Jermaine and Tito was too fine, but that music just made my heart move too fast.

Herbert Kelly kept following me home and I think he was looking for more than carrying my books. He liked my hair. I caught him trying to touch it once and I wasn't about to let him put his dirty paws in my relaxer.

"Herbert, don't you have some basketball to play?" I gave him a good eye rolling. "Something?"

"You trying to tell me to go home, Patience Jan Campbell?"

I could have dropped my books and ran home screaming. Who told him my full name? That fat butt Sheila Flowers. The spit in my mouth was sour. I had given her a pass too many times. The next time she got in my face I was going to light her up like a Christmas tree. But I was not going to run or act like my own name bothered me.

"If I wanted to tell you to go home, I know how to say that, Herbert Kelly."

"Want to listen to some records with me?"

Lord, Lord. Some folks make you go straight to Jesus. "Herbert, I don't have any records you want to hear and vice versa." It was my first time using *vice versa*.

"Versa vice, bet I do."

Versa vice? Herbert Kelly's sister might be intelligent, but he was a retard. His nose was as big as a normal person's chin, his eyes sat back too far in his head, and his forehead and cheeks could have used some pee.

"What kind of records do you have?"

"Well, I ain't got none." At least he didn't lie, 'cause he and Geraldine lived in Old Moleen and their house was raggedy and didn't neither one of them ever stop at the corner store, Mr. Sam's penny candy, or Joe Riley's meat counter, where you could get a thick piece of souse and a slice of spicy hot head cheese both for a nickel.

"You mean you haven't got any." I corrected him and he kept right on talking crazy.

"I ain't got no records, but my daddy do and I bet he got some cool-cat, get-down-daddy music you ain't never heard."

Herbert Kelly started to hum something that sounded like jazz, but not the jazz I was used to. Then he started yelling, not singing, "A love supreme, a love supreme." Then humming again.

It was a good hum.

"My daddy got John Coltrane and Miles Davis and a whole bunch of sounds you ain't never heard."

"Bye, Herbert Kelly." I wasn't going to argue when I couldn't win. I'd gone through every album in my house and those were two names I'd never heard. I walked ahead of him; if there was a door around I would have slammed it. Coltrane and Miles Davis. I wanted some of that. I had money, Mama let me have some of the change left over whenever she sent me to the store. All I had to do now was get to a record store.

"We got Smokey Robinson and the Miracles, too. Bet you ain't heard that," Herbert called after me.

I kept walking. I knew about them, everybody watched *American Bandstand*. Herbert Kelly was a nut fool.

A Love Supreme

I talked to Ada and she told me about Miles Davis and John Coltrane, but hearing about them wasn't the same as hearing them and she didn't have any of their records, either. So, I avoided Herbert Kelly and made my supplications known. I prayed for jazz albums for Christmas, 'cause I knew no fat white man was coming into Moleen to bring anything to anybody. Especially since, the way things were going, he'd get beat up just for crossing the railroad tracks. Black and white people was having themselves a row, race riots were breaking out all over, and nobody was looking forward to summer coming. My mama said she was surprised it was taking this long for Negroes to get fighting mad and that when Rosa Parks sat down on a bus in Montgomery, Alabama, over ten years ago, everybody else got up off their behinds and started doing some things they should have been doing all the time.

Now, the white people didn't want us to go to their schools and they had better books than us. We were tired of reading Dick and Jane from first to, and through, second grade when it was a kindergarten reader. That's what I heard. So I'm repeating it. We did have Dick and Jane two years but none of us went to kindergarten anyway. I would listen to my mama and daddy talk about this. They were talking, but not together.

My daddy would talk to the men in the garage and my mama would talk to Mrs. Mont T. I learned about riots, marching, and the KKK. My mama and daddy wanted to integrate our schools. They would change their work shifts for different hours so they could go to meetings.

"Time brings on a change." Mrs. Mont T was hot curling my mama's hair in the doorway between the living room and the kitchen, so we could watch the television. I kept watching Mrs. Mont T and wondering if she was burning more of my mother's hair than curling it. I once heard she did Betty Lou's mama's hair and left it in little rows of curls. The next day when Mrs. Perry combed her hair out, the burned curls fell to the floor. Madam C. J. Walker's hair oil was sizzling, smoke was rising, my mama was holding her ear, and hair was smelling up the whole house. The television was on and they were watching Walter Cronkite.

"Oh, my God! Help me, Jesus!" my mama screamed and Mrs. Mont T stopped with the Marcelle iron in her hand, walked back to the kitchen, put that curling iron on the stove, and came back and sat next to me. She held my hand but hers was the one trembling. Black folks was rioting in Detroit, burning stores, and Cronkite was talking about jobs and housing. My mama started talking about the hoses policemen used to use. I didn't see hoses, I saw people running and screaming louder than my mama, but Mrs. Mont T explained, "Child, wasn't that long ago that white folks was hosing us down with water so strong Negroes was knocked off their feet and sliding like they was at Riverview. And that kind of slidin' ain't no amusement ride." My daddy and a bunch of coveralled fat-meat and car-greasy men came running in the house.

"Turn on that damn TV, Jessie."

It was on. An announcer was saying something, but nobody in our living room was listening. It didn't matter what he said, we could see it, skin feel and touch it. Store windows disappeared, we felt the heat from fires and smelled the hot musty breath of barking dogs on our legs and near our faces. White folks wanted to kill us 'cause we wanted to learn how to live better than we was living and we were all marched out and ready to fight.

I got up and went to my mother's room and called Ada. Uncle Albert answered the phone.

"Yeah, baby. We saw it, nonviolence just lost the 'non.' Ada gonna call you back. She's on her knees prayin'."

I hung up the phone and did the same.

For Halloween I was Billie Holiday, and Herbert Kelly was the only person that knew who I was. I wore one of Ada's old dresses from her days at Club DeLisa. I had my hair pulled back in a French roll with a plastic flower to one side and held a microphone made out of Reynolds Wrap. I had memorized the words to "Strange Fruit," but I didn't have the voice or the nerve to sing it. Herbert Kelly was Barnabas Collins from *Dark Shadows* and kept chasing me, saying, "Hey, Billie, I want to suck your blood." He really was touched. That boy couldn't even keep the lines to *Dracula* and *Dark Shadows* from getting confused.

When we bobbed for apples at the church, I wouldn't go after him and he followed me home asking how come I thought he was a germ or something. That was funny, he did describe himself accurately, but I told a white lie.

"I don't think you're a germ. I just don't like bobbin' for apples anyway."

"Then what do you like, Patience Jan Campbell?"

He took to calling me that from time to time and I ignored him.

"Want to walk up to Gino's Pizza, they giving out slices?"

"You must be crazy." I never heard of Gino's giving out slices. Geraldine walked up and said it was true and Marie Perkins appeared out of nowhere and said she wanted to go. Geraldine was dressed like Angelique from *Dark Shadows,* she even had a blond wig. It looked silly on her blue-black self. The Kellys must've got hold of some money with store-bought costumes. I would've had five new albums.

"Real nice costumes," I told Geraldine and Herbert, lying a little to be polite.

"Thank you," Geraldine said. "Who are you?"

"She's Billie Holiday." Herbert gave her the hick eye. "Can't you see that?"

Marie Perkins said "Billie who?" louder than she needed to be.

"The famous jazz singer." Herbert was trying.

"Oh yeah," Geraldine said.

"Girl, you is sickenin'. Ain't no jazz singer suppose to be a Halloween character." Marie, dressed like a witch, which was as common as a cold, seemed like she wanted to call me out over a Halloween outfit.

"Well, it is now," Herbert Kelly said, and huffed up in front of Marie.

"Herbert, you would hit a girl over that bony yellow thang!" Marie dropped her bag and put her fists up.

"Nobody said anything about hitting you, just 'cause you like Herbert and we know he doesn't like you." Geraldine stuck up for her brother. With all that going on, I was starting to feel sorry for Marie. Then she picked up her bags, turned around, and said, "Billie Hollinbay, go get yo' pizza with your husband and yo' sister-in-law."

The three of us stood there and watched her plastic black dress fold into the darkness. The top of her tall pointy hat tried to kiss the streetlights, then I said I couldn't walk all the way up to the railroad tracks for a slice a pizza and started walking home.

Herbert didn't follow me, but when I passed him he looked embarrassed and Geraldine looked like she was trying to think her way out of something that was already done.

The next day when I got ready to leave out the side door for school, a record album was inside the storm door. It was an old worn cover with John Coltrane on it, *A Love Supreme*. I played it as soon as I got home from school and every day after.

My daddy and his friends had to build fires in garbage cans outside the garage to keep it warm enough for them to scoot underneath cars and change oil, prop up hoods, take out carburetors, and patch up radiator hoses. Some days I would dress warm and go out with them for a spell. They'd put their pints and half pints up and look at me with eyes that made hiding their liquor unnecessary.

"Out at the mill, you should hear them white boys putting down Reverend Doctor Martin Luther King."

"Shoot. You ain't got to go to the mill; that integrated church up in Bellevue, heard tell a white pastor quoting scripture about a passage in the B-I-B-L-E saying a man will come and say I have a dream, I have a dream, and not to believe him. He the anti-Christ." They started laughing then and Mr. Barnes took out his half pint and slipped a taste before he noticed me.

Race was everywhere. People were wearing Afros and shouting, "Black is beautiful!" Everybody at school tried to dress like Diana Ross, and the high schoolers were puffing and flipping their hair up. The rapscallions that did have a car would ride around the block with their windows down, cold as it was getting, playing James Brown, "It's a Man's World," and shouting

"Black Power." I didn't agree with James Brown but wasn't sure if I agreed with Dinah, either, so I stayed inside and listened to John Coltrane. Without one word, he said everything.

One day when my mama was working overtime and my daddy was at work too, Herbert Kelly came knocking at my door.

"What do you want?" I asked him, looking through the screen door.

"You never said you liked the album."

"You never said you left it at the door." I knew he had left it, but since he'd stopped walking me home, I was kind of mad at him. I wasn't supposed to, but I let him in and said, "Want me to play it?"

He walked in all careful. I could see our house must've looked better than his. The Kellys had to be poor. We listened to Coltrane and then he got all nervous and said he had to go. I was glad, but he came back in a few days with Miles Davis. Miles was different and I wasn't sure if I liked him. Herbert acted like he was proud of knowing something I didn't know and he started walking me home again.

Marie Perkins would roll her eyes at me and I heard she said I was "copped" after school, but when I saw her I would pat my butt and throw my hand in her direction, or jut out my neck, then turn it slowly to the side and she left me alone.

I played some of my songs for Herbert and even dressed up in my Billie Holiday outfit and used my microphone like I was singing, but I only opened my mouth. When Herbert told me to sing, I told him I was "lip-syncing and pantomiming her performance." He didn't know what I was talking about and changed the subject. He told me he heard about my parents' parties and wondered why they didn't give them anymore. I didn't want to think about that but I described the parties to him and he asked me to dance. We tried dancing to "Miss Brown to You," and then when it got slow with "No Detour Ahead" he got too close to me, pressed my shoulders into his chest, and kissed me.

"Herbert Kelly!"

"I'm sorry. I swear 'fore Jesus."

He was really dumb. "You're not supposed to swear like that, Herbert, and you ain't got no business putting your ol' big lips on me."

He started for the door shame-faced. I let him go, but sat down and didn't even change the record when it stopped. Just sat there hoping it didn't scratch. Kissing felt good.

Winter Knives

"*The* eagle may fly on Fridays, but the hawk got the best of me." My daddy would come in the door with some crazy saying like that every day, shaking the snow off his boots, rubbing his hands, and trying to get back in my mother's room in the early morning when she came home.

I guessed he missed her kind of kissing, like I missed Herbert Kelly's. Every time Herbert came over now, we would play party and end up kissing. I bought *True Confessions* at the store across the railroad track and I knew where kissing led. They gave the details of how "it" was done. Xavier Hollander had a column and it told you to do things like close your eyes and feel cotton balls, Jell-O, and feather dusters to make yourself more sensitive. I did all that and dreamed about it. Boys aren't the only ones that have wet dreams. I had never been so wet and warm between the legs before and I knew it was wrong. But I didn't want to stop it. If I wasn't supposed to be wet, how come God let me get wet? I didn't want to ask Ada and I sure didn't want to pray it away.

One day when Herbert Kelly came over we kissed too long and his thing got hard, felt like something hit me and when I started to jump back he put his hands on each side of my butt and pulled me closer and started moving around. I should've said something but I didn't, I moved back and got so wet I had to sit down. Herbert and me ground up on each other until I thought I was going to faint, then he started touching my breasts and they started tingling and I had the good sense to start yelling, "Go home, go home!"

He pressed on me some more and I was pressing back and still yelling go home and I wondered if this is what Paul was talking about when he said all that stuff about the flesh and doing what he didn't want and what he did want to do he couldn't, all that made me think about Ada, Abel, Cain, Hester Cochren, my mama and my daddy and even Hannah. I started calling Hannah, whispering for her at first. Then when I got loud, Herbert Kelly said who is Hannah and jumped like she was a real person.

"Hannah is my grandmother. She's visiting us and sleeping downstairs," I lied.

"You lying, P.J." Still, he jumped up and made it out the door. "You lying."

I just kept calling Hannah. That night I prayed but I had gotten the way to do it all jumbled up and I just kept asking God to send Hannah to help me. *Please send my granny. I can't talk to Ada, can't tell my mama or my daddy, send Hannah. Tell her to help me.*

I don't think God heard me, or maybe Hannah couldn't come, because I kept seeing Herbert Kelly. He met me in the garage and we sat in the back of an ol' broken down '58 Cadillac, kissed, grinded, and went all the way. He even wanted to do it when I had my period and that made me remember something because in January, when it was time for my monthly, I didn't see a drop of blood.

I told Herbert Kelly and he picked up his father's albums and stopped coming over my house and started walking Marie Perkins home. All that in a week. I thought about dying. Not killing myself, just dying. I filled the bathtub with completely hot water and eased

myself in screaming and crying, I prayed and called Ada,
but I couldn't talk to her long like we used to. I wanted
to hear that passage about a man leaving his mother and
father and cleaving to his wife, but I couldn't ask about
it either. Herbert Kelly must've never read the Bible and
we wasn't married. I thought Ada could see through the
phone, hear my worry, know what happened.

"Mama Ada?"

"Hey, baby. Long time no hear from but always see."

She said that a lot and just meant she could see me in
her mind's eye. I would have fainted ten times if she
could really see me. "Daddy won't bring me."

"Baby, Daddy won't bring himself. I am my brother's
keeper and I got enough bones to pick with your father
to make a skeleton and he knows that."

I knew about some of the things my daddy was doing
wrong. But he came home, not every night, but he came
home. Herbert Kelly was supposed to come back and
help me. At least my mama was with my daddy and a
long time ago they probably loved each other.

"Mama Ada, did Daddy and Mama ever go with you
to the jazz clubs?" All those albums had to mean something.

"They went to speakeasies more than I did, but we
didn't go together much. Your father is younger than me
and I had a different crowd. Steel sharpens steel and so
does a man's countenance amongst his friends."

"*Countenance* I know, but what does your face have
to do with steel?"

"People show their faces amongst people that are like
them, talk to each other and try to get sharper and wiser
together. Even then you got to be careful not to get cut."

Ada knew about what happened to me. Herbert Kelly
didn't make me do anything I didn't want to do. I got in
his face as much as he got in mine, we both got cut, but
my scar is deeper. I wanted to tell on myself, just spill it

out and tell it. But I didn't want Ada to stop talking to
me. What if she didn't know and I up and told her and
she stopped talking to me? I wouldn't have anybody to
talk to.

"Why would people who love you cut you, Mama
Ada?" My mama and daddy were all but dicing each
other up like onions.

"Everybody's got their own knife, Jan. You can defend yourself by hurting others or by cutting out things
you see in yourself that will hurt you. And everybody's
got a light so they can see which one to do and when.
But"—she was sighing like she did every time she talked
about my father too long—"it's easier to cut on somebody else instead of doing your own surgery."

I took a hot bath every day I was late, sometimes two
a day, and then I started taking Epsom salts. I don't
know what I thought that would do, but I ate whole tea-
spoons of it and then decided to add baking soda. I was
in the bathroom throwing up something awful when I
heard my father's car. I grabbed my smelly clothes,
wiped the vomit off the floor, sprayed Lysol, and ran to
the basement to put my things in the wash. Halfway
down the steps, I tripped on the clothes and fell down
the stairs. I don't know how long I was lying at the bottom of the stairs. When my daddy came in, he didn't
even look down the stairs. I held my breath and when I
woke up it was dark. Before my mama came home, I
made it upstairs and in my bed. I started bleeding the
next day, with lumps, and passed a little piece of something that looked like chewed-up hot dog. I hated Herbert Kelly.

I wish I could say I hated doing it and being on a boy's
arm, but I can't say that. I wanted to find another arm to
be on as fast as I could, but the closest I could come to
being on somebody's arm was getting to Ada. I wanted
to go to her and see if Hannah had been around and find

out what was taking my grandmother so long to come see about me. If she'd been around and loved me enough to drop me off a table and tell me not to trust anybody, maybe I wouldn't have to hate Herbert Kelly.

I got in my mother's bed underneath the covers and called Ada, and asked her to tell me about the times when she was growing up. Sometimes she talked me to sleep, but mostly I stayed awake listening to the stories of the days before I was born.

"In the South, when mothers or fathers died early, when men left, or when grown folks stood around with broken spirits, we prayed and cried out with our hearts for answers. We learned to see more than rain coming in the clouds. We knew one day would lead to the next and if we made it we had hope. We didn't just walk, we felt the grass and dirt under our feet and we listened to the wind. We listened until we could hear our own spirits."

I thought about the bad spirit on the willow. If I'd listened hard enough maybe the wind would've spoke, but I didn't think so. "Hearing a spirit?"

"Intuition, conscious, whatever some people want to call it now, we knew it for what it was and is. We listened deep, until we were guided and led by all that was inside."

Every time I looked inside myself, I wanted to look away. I saw Herbert Kelly and what I had done. I heard that fool talking about how we had a love supreme and it seemed like Miles was laughing at Coltrane and Dinah was laughing at me. But Ada kept talking and kept telling me about seeing good things, like she never did nothing wrong. It made me hot and almost angry.

"Mama Ada, was there only good to see? How could you see good through the bad times?"

"We listened closely and life brought us back. We used the knife of our will to cut out people that couldn't hear and see. We had to. Young people have so many things now to distract them, but we didn't have that."

"I don't have that much to do, just eat, sleep, go to school, and study. That's it. I know Daddy didn't finish school, he had to work the fields. Didn't you?"

"I was supposed to, but when I was young and able to know the fields for more than a place I could walk past or play in, a place where I would soon be, something inside of me just came undone. It made no noise and had no voice, but it burned a message to my soul. I hated the field, white puffs of cotton with those dried brown cracklings. Picking cotton looked dumb to me. All those heads bobbin'. All those people singing and roasting in the sun when slavery was supposed to be over. It looked so foolish and I felt hopeless going near it at all."

I sunk down in the covers and made a warm den in the bed. I had revved Ada up till she felt like I did. I'd taken her back to the past and she was letting me look at it, too. We were alike. "I know, Mama Ada. I know." Doing something and feeling hopeless and still doing it, I didn't want to be like that either.

"The field was my mother when I wanted her to be with me. It was my father's undoing since no matter how heavily he planted, it would never yield enough. It depended on more than God's rain and His sun. Even when God gave it the best of His nature, the crop fell into the hands of a white man with no fairness in him. So I went inside myself and prayed."

If Ada hated the field, I hated it, too. Never could understand why my mother spent so much time in the backyard garden trying to make something up that had everybody else running North to get away from it. My daddy spent as much time keeping the grass green, even if he did say water was "white gold" and I should stop filling the tub to the top. He used a whole bunch more making brown grass green in the summer.

"Mama Ada, did the prayer work?"

"Sure did. After my first day picking cotton behind the grown-ups, I guess I was eight, nine maybe, I begged my mother. 'I can do all the household chores, all the clothes washin', cookin', and watching the children too, yes I can. Just don't send me out to the fields. Plenty in the field.'"

Ada's voice fell around my shoulders in big clumps, soft like hair. It started rocking me to sleep. I remembered my father's stories and dug them out of her own. Ada had moved North first and when he had enough money, he'd come to live with her. I moved down deeper under the covers, closing my eyes, and thinking of Ada trying to reason with Hannah.

"I didn't pick cotton, but I tell you I worked harder than anyone else not to. I chose the smell of bluing and lard soap, the rising of bread and the voices of children. I found a piece of myself, by looking hard, pushing my heels way down past the red dirt I had to stand on, putting my finger on what I hated and asking for something else. It was my first calling out for the Spirit. I couldn't see exactly what I wanted, but I knew what I didn't want. And I asked, down low. Are you asleep, baby?"

"No." It was the lace of a lie. "Don't stop, I'm still listening." Some afternoons I did wake up with the phone beside me. I would call Ada back and apologize, but it never seemed to bother her, she'd just ask if I had a good catnap.

"I guess I didn't even know I had called the Spirit then. But the South served tears for breakfast and every day there was new hunger. I stirred clothes in the wash kettle for many years, chasing after the brothers and sisters that kept coming until Mama died."

Ada took a deep breath and let the truth escape. "Now, if I'm a tell it, I might as well tell it true. Your father was as

hardheaded as his hair was long and when he was growing up, he wasn't my favorite and I wasn't his.

"People been favoring since Isaac and Esau and I did
too, like now." I knew Ada was talking about me and I
pulled the covers tight around me. It felt like a hug.

"Verga was your father's favorite. They played in the
red dirt, kept as close to each other as ninety-nine to one
hundred, while I stirred that wash kettle. I remember the
promise they made one summer evening at supper before Verga had turned thirteen.

"'Charles and me got something to say.' Verga stood
first and Charles, three years younger, grabbed her hand
and popped right up beside her. 'Whether Charles dies
first, or if I do, don't matter. We're gonna see if we can
come back. And if we can, we coming back and tell the
other all 'bout it.'

"'Yes 'um!' That's what your father said, he was
Verga's echo. Papa told them both to sit down and eat.
But I watched Verga's and Charles' hearts trying to join.
In a few years Mama died and it wasn't long before
Verga moved and got a room in the colored part of
town. No sooner she got there good, Charles up and
left. I heard tell he slept at the foot of her bed."

I tried to imagine my daddy young and so close to a
sister that he would sleep at the foot of her bed.

"They planted their own crops. Verga kept white
folks' houses and Charles worked the fields. They lived
that way and didn't care that people spoke all kinds of
manner about them. I heard they spent most evenings on
Verga's porch rocking back and forth, calming themselves. Both of them were born with an extra dose of
anger so they understood each other, talked for hours
about anything from the day's chores to nonsense, I'm
sure."

"Why doesn't Daddy ever talk about Verga?"

"Hmmm." Ada was thinking too long and I knew she was trying not to tell something. I waited.

"Verga didn't live long. A few years later the Spirit called me to both of them.

"I was stirring clothes in the wash kettle. And a pain forced my hands to my bosom like I needed to hold my heart in place. 'Who is it, Lord? Where is it, Lord?' I asked, then I saw her go. We didn't have telephones, most of us could barely read or write, so we had to develop parts of ourselves people don't even bother to use now. I knew it was Verga. A rush of wind passed the field and reds like her anger and blues like the calm that never quite settled with her lit the morning sky.

"I shoveled dirt over the fire under the wash pot, got the oldest to watch the youngest, and headed to town. On my way to Verga's, I thought about your father, how bad off he would be. Verga was his heart. Without her, no mother and no father to speak of, I worried about him and wondered how I was gonna tell him. But your daddy was in Verga's room when I got there. I asked him how he knew and he said he watched Verga pass over the field where he was working."

Ada's voice seemed faint and far away. I wondered where Hannah was.

"Charles pointed at her body and said what was left in that room was bones, flesh, and on its way to dust. Nothing to hold on to, not a thing ever meant to last, but I think he would have been a different man if she were with him now."

I peeped out from under the covers and looked around my mother's room. Nothing that belonged to my father was near me, not even the scent of his cologne. He never would have slept at the end of her bed just to be near her. He just got a bed of his own.

"Most of us, including your daddy, saw the spirits of people. In our own way we understood them. Now,

Charles may have made some foolish choices with his life, done wrong and got caught like the rest of us. But he can reach out and make his peace, choose to see the other worlds around him whenever he wants to, and so can you. The key is desire, Jan. All you need is the desire to know yourself so much you burn. The willingness to light your own lamp to see all the worlds that live here with us and the courage to get rid of anything or anyone that don't belong."

"Ada?"

"Mmm."

"I want to see Hannah."

"I know you do. Keep praying."

Earth Folks

When I lived on earth, old folks used to cut their eyes at young mothers and their children, the elders pronouncing most of those observed as "wise and otherwise." Now, it's true, some mothers simply lack the courage of love. Operating in a spirit of whimsy, they never learn to love a child strong, gentle, and past their own pain. So both the child and the mother often look more otherwise than wise. But to be a grandmother, now that's double love.

Since my earth time ended a half-century ago, I can see past old folks' sayings. The knowledge behind their phrases of truth is considerable and much respected. Often, what you think is rumor, especially the one they keep spreading about heaven being a place where "the streets are paved with gold," is just simply a truth so plain. Now that I have roamed heaven, and traveled on a thought to earth, I am a witness. Heaven's streets are made from a gold so pure, you can see right through them onto the earth and into the hearts of those you love.

Sometimes that love goes both ways and grows hurt deep until, if you are called, like I was, the angels will plead your case to return and help you guide the object of your heart into their own. See, earth folks hold a power in their hearts, loosed most often by the prayers of mothers and children. The strength of their fevered words pierce the clouds, the sky's blue, and finally the gold until it shines the floors of heaven with flickers, rays, and sometimes full beams of light.

Angels scramble to grab snatches of that light and answer the prayers of earth folks and we, the living dead because we are still remembered, wait to see if our name is whispered true from a heart below. Whipped by living into wisdom, young mothers call for us with all manner of prayers. They ask God for the strength of their mothers, aunties, and all the mamas and papas who've raised them and passed on. Somewhere inside they know the love of the dead is strong. In selfless desire, they cry out. Most times their pleas for help usher in needs they would seldom ask for themselves. And children, fresh from the place where they were created, pray simple prayers that rise with such clarity, many of us stand still to absorb every word and watch colors that shame rainbows. Often, in unassuming phrases that light our laughter, their wants for wisdom, love, and understanding beam forth, cleaning the floors of heaven, polishing them with youthful light. These prayers beam and in faith linger, until an angel grabs each request with both hands and is dispatched to answer.

That's what happened when Patience Jan Campbell, the daughter of my son, the girl-child who calls herself P.J., prayed. The child prayed me a second dance on earth, and long before her first word, I heard the music. You see, from birth she held the passionate embers of my bloodred fire humming in her thoughts, not to mention a full crescendo of my common sense and mother wit. Pulling up on the side of a crib, she tucked calm mixed with melancholy and the anger of her father into her heart. When she was tall enough to peep over the cutting board, she asked to be lifted up to peer into pots and I saw the cooking skills of both families sear fruitful hands. When she grew ears deep enough to listen to grown folks' conversation and form an opinion of her own, I witnessed the part of her mother she really didn't like—the desire to eat words instead of speak them—take on a new note in her own spirit.

So my double love was with the girl. I spent the beginning of my eternity enchanted by the freedom she had to study people instead of rows of cotton. I knew that if she ever called my name I would take whatever form I needed to come. And this I told to Ruth, Moses, the angels of the Lord, and any heavenly being that would listen. In the meantime I flew, danced, sang, and sat, just taking in that girl's ways.

Her voice became louder, her mind nimbler, and when she used them both at once, I would have disagreed with the old folks and said she was more wise than otherwise; that's if I had gotten a chance to be earth old. Less than forty years on earth's calendar and not yet a full half-century on the infinite one, Esther, Abraham, and especially Methuselah tease and consider me young. But I'm still the child's grandmother, named after that woman in the Bible that wanted a child so badly she prayed, lips moving with no words coming out, until the priest thought she was drunk. Like my namesake, Hannah, I never fooled with spirits, at least not the man-made kind. But I did, can, and do pray. Oh, yes, we still pray. Every word is a prayer in heaven and, truth be known, I believe that it's the same way on earth. Every being prays except the Devil. It's just a matter of whom you're praying to and how much you believe. I spouted this truth in all three heavens and received the nods of multitudes.

Now, Godly prayer was the heirloom I passed on to Ada and she gave it to the child. So when the child did what was natural and called my name it was no surprise. As soon as the prayers left her lips, the gentle push of angels began my journey. Gathering colors and gifts from the ancestors I came, a grandmother that had not lived long enough to be called grand. I rode on the cushion of blue God spread underneath the floors of heaven to become the delight and inspiration of those on earth. And I carried my color, the one earth folks had mistaken for anger but held the deepest love, bloodred.

When Jan walked in Jessie's garden, I stretched my love across the bean vines and sprinkled it on the flowers, kissing it true into the collard greens. When she played her jazz, I danced hope through the prisms of crystal and wove joy through the shingles of the chandelier lamp, spinning it all around each vinyl disc.

I saw the wax of the world fall from that child's ears. And Jan had sight. She could look through Charles and Jessie until there was nothing left to see. But I knew the real reason I had to come. The child needed to fight for her voice. Her mouth was too busy weighing words to cover the secrets she saw hiding behind her parents' eyes. Guilt can last through years on a single morsel and its first captive is the tongue. I watched Jan's pain rise like morning, with optimistic promise, and both the fragrance and the stench of its possibilities.

Jessie had lost too much strength. By swallowing before it was time to chew, she had grown sluggish when it was time to plait the child's hair in majestic braids, talk, hum, sing, push into her mind the wealth of older days. When Jessie tried to speak, her mouth filled with crumbs. Charles' slim smiles pretended to laugh the pain away, but his secrets cradled him in their arms and rocked him in his sorrow. I ached for my son, but Jan was my charge. I could only pray that help for one would lead to the salvation of the other, and that's the way we passed the years.

Now the child thinks she's a young woman. Jan has moved to the city and although I cannot speak for her, or tamper with her own free will, I can fight the evil spirits with my love. As her voice wanes I will tell the story until her true sound comes back. And it will come. All she needs to do is use her lamp and her knife. I can hold one until she is ready to wield the other. Most times, I sit across her shoulders, whispering enough wisdom in her ear that it finds a way into her dreams. One day, when my voice meets hers and we recognize each other, I'm sure I'll hear all the music that is being composed inside. I know she has a song and I understand why she loves to listen to the women who have the courage to sing their own. The girl has already stumbled on what being an earth woman is all about: singing with your own voice, and not giving a you know what if somebody else thinks it's off-key.

Patience Jan Campbell is more wise than otherwise, I'll put my double love on that. That's why, as she waits on her change to womanhood, I stretch my arms out. Unlike earth arms, they cannot grow limp or weary. And my aim is to hold the lamp in front of her. That girl is going to pick up her knife one day, and I want to make sure she can see.

Shadows and Shade

"*E*xcuse me."

Our attention is drawn to a handsome, even if he is prematurely balding, man, almost camouflaged behind a set of tables in the shade ahead of her. I see orange hues of trouble. Jan senses it too, but her feet still follow the voice that pours past the awning of a boutique and into the sunlight. Its low pitch joins the sounds of cars, buses, and people lagging along.

"Excuse me, Sis."

Jan peered into the shade. Two tables were filled with rows of clay busts.

"I've already sold some ladies today, so all I'm looking for is an opinion." Jan moved closer. Sculptures of black women stared from the front row, while those behind seemed to peep over bare brown shoulders. The man stood. His arms were lined with muscles more than were possible from just sculpting clay.

"See anybody you know?"

Jan looked at the palette of blues, reds, purples, and yellows he used to mix skin tones.

"What about that one?" He drew her gaze to the hardened clay shape of a young, rather proud-looking woman, but it was the sculpture next to it that begged her attention.

"I like this one." The child saw Ada in everything wise. The artist took her hand and placed it on the bust.

"It's okay to touch them. Pretend you're blind and try to see with your hands. Before I paint, that's what I do. Just feel and think."

Jan's fingers began to fall into the contours of the different sculptures, but I watched her mind drift past the women on the table and toward the women of her childhood. Some sat at shampoo bowls in Ada's basement hair salon, others whispered in Moleen kitchens where the smells were so different from the scents of Mexican, Greek, and Chinese food surrounding us, pressing against each other, and filtering through the summer air. Noon's beams feathered down until they reached the place where pots and pans bore witness, along with her quiet, too-young-to-be-listening body, while women were stringing beans, shucking corn, or performing some such task. Their actions diverted attention as the child digested stories, some wrapped around lies or the sharp pieces of shattered hearts, and others dropping morsels, tasty bits of love.

One of the sculptured figures underneath her fingertips was missing the telltale hat on its head. Still, large bulging eyes pulled the face condescendingly upward. The sculpture seemed to wish for arms in order to grab branches from the low-hanging trees and create some adornment for her head like her church-bound sisters in the row behind her.

Jan moved her hands to the next bust. The face was younger, timid, longing, and I knew it reminded her of the earliest hours of the morning. Before her run on the lakefront, humidity had crept around the girl until her studio apartment was reminiscent of the room overlooking Jessie's garden. Going to see Ada last week had helped, but now some of Charles' indigo crept into her spirit again. While she fingered the sculpture, her watch accidentally scraped against the clay.

"Did I scratch it?" The finish of earthen-colored paint

didn't appear damaged. Looking up, she saw the curl of the artist's chin. He didn't seem too concerned with the welfare of his artwork.

"Don't worry, it's hard to hurt the ladies," he said, rubbing the cheek of the sculpture with his thumb, slowly. "Too bad it brought you back. Art can take you places. Want to tell me about it?"

"Sorry." Jan's smile hid thoughts that mingled with his. "I've got to go." When she adjusted the purse on her shoulder, the gold tone of her bracelets caught the sunlight. I watched the artist observe their dance.

"The ladies have a way of doing that, especially with other artists. You're an artist, aren't you?"

"No." Jan shook her head and frowned. "Good luck with your work." She stepped backward, but before she could turn, his eyes mixed a palette of gold and sun into her skin color. "Here." He offered a business card. "Take this with you."

When she reached for the card, he pulled it back a little and repeated, "You're an artist, aren't you?"

"No, I'm training to be a disc jockey."

"What kind of music?" he asked.

"Jazz." The word swirled around her tongue, *zzs* hovering, keeping her mouth open until it formed another smile. She considered the sculptures, wondering what songs the women would've sung. "Have you ever sculpted the women of jazz?"

"Mmm." He stroked the shoulder of one of the women. Jan watched his fingers, flat and smooth from the clay. "Never thought about it, but I tell you what I do think. I think you're an artist. You just don't know it yet. I can always spot another artist."

He put the card down and extended his hand. "Don Obatunde." His hand seemed twice as large as her own, and cool.

"Jan Campbell."

She should have used her full name, Patience Jan Campbell, but she didn't.

He spread his arms to encompass the tables and announced, "These, as you know, are the ladies, and I'm looking for a model. Been watching women as they pass by, and I noticed your lips. That's really why I stopped you."

The child had told enough lies to know when she'd heard half the truth. "Billie Holiday has great lips, try hers." He laughed. Jan slipped, then fell into the laughter. "Your work is good, but I'm not a model and I'm late for a visit." Jan avoided the card that sat on top of a few papers. "Got to go," she said, turning.

"Then, please, take these articles and my card," he said. "The articles are about me and the girls." His voice lowered, settling against her back. When she looked over her shoulder, his eyes softened. "Your lips are from the Ashanti tribe. That's why I'd like to sculpt them. And I like the way you got into the art. I got a few friends that spin records. So, call me. Maybe we could help each other out."

Jan noticed that his eyes seemed far apart, as if he could see more than he was supposed to. His own lips were just slightly darker than his skin, like the flecks in a pecan shell.

"I'll think about it." She accepted the articles.

"Sounds fair. Call me."

He hadn't asked for her number and I was surprised she didn't fully understand this. She was always curious and earth folk still have a pretty good saying about a cat, curiosity, and a killing.

Jan walked the block down to Belmont and headed east. Spouting out little hums, she turned into the familiar apartment buildings that formed a horseshoe around a large courtyard with a multiple choice of evergreens and agreed, playing jazz recordings was an art.

A Friend

*J*an's color deepened as she climbed the stairs of the three-floor walk-up. Windows at the base of each landing offered light where particles of dust flickered and I used them to ride back to the times when Jessie was ill and Ada had kept the child, then a baby. We kneaded extra love into her knowing it would find its path. Now, Sarah had a piece of it.

"Door's open," Sarah called.

The apartment smelled of cigarettes, beer, marijuana, and something fried. Sarah, framed by walls painted a light green and trimmed in a dark wood that nearly matched her skin, sat on an oversized pillow on the floor.

"Hey, girl. Has the zoo started?"

The child knew Sarah avoided Saturday crowds on Broadway.

"Yep, and I was one of the first victims."

One eyebrow arched upward before Sarah returned to the sewing on her lap. Jan noticed her friend's face was puffy. We could both tell something had happened, but a swiftly lowered brow cautioned Jan not to ask.

"I met an artist on Broadway."

"Who hasn't?" Sarah wore a sleeveless bodysuit and nodded toward a milk crate. Jan sat down. Sarah knotted the thread from the pants she was hemming. "What kind of art?"

"Sculptures of black women in clay, painted all different skin tones. Detailed. Your mama, my mama, our friends. It was interesting. I told him what I thought about his work and he asked me if he could sculpt my lips."

Sarah looked up from her sewing box. "Was he attractive?"

"In a way. You know, muscular, tall, that pecan type of brown."

"About how old was he? My age or yours?"

"Older than both of us."

"Were you attracted to him?" Sarah's tone implied that since there were eight years between the friends, anyone older than she was too old.

Jan swallowed what she felt and I remembered this world where so much rests on rules, like see and don't see, talk but don't tell. The child had chosen a good friend, one who spoke her mind. But people don't come perfect and I saw both their needs. Struggling to be grown, having grown up too fast, they passed a balm between each other.

"He says he knows a few deejays." Jan told herself that maybe too much beer, too many tears, or a combination had caused the swelling around Sarah's eyes.

"Please." Sarah fidgeted with the pants then breathed hard and let her truth go. "Jan, most of these artists are hounds. The one you met is obviously after something more than lips in clay and you have to decide if you want to get involved. If he's older than both of us, then he's probably carrying more bags than we are, and who needs that?"

Sarah shook the pants, stood, and snapped them in the air, trying to shake off the ill feeling that settled around her. "These street artists are either young and getting started, which means they don't know from nothing about women, or they're too old to be out there on the street, which means they're probably losers across the board. What do you think?"

The girl would not call anybody a loser and loved men too much to see them as any other animal. Charles had taken care of that. He could capture a heart despite his sins, lean into your soul with his need to love until you loved him whether you wanted to or not.

"He seemed all right, just interested, and he wasn't wearing a wedding band."

"Not wearing a ring doesn't mean a thing. He sounds smooth, too old, and if you don't want to find yourself taking Men 101 over again, pass."

"Sarah." Jan started to ask what was wrong and why she had to smoke so much pot to deal with it, but stopped herself.

"Sorry. You're smart, Jan, but men throw you and you're not smart enough to tackle the old ones. Trust me." Sarah pulled her pants on, zipped them, and walked over to a full-length mirror on the back of a door. "Hot off the sewing machine," she said, turning, showing a figure almost as perfect as the bite of her tongue. "I don't want to walk all the way to the beach, let's take the bus."

Settled on the Lake Shore bus, Jan wondered about Ada. Less than twenty minutes away from this view of the North Side and the wealth of Lake Shore Drive was the West Side she'd driven through last Saturday. She recalled the blocks around Ada's home, run down from a decline that had started some years ago when she'd been too young to notice.

I knew it was the way Ada made Jan feel that had all but erased the slow creeping blight. Now, she watched the view of buildings that appeared to be cleaned brick by brick and tried to fight an anger at the boarded-up homes leading the way to Ada's.

Jan looked to the other side of the street, where a pale

blue sky melted into various shades of its reflection in the lake. With few exceptions, the street that would eventually become Michigan Avenue was scattered with couples jogging, riding bicycles, or holding hands. She remembered her jazz. "Sarah, I've got that assignment due next Friday and I still haven't found a guest. Can you go to the clubs with me tonight?"

"Uhn, uhn, uhn." Sarah shook her head and looked out the window.

"If we had men like those women"—Jan pointed toward the couples—"then I wouldn't ask you."

"You have no idea what those women are putting up with to walk next to those men. This is public. I'd like to see what goes on in private."

"Are you going to be like this all day?"

"Like what?"

"Thinking everything has to turn out bad, like everybody is out to get everybody else. Some men and women still know how to care about each other."

"You've got that man on your mind. If you want to dream, dream for yourself." Sarah turned her attention to her purse and began to rummage. "All I want is a cigarette and I'll have that when I get off the bus."

Bitch! Jan thought. If Jan could have heard me, I would have told her to clean up her inside tongue. Girl needed to watch her thoughts, which were busy musing on how it was getting harder to understand Sarah's attitude lately. "What's wrong, Sarah?"

"I'm in a mood." Sarah's hand was still buried in her purse.

I stayed with Jan's memories of the women in Moleen, always saying they had come for one thing when they were after another. Then I moved to her thoughts about meeting Sarah two years ago. They were employed at the only company the child could find willing to let her schedule work hours around college courses. Most of the women in the office were older and settled into cliques. Few had been to college, and most would tell her where the coffee was but never offer to sit down and have a cup. Sarah had been different.

Over brown bags, fast food, or an occasional splurge, Sarah had told her how she putzed around on weekends, mindful of a budget that was slimmer than most since she had custody of her son, Jonathan.

The first time Jan met Jonathan, Sarah introduced them by saying, "Jonathan, this is Jan and she's going to be a friend." Jan had tried to live up to that greeting while watching Sarah raise Jonathan alone. Some days she could almost understand Sarah's bitterness, which occasionally sent her on a weekend binge of tears, cigarettes, beer, and pot. The bus stopped and Jan took a last look out the window, confident that Sarah's experience was not the blueprint for her own.

Charles had done half his work. I considered the endless strata of time on one side, the shortness of life on the other, and picked indiscernible lint out of the child's hair.

"The beach is already crowded," Sarah announced, getting off the bus.

When they finally found a spot, Sarah lodged a cigarette in the side of her mouth and tugged at the crumpled towel in her bag.

"Jan, you've got looks and lips that got a Negro you don't know from Adam trying his best to get a chance to check you out. I know you're still thinking about him, but you better be careful."

"Sarah." Jan put her hand on the slim swell of her hips, half teasing. "Stop trying to tell me what to do." Then the child pushed hard against a recent past, peppered with boyfriends that most parts of her had forgotten.

Sarah took the twisted towel and popped Jan. If I had

my earth voice, or they had spiritual ears, they would
have heard me laugh. The child's friend pranced around
with more calculated snaps of the towel. Jan shielded
her head and asked Sarah to start acting like she was
thirty, which sent Sarah into a flurry that lasted a few
seconds and ended with them both flopping down in the
sand.

"Are you going to call him and ask if you can interview him on the radio program for your class?"

"I hadn't gotten that far yet."

"Unh, unh, unh. Look, this does not sound like Mr.
Wonderful. The best the boy could do is save us from
having to visit all those jazz clubs tonight. I'm tired of
begging deejays to do your program for no money and
no sex. You got to learn to use men for what they can
do, not for what they can't."

"Thanks, Sarah. Now I really feel like asking you to
come with me tonight." Jan stretched out on her towel.

"Let me complain a little. You know I'm going."
Sarah retrieved a half-emptied pack of Kools.

"You're chain-smoking." Jan reached for the pack,
and Sarah let her take it. "Slow down a little," Jan
added, remembering that this was the first weekend of
the month and the apartment had shown no sign of
Sarah's son, Jonathan. If David had picked up their son
for the weekend, his visit had probably left some debris.

"Rough night?"

"Yep." Sarah ran her fingers through her hair, only a
few gray strands mixed with dark brown curls.

"Bad time with Jonathan?"

"Jonathan and David. Yep. Bad time with them
both." Sarah followed the smoke from her cigarette
until it disappeared. "When you get involved with men,
there's so much to put up with. You can try to get rid of
them and start a new life, but sometimes a divorce

doesn't do any good, especially when you have a child. They keep hanging on."

"I'm sorry it was a bad night."

"Well, I'm glad you came by, it helped get me out of that apartment. There was a lot of shit hangin' in the air the beer couldn't get rid of."

The mouths of babes. I wished they could see what was really in the air.

Sarah put the cigarette out in the sand, then wrapped the butt in a piece of tissue and put it in her purse. "I hope you don't mind if I nap," she said, stretching out on her towel, limp from an exhaustion Jan didn't know a thing about.

We watched the wrinkle lines that had begun to cross Sarah's forehead and followed others as they creased the corners around her eyes and crept into the space between her chin and cheekbones.

I liked them both. Even when they played their gentle tug of war, pulling against each other, they were still trying to reach the same side. I joined the sun and stretched goodness over their feet and tucked mercy comfortably around their chins.

Jan took the artist's card out of her purse and traced the raised bust of a woman with an interrogating forefinger. Don Obatunde, Visions of Women. How old? Forty at the most. Married? Probably divorced. Children? Maybe. What would Ada say? She could tell by looking at Sarah, but the child still took the articles out and began to read.

Lingering Voices

$\mathcal{D}$espite all the lessons I had pressed into the child's dreams, her apartment still held the heat from last night and carried it into morning. She was fighting herself, stirring the air until it rose against the ceiling. I sat in the small corner window with its view of the lake. We both looked out, then Jan decided to break her routine. Running along the lakefront was the last thing on her mind.

Jan tugged the sweat-dampened gown over her head, feeling moist air cling to rising degrees. She seemed grateful that one source of heat was on the outside and headed for the bathroom, fighting the other.

When she stepped into a cool shower, I looked out the window and we both remembered the evening before. As soon as she'd entered her classroom, Don left a cluster of students and walked over to her. "I'm glad to be here, babe. Got everything under control. Just go get your stuff together."

"Don, my stuff is together." She'd disliked an attitude that assumed they'd been seeing each other every day for a month, and entered the recording studio expecting an interview with a know-it-all. Instead, he changed his tone and she found herself relaxing at his ability to anticipate her questions and weave his answers around them. He spoke about the female jazz artists' influence on many forms of black art and when he talked about his sculptures, she sensed he'd studied women until his hands molded both features and personality into the clay.

I knew the same, but his street-smart mannerisms intrigued the child and left me wondering when she was going to develop her own.

Jan scrubbed her shoulders, reminding herself that intrigue wasn't enough to erase the articles she'd read. An ex-convict and former car thief whose art had been discovered in prison wasn't exactly what she'd been looking for. Still, she remembered the night. Before the interview was halfway over, both she and Don had become cautious, guarding the voices entering the microphone, careful not to speak directly to each other. Whenever he moved closer to her, she sensed the same energy growing between them. Now it returned, in folds of heat, despite the cool water.

I thought about the earth time it takes to see one's own beauty and I was hoping Jan would look in the mirror, see her own face, and speak to her heart. But she just kept thinking of that evening past. I sat while she contemplated what was and is, then twisted the thing into what would be.

This morning she was going to Don's loft to pose for his sculpture of her lips. She'd figured she'd shorten the visit by telling him about her plans to get together with Sarah. If she'd looked in the mirror, she might have seen the reflection of a young woman trying to find a way out, before getting in.

The world misuses retrospect, always waiting for something to happen then figuring a way out of the double load. In the spirit we use discernment, seeing the branches of the road before we walk down the path. I entered the steam and tried to tell her so, knowing full well my words misted into the moisture, ran down the sides of the tile, and drifted into the drain. Jan pushed the shower knob in, cut the faucet off, and told herself that she could handle Don and any conversation he wanted to have.

I sat on the sink. She dried off, then lotioned her legs, trying not to imagine Don between them. After months of self-control she was going way too fast, and with every thought she used to slow down, she only found herself racing forward. We both knew what it was, but I could see it.

Lust has wings, feet, paws, hooves, and antlers. It burrows low deep, soars, runs, and fights for its freedoms. Love can help, but only the owners can wage its war. The child was confusing the beginning of lust with the possibility of love. One fought, one conquered. One settled, one saved. One came like the cobra, from the ground up, belly down and underfoot, where all the nerve endings rest. It sought a soft spot, a nerve unraveled or fettered, then entered to guide the feet, moving up the legs, wrapping tight and squeezing through thighs, shooting its poison into the genitals so the fire could burn. Um hum, just nibbling at the heart, so excited to tease the place where love lies, taking the breath from the lungs and easing into the brain to sow seeds that fall out of the mouth like so much nonsense.

I needed to see Ada, tell her to miss a few meals; fast, pray, and tarry for the child. On her shoulders, I reminded Jan of all that I had pressed in her dreams, but she couldn't remember. On this side it's so hard to get an audience of even one. It would take time. Fortunately, we both had some.

Works of Art

(M)ichigan Avenue's Tiffany & Co., Millionaires Club, Saks Fifth Avenue, Brooks Brothers, and all the places some folks thought made them, others were indifferent to, and still others despised, disappeared. They were replaced by skimpy storefronts, clubs that didn't open until the sun slept, and warehouses that only carried half the things they claimed they did. Jan walked west of downtown into the artists' district. She reached the address on Don's card, stood in front of a large four-story, its bricks weathered to a muddy brown, and searched the buzzers until she found Don Obatunde. No sound; no answer. The main door was wedged open with a brick, so she stepped inside.

We took in the floors lined with scuff marks and uneven from wear, dingy gray walls, and a smudged door leading to the stairwell. Jan chose a large freight elevator instead. His loft was midway down the hall on the second floor.

"Hello," Jan called, pushing open the cracked door. Inside there were hills of clay wrapped in plastic, long tables, high ceilings, busts of women—complete and incomplete—on shelves around the walls, crates, pedestals, a large kiln in the corner, and the pungent, slightly musty smell of wet clay.

Don stepped from behind a tall screen wearing a T-shirt that barely stretched over his biceps and faded blue jeans covered with paint and clay stains. He walked toward her, wiping his hands with a towel. "Well, if it isn't the deejay for women only." Closing the door behind her, he ushered her to the middle of the room.

"Sit down." He pointed to an empty stool.

"So this is where you work?" Jan looked around the studio again and thought her apartment would have fit into it five, maybe ten times. Seven.

"Yep. This is where I try to make it happen," he said.

Don walked Jan to the stool and set the towel on a counter cluttered with tubes of paint, brushes, and chips of clay. He lifted her chin and studied her face for a moment, then readjusted the lights.

"Your lips are from the Ashanti tribe. I'm sure I told you that, but I don't think you know what it means. A person's history can be traced by their features." He turned her face to view it from a profile. "Your folks did an excellent export job on these."

Don traced her lips with his finger while Jan tried to keep them from trembling. She thought he seemed less interested, more clinical and in control today. Taking a pad off the counter, he handed it to her. It was a rough sketch of her face in pencil; the lips had been erased and redrawn several times.

Don handed Jan a mirror. "Did I come close?" It was another chance to see herself, but the child only looked at her face in relation to her lips.

"Yes." Jan stared at the pad, then the mirror and at the pad again, frowning. "But you made the lips dominate my face."

"Exploiting features is my business. Don't worry, I won't let the lips overpower all that sweetness." He grinned. "See the bust I started over there?" Jan's eyes joined his. Grasping her hand, he led her to the shelves. Fingers and desire sunk into his palm.

"How long does it take to finish these?" The bust and several others were wrapped in plastic.

"Depends on the model." Jan felt his hand tighten around hers.

Shelved, in their rightful place, I could see that the busts represented many women. Parts of their spirits, almost transparent colors, had been left behind. I moved closer to the busts and cast hope over my shoulder to land on the child and prod her to recall dreams lost to the night. In front of me, spirits sighed, fidgeted, some still charmed, others fading away. Slowly.

"What do you think about this one?" Don asked. It was a profile of her face, but what she thought had nothing to do with sculptures. In her mind, Don was offering her a ride home after their interview last night. As they walked along the lakefront, they neared the place where she usually watched the sun rise. She envisioned them sitting, then lying down, his hands then his body matching the motion of the waters.

"I think it'll be fine."

Don let go of her hand and held her face up to the light.

"This bust is you, babe. I'm thinking of sculpting all your features, but I'm still going to call the piece *Lips*." Don released her face. "So, let's get started."

"I only agreed for you to sculpt my lips. I don't have a lot of time."

"Still turning the control buttons, D.J.?" Lifting the partially finished bust off the shelf, Don walked back toward the counter. "What y'all call it? Riding pots, keeping 'em in the black, don't dip in the red, too much gain."

Jan stared at the sculptures. I blew her kisses, but they were not the ones she wanted. So, I settled near the clay busts knowing that mistakes are often the best teachers. What was left of the other spirits agreed.

"No radio for you, Don. Stick to ladies in clay." Jan laughed, returning to her perch on the stool, unable to walk off the curious desire to enter Don's life. I'd heard her tell enough would-be lovers that movies with stale, butter-drenched popcorn, and the expectation of sex in exchange for a few dollars and a little time spent weren't going to work, but this was different. He was not a young man and she would have to see, hear, speak, and use all her senses.

Jan watched Don's hands carefully pick up a thin wire and begin to add texture to the lips. He pinched the clay with his fingers, then used a fine wire to imprint almost imperceptible lines.

"I can read parts of the face like a fortune-teller reads hands," Don said, his breath so close to her face she inhaled his exhalations. "Every line, every smooth stretch, the corners, creases . . ." He continued to talk as he walked away to adjust the lights again. When he returned to the stool, Jan noticed a perspiration that hadn't covered his chest before. It caused his T-shirt to cling to the well between his muscles. When she followed the swatch of perspiration up to his face, he didn't look away.

Don wiped his hands and traced her lips with his thumbs, starting from the middle peak and circling outward until his thumbs met underneath her bottom lip. Jan couldn't hold her lips still.

He leaned back against the counter and rested a hand on each of her shoulders. "So, D.J., will we play this straight, or will we take this thing where it wants to go?"

Jan didn't avoid his eyes and eased further into the desire. What she wanted to do was wrap her arms around his torso, take a deep breath and find out how he smelled, see if his body was as firm as it looked and find out what the hands of a sculptor felt like. By the time she realized she hadn't answered, Don's voice did the same thing it had done at the street fair, poured through the space between them until it reached inside.

"What I mean is, we lasted through one night wondering what today would be like. Am I too old? Is she too young? What about how different we are? But the truth is, I'd rather taste your lips now and sculpt them later no matter what we decide. What do you want to do?"

Jan looked at the clay women on the walls as if their expressions could offer opinions. She thought past their cold faces and asked what would they do. From the front row I told her to remember herself, but her tongue was lost and her ears and eyes had followed. She groped for Ada and Sarah, knowing they would have told her to leave, then stood, walked over to Don, and felt the heat from his face as it came closer to her own. This time he traced the outline of her lips with his tongue. His perspiration touched her skin. Before his tongue reached the center of her lips she parted them. He reached under the cotton blouse, put his fingers underneath the tube top and rolled it down. A thin layer of perspiration covered his hands and aroused the nerves beneath her skin. When her lips closed, so did his. His mouth opened again and followed the path of his hands. She was aware of the lights, intense colors, heat, the awkward movement to a pallet on the floor, and sounds drifting back and forth between them. It sounded like a mixture of Miles' and Armstrong's trumpets.

Friendship

Sarah shook her head and put the articles down.

"You knew all this about his past, nothing about the Negro today, and you went over to his studio and screwed him before you had a chance to figure out how he would fit into your life?"

"It was more than sex. Last night at the taping his art and my music came together. He has a lot to say about jazz, my career, his future, and I liked him. I didn't expect to, but I did."

Sarah lit a cigarette and quoted the article. " 'In the projects we had some people who were barely making it trying to live the right way, but for a lot of us, life was raw. Steal. Live. Take. That's the way it was. In prison I was forced to think about my life. There were times when I thought I was drowning and I learned to save myself.' Excuse me, Jan, but that's one of the worst bullshit, feel-sorry-for-me lines I've ever heard."

"Sarah. It's an article about his art and his life, not a line." The child bit her lip so hard, she had to stand up.

"Believe me, the man has five different takes on these." Sarah held the articles up. "I bet he repeats them three times a day until he hits bingo. These street artists are like that." Sarah's face was contorted behind a veil of smoke. "Jan, it's a free country and I like to get some like the next person, but you're in over your head. I think you better get out of this one before it goes any further."

Sarah turned a page, shook her head, grunted, and read more quotes. " 'I think I have always loved women.' Yeah, I bet. 'To draw, then sculpt, their faces became a way to express those feelings.' Uh-huh. 'I've never seen a woman without beauty. It could be the eyes, the lips, the cheekbones, the earlobes. Each feature has a range of its own.' Unh, unh, unh. He's a sculptor, all right."

Jan stood, picked up the articles. "I'll see you at work Monday. I'm going home." The child had dander.

"Don't get pissed, Jan. You asked me to be honest. What are you going to do about Don Juan?"

"I haven't decided yet. I like him, Sarah." The words hit the inside of her teeth, but still squeezed through. "You and I disagree about what he's after, but what about what I'm after? Maybe I haven't been so honest about that. Of course I want perfect, but what if I just want something right now?"

"Something, Jan. Not even someone? No wonder you never use your first name." Sarah lit one cigarette off the other and cocked her eye up to meet a widening brow. "Do you think he lives in that studio?"

Jan picked up her purse.

"Where was the kitchen? And wasn't he a little too hard to reach all week, until his last-minute call and that grand appearance at the taping?" Sarah ground one cigarette out and puffed on the other. "If that ain't enough, every other Negro I've ever heard talking that African, Ashanti, whatever, especially them ones with those half-African names"—she flung the free hand up in the air—"usually follows it with how it's natural for a man to have more than one woman and how men in Africa have six wives and all that mess."

"Sarah! Who laid down with who?" Jan walked to the door; Sarah didn't bother to get up.

"Shit, Jan. You're right, you're the one screwing him. I'm half-sorry, but it feels like my fucking life all over again. You said I could be honest. Well, it feels just like my life."

Outside, Jan fought her way through the air, still hearing Sarah's voice. I stroked her ears to make sure they were open wide. And I whispered too, told her where love lived and gave her the route to find it. Then I held the lamp close and wondered when she'd start to use her knife.

New Moleen

Wounded? Yes, but at least the child had started to show some color. Faint red beginnings of anger settled around the apartment so I tossed kindness over its root, hurt. What was left turned into so much dust, which I blew into a crevice. A little work done, I sat in the small corner window with its view of the lake. Jan played the tape she'd used in class the night before and wondered what Don would think of her apartment. True, the place is small, but insignificant was a poor description. Jan is surrounded by everything she loves.

Sand-colored grass cloth covers one wall with all the shades of lakefront mornings. In front of the wall, a platform she and Sarah built is covered in chocolate carpeting. On top of it, milk crates turned sideways are filled with albums a collector would fight for. A small table, from a garage sale, holds an old reel-to-reel with razors and a cutting grid for splicing tape. A long étagère shadows the wall in front of the two windows that look over a courtyard filled with towering oaks. Dried flowers, once fresh from Jessie's garden, are arranged in vases Jonathan made. In my corner there's a table for two with a view of the lake. A cute little Pullman kitchen is hidden by sliding double doors. Ada would be proud of the spices the child stocked. A sofa sleeper is sandwiched by end tables overflowing with books that call her hands some nights and take her into the early hours, where the sun may find a finger or two still between the pages. Small, but not empty, the emptiest space is the child's heart and only a growing spirit can fill that.

I watched her thoughts switch to Sarah and knew by the way the red deepened past anger and into love that they would last the argument. The points made by her friend were not forgotten, so I listened to the chatter of Jan's mind.

If that was only his studio, where did he live? She took Don's card out of her purse and dialed his number. After two rings, she hung up and stared at the receiver. She didn't want to unravel the morning and she didn't want to wait for her phone to ring, either. She remembered telling Jessie she'd come to Moleen on Sunday and decided she might as well leave now. She gathered a few things so that she could spend the night, and we headed for Moleen.

In the car, Jan switched radio stations until she found the old jazz station she'd listened to years ago. She wondered why love was always sitting quietly under the words the vocalists sang and sex was often the chair it sat on.

Jan eased her foot off the gas pedal, recalling the voices of women from those times. They formed words that bumped clumsily into one another. *Believe, and ask for what you want. We trusted ourselves. Be careful, he treated her badly, chil'. Humph, she didn't look out for herself. A hasty fool, that girl, walking around looking live but been long dead of a broken heart. . . .* Whispered bits of long drawn tales choreographed the tellers' lives. Pieces of the stories passed like cars in the lane beside the child. She'd heard these tales while women combed each other's hair, spoke carelessly into telephone lines, or delivered revelations in hushed tones as they handed a dollar or two out the side door for a woman in need when there was no man, or when a man had made no provisions. As far back as she could remember, women had helped one another with fifty cents for dry beans to go with salt pork, sent school field trip money down the street, offered encouragement that stayed past the gossip, but they hadn't been able to fix each other's hearts. Sarah was like that for her now.

Jan put on her turn signal and thought of Don. He was responsible for the memories so close she could smell hair frying and yeast rolls baking, and could hear the low rumble of black-eyed peas in the pot. She tried to see him in his studio surrounded with the busts, musty smells, and the damp, cold touch of clay as she took the exit to Moleen.

Only a few modern signs joined the majority of hand-painted advertisements—Sammy's Bar-B-Q, F & G's Groceries. From cracks on the sidewalks and along the median strips, grass grew out of the concrete. Trash collected against the railroad tracks. Old Moleen came first. Its taverns and liquor stores, busy in the late afternoon, caused Jan to remember early fall mornings. Corners would be cluttered with children on their way to school. Now the corners served as sofas, chairs, and walls for a sprinkling of adults well on their way to practicing a different type of education—how many drinks, guzzles, or swigs from a bottle covered in brown paper and tightly held would get you drunk enough to forget life in Moleen. She saw a few of the young boys Charles would have called rapscallions and the older ones that would make Jessie say, "I told you some of these Negroes would never get off of two heels and onto four wheels." They still balled their fists up tight, dug them down hard into the air beneath their hips, and swayed their thin chests from side to side. They called it pimping. Jan called it a lot of work for not having a car. I agreed. Old Moleen stretched its gray wood lean-tos, small brick three-room houses, and coveted two stories ahead of us. It was keeper of the fish house, taverns, and the corner store. Braking at the four-way stop sign, Jan avoided the eyes of the young men and looked straight ahead. "Hey, baby" called from a corner was the last thing she wanted to hear.

Jan turned down Fifth Avenue and passed the familiar streets: Rose, Berry, Stanton, then pulled up in front of her parents' house. Charles was in the driveway under the hood of his latest reinvention: a sky blue car with one white door. He lifted a hand and she returned the wave. It would be at least another hour before he admitted his eyes were too old to compete with the effects of a sunset. Jan entered the open side door of the house.

"What you coming back for? Fix that damn car so you can go. And I don't give a damn where you go or who you're with, either!" Jan stopped in the small hallway before the kitchen. Jessie's body filled the doorway, her wild eyes focused, she retreated.

"Jan." Dishwater dripped from her hands onto the floor. Jessie followed Jan's gaze to the small pools of water forming and began to wipe her hands on the white apron stretched tight across her body. "I thought it was your father." She fumbled with the apron so stained from use that, although clean, it appeared dirty.

"Mama, what's wrong?" Jan walked into the kitchen. As usual, boxes were in the corner, old newspapers were stacked high in two separate piles, and dishes almost toppled from the sink. Food was kept warm on the stove and a cake sat on the counter. Half of it was iced—chocolate swirled in intricate curlicues—the other half was plain. Two dark brown layers connected by unfinished icing.

"Sit down." Jessie's words came out in uneven tones. She brought the cake to the table. "Nothing wrong time ain't already fixed. Sit, sit. Don't worry 'bout me."

"What's wrong between you and Daddy, Mama?"

"Bet you're tired from that school and job. That'll be over soon." Jessie sighed.

"I know you don't want to tell me what's going on, but I want to know." Jan looked at her mother and around the kitchen, drifting back and forth in time. Moleen, her parents, and the house had the power to reduce her to a teenager, preteen, or even a toddler on a simple visit home.

"Two more years and you'll be finished." Jessie's voice bore into her thoughts, trying to change the subject. "I wished I'd done the same. You know, I finished high school and I really wanted to go to college, but you know how that went."

"No, I don't know how that went. What's wrong with you and Daddy?" Jan fixed her immature mouth and squinted her eyes just like she hadn't heard what Jessie was trying to say. She was thinking Jessie was set to ramble on about something in the past and was about to miss what linked her past to this day. Jan was just thinking what she could do to keep two old people together, like that was her job. If I could have talked to her outright I would have told her too, but mine was not to tell, and her time was like mine, a time to listen.

"Jan." Jessie sat down, relieved to be off her feet, her thoughts fluttering between Jan, herself, and Charles. She noticed how much Jan had grown up and consoled herself. The child wasn't yet a woman. Just 'cause you did some woman things don't make you no woman, she thought, smiling to herself. Life makes a woman. Its scars and how you take 'em make you a woman. Jessie decided she'd tell her story again and this time add the truth where she normally left cleaned-up tales. She'd told enough lies meant to save Charles and the fairy tale that Jan had built around him. "I wanted to go to college and I was smart, too. Everyone in Crawfordsville knew that, starting with my daddy. But when I moved up North, I found out you had to be more than smart."

Jan heard the tremble of her mother's voice, nudged back thoughts of Don, the morning, and the anger that was beginning to build around what she thought was Jessie's deception.

"Truth is, the Jews I worked for would've sent me to college, but I met your daddy and he didn't want me to go."

Jan remembered Jessie dropping hints when Charles was near. "If I had've gone to college like I planned. Would've been different if I got that education that was mine for the taking."

Now, Jessie stopped staring at the wall and turned to Jan.

"That's right. I guess you think your daddy is the world on a silver platter. Daughters do that. I did it myself, but I had a good daddy. Your father saw me coming from Georgia. I'd never been to the big city. He'd been in the city for enough years to have him a woman who knew more then than I know now. She treated him like a country bumpkin and I got stuck with what was left." Jessie grunted. "Truth is, what did I care? In a lot of ways, people do what they got to do, even if it means settling. I wanted to leave my aunt and uncle's house and I thought your father was my ticket, but I got on the wrong damn train." Her voice was low, coarse, almost growling.

Jan stuck a fingertip into a pool of icing on the plate near the bottom layer of cake but couldn't bring the sweetness to her mouth. Her spit turned sour and she tasted the way her parents had used each other to run from their own lives.

"What do you think of that, Jan? Does the truth help you any?" Her mother's voice began to steady itself. "It sure helped me to say it."

"Mama. I always knew something was wrong between you and Daddy, but I didn't know about school and what you wanted to do with your life. I don't think you should've let him stop you."

Jessie pushed herself back from the table and stood up. Jan watched the tears drop from her mother's eyes until Jessie put her hands under the apron and brought it up to her face. "All these women and their 'we can do anything' selves today, burning bras when it took some of us months to buy a brassiere. They didn't live in my time. Life wasn't yours for the taking and it really ain't like that now. I studied under the tree near the kettle with my daddy. You hear me? My daddy was called Professor Jack to everybody, including white folks. And he knew what any white-lawyer, half-brother, nigger-loving father knew 'cause he was taught. After I married your daddy, I still read and read into the night. I read books and I knew more than them bra-burning marchers know. I know all fifty-four volumes of *Great Books from Homer to Faulkner.* The shit I don't know."

Jessie walked over to the sink, turned on the hot water, and watched it rise around the dishes. Jan stood and rubbed her arms, hot as it was. She walked toward her mother. "What's going on now?" Jan reached for Jessie and Jessie pulled away.

"Your father cheated on me then, now, and I expect he'll do it in the future. All the while holding me back. Breaking me down and holding me back. Being cheated breaks a woman down, Jan. Just breaks her down." She tried to replace the words with nervous laughter.

Jan heard her father open the door.

"Look what the Windy City blew in." He joined the last bites of a laughter he didn't know the motivation for, holding up his oil-stained hands like trophies. "You need some oil? It's still light outside."

"No, Daddy. I don't need any oil." Jan tried to look at

him as if she were not his daughter. He was still attractive, too heavy, but handsome. *Who would he cheat with? A neighbor? A church biddy? What did it matter? Who wasn't as important as why, what would make him stop, and what they were going to do.* Jan wanted to know his side of the story and ask them both how much longer they were going to live in the same house without living with each other, but Jessie's hunched back hushed the questions.

"Girl, you know you ain't spent a dime on no oil or oil change. Did she, Jessie?" Charles didn't notice Jessie's back was trembling from a mixture of anger, grief, and lost pride. He didn't wait for an answer. "Pull that piece a car 'round to the driveway and let me change the oil before I wash up now." He turned and walked out the door.

Jan stroked Jessie's back, and both felt the goodness of touch, soft and hard at the same time. There were no new tears. "Mama, I'm sorry."

"I know you are. Me and you both. Remember I ain't no picnic and he ain't the worst man in the world; a helluva lot of 'em got him beat." Jessie wondered if she should tell Jan the rest of the story, then decided it didn't matter that she'd only told his side since he was the one with the most shit in the bag.

Jan walked over to the table, picked up her keys. "I'll be back. I'm going to take my car around to the driveway."

Outside, Jan started her car and considered the house, the yard, then a run along the lakefront, and the quiet of her own apartment. When she pulled away from the curb she thought about driving back to the city, then pulled into the driveway.

"Your car sounding like a truck, girl." Her father frowned. "Looks like I got my work cut out for me. If you got a boyfriend, he don't know nothing about cars, else he ain't trying to help you with yours."

"I don't have a boyfriend." Jan knew *boyfriend* was never going to be the right term for Don. "Daddy, how'd you meet Mama?"

Charles lifted the hood, hung a light underneath it, and used the time to aid him in the decision of where to begin. He wiped the dipstick, then pushed it into the motor to check the oil. He'd made so many rungs out of lies through the years until he'd climbed where love couldn't find him. I kissed the dimple in his forehead and hoped for courage.

"In my day, a southern woman knew how to make a man feel tall as an oak tree." Ruminations about his courtship days and the southern women he'd known played in his memory like bittersweet candies that begged to be savored. "Uhm." A low sound escaped and he decided the truth would have to be measured. Charles busied himself under the hood. Instead of the heat of the motor he could almost feel the hot, needy breath of women from days gone by, almost hear the voices that spoke as if they were willing to clear a path in front of him just for his being near. He looked good then, worked hard, and they wanted him.

When Charles had traveled back in time until he was close enough to step onto the hearth of so many yester-days, he recalled how he'd also learned about the opposite of a backwoods southern woman. A northern city woman could slick a man, run her fingers through his hair, wrap them tight, and politely snatch him bald-headed. Then she'd toss him away with her palms stretched out, ready for the next one. He shook his head, pretending to show his displeasure with the amount of oil in Jan's car. As his head moved from side to side, he mourned a greater loss.

When he met Jessie, he'd already been slicked. A city

woman with liquor on her daytime breath had stolen his
heart. She didn't cook, hardly cleaned, and could sit at a
card table all night after drinking him into the linoleum.
"Put Charles to bed." He'd hear her slurred speech. The
sound of cards slapping against the table and men, half-
or full-blown drunk, dragging their feet came to him as
plain as the wing nut in his hand. A couple of men
would walk him to the bedroom Lola shared with him
and God only knew who else. He shuddered a bit and
looked at Jan. He'd never wanted a child by Lola. If
she'd ever had one there wouldn't have been a coin with
enough sides to flip on who the father would've been.

Carefully, Charles tucked parts of the story away. On
Monday mornings, after the big card parties on Sunday
night and before he'd go to work, he'd look out the window while he shaved. "Yo' mama was a pretty girl," he
told Jan, "and I watched her from my window in the
morning. Figured she was nineteen at the most. Dolled
up in them light-colored suits. From my window I could
tell she wore real silk stockings by the way they caught
the light. She'd be strutting her way to the bus stop with
them skinny legs. I figured her up to be a 'Bama girl. She
walked that Alabama walk."

He laughed, paused, and pulled his crowbar out of a
crowd of tools. "Jan, I'm gonna have to change this oil,
not just add some. You running this car on mud." He
jacked the car up and remembered Lola snoring to beat
out a lumberjack. Then, he'd look through the part in
the curtains as much as he wanted. At first, that was all
he'd had the nerve to do. He imagined Lola and the
'Bama girl fighting over him and knew it would've been
too bad for the 'Bama girl. Lola woulda whipped her
right and left. And she was a high yellow, too. She
would've been black when Lola got finished with her.
The thought made him laugh out loud. "Oh, yeah. Yo'

mama was a fine piece of work, then." He covered the reason for his laughter.

Jan remembered pictures of Jessie. In formal attire, her perfectly manicured nails were showcased in gloves without fingertips. In most of those photographs, Charles wore a black suit or a tuxedo. His hand relaxed comfortably around her mother's waist or an arm draped protectively, even jealously, across her shoulders. They were always dressed well and their smiles, Jan was sure, weren't only for the camera. They must have loved each other, Jan thought as she ran her fingers through the grass. Charles lay on the crawler and scooted underneath the car, pushing his oil pan alongside.

Instead of the clinks in the pan and the draining of the oil, Charles heard the voices of those days, mornings when he rose early, dressed his best, and took to walking past the bus stop. At first, passing Jessie, he'd lift his hat polite-like. When she smiled, he thought of her as someone who needed protection. One good glance at her clothing told him she could afford to dress better than he did and it made him feel smaller than his robust frame. He'd tried not to think about that, but began to save for a new suit coat. He sized her up as a sophisticated colored girl, neat and proper. Her hair was combed as well in the back as it was in the front.

She wasn't the shortcut type. From her smile, he could tell a cigarette had never hung between the lips trimmed in just enough red lipstick. Charles began to practice his best English in front of the mirror when Lola wasn't home. When he finally mustered the nerve to speak, he asked Jessie where she was on her way to. He liked the way she didn't chop him up and say, "To work," but made a complete conversation out of the question.

"I took to changing my schedule. I'd stroll past the bus stop, tip my hat, and keep on. One day, I nerved my way up to speaking to yo' mama. She told me a whole truck full. 'I'm on my way to work at the Dotson home for children. I help the handicapped there.' Something like that." He recalled her words being clear and sailing smoothly through educated lips. After that they talked most days until her bus arrived. He found out she lived with her aunt and uncle and pictured her helping other people all day. He knew she must be kind and he developed a taste that grew into a hunger for some of that kind treatment.

Jan stretched out on the grass, pulled its blades, and watched her father's face. He'd elected to recall the good times, when a young woman and his youth had seduced him into happiness. Beneath the car, squinting to see what he was doing while his mind traveled back in time, his expression was so different from her mother's tears.

"I started to take her out after that, showed her the town like she didn't know then and ain't known since. Them was the days when we was young and, like they say, loose on the foot and fancy free."

He rolled out from under the car. "You sure don't know Tracy Dick about taking care of a car."

"It's Dick Tracy, Daddy."

"Not when I'm saying it. Archie Bunker ain't the only man can mess up a word or two." He grinned and walked into the garage, set the oil pan on a shelf, and reached for a quart of oil.

"Tell me about the footloose days, Daddy." Sitting up, Jan watched his face. "Were you in love?"

Charles looked down at the oil can and fumbled with the pull top.

"Were you in love?" Jan repeated.

"Oh, yeah," Charles said. "You don't marry somebody if you ain't in love." It was the first outright lie he could remember telling his daughter. But he rocked himself and thought that at least he'd done the things people in love would do.

He poured the oil, but saw beyond its thick blackness the young girl in bright suits who became his wife. Before the city slicked them both, he'd plotted their escape to the suburbs. By the time his daughter was born, she was growing up in a better place than anyone else he'd known. That was love, he told himself, and watched Jan pulling up the grass. He remembered her doing that same thing when she was little. Sit like that for hours, uproot grass, and think. He used to say, "If you'd move around, I wouldn't have to mow the lawn." He capped the valve cover.

"Get in and turn the ignition so I can check this oil." Jan crossed over to the car, opened the door, and started it. He watched every move and sway. Jan's gait jolted him. He knew how to watch a woman. He'd watched enough in his day. Done more than watched, too. He'd both picked cotton and planted the seeds. He knew when a woman would say yes, and when she was most likely to say no. He knew when a woman was ready to be picked and when too much picking had been done.

Charles bet himself Jan wasn't pulling up grass in the city with her spare time. She had a boyfriend quick as she said she didn't, and he must be no good or she would have been proud to tell about it. Some things you guessed and some things you just knew. Like he knew Jessie would treat him much better than city slicker Lola. But he hadn't figured on not being able to treat Jessie the same way. When he'd tried to treat her well, he couldn't. He'd never known a woman since Verga to give him such a gentle touch. Something inside of him snapped after a day or two of kindness.

Nowadays, Jessie didn't treat him well anymore and she really didn't look like something you wanted to be nice to. Fact was, she looked like hunks of lard before it was smoothed. She didn't dress well, put on whatever covered her skin, and he was sure she'd forgotten everything she knew about being neat. The house was a collection of junk and rags, barely a step up from a barn. Something edged up and asked him, had he done that to her?

"No," he answered aloud, opening the engine valve cover and pressing the darkness back. His voice was lost in the sound of the motor. What he'd done was move her to the suburbs, and that was an improvement over the life she would've had. The parts of the city he could afford and those that coloreds were allowed to live in would have been too rough. His family would have been different people if they'd been bound to a city life, his daughter talking street talk to survive. There, they'd never have been able to afford a nice free-standing house with a basement and a backyard. No. They would've lived in one apartment after another. "Okay, cut it off."

He checked the dipstick. "Damn car—needs more oil," he said, loud enough for Jan to hear. He wiped a drop of perspiration traveling down the side of his face with his sleeve, closed the hood, and took in the town around him. Moleen was not the city. It was quiet here. Charles, he thought, you didn't do so bad for a little black boy from the backwoods of Mississippi.

Behind the windshield, he could tell Jan was lost in another patch of thought and he added some of his own. Girl could've stayed right here at home, got all the education she needed, and slept in a decent bed at night. But she couldn't wait to run to the very place he'd tried to protect her from. He imagined her in the city now. The men she must've had already, how they'd used her. She didn't tell him this, but she didn't have to. He could see it in her eyes, in the way she moved. Every now and again, she would bring a scraggly home for him to meet. What the Sam Hill was he supposed to say? He knew what they were after. He'd wiggled his toes in those same boots.

I watched Charles shut the hood and ponder the child he wanted to tame, conceding that it was out of his reach now. Her day to day had been none of his business for a long time. All he could do now was hope she got that heap of education she wanted so bad. Maybe then she could find a man with as much or better education and who knew how to treat a woman. Yes, sirree, he thought. Since she wanted it so much, he wished for her the two things that seemed to be on her like a cocklebur: a big-time education and a man to match. Long as she didn't quit school from the pressure or get snagged by a no-count, she might make it.

I agreed for the most part, but there was something more he could do and I waited to see if he would do it. We felt the moment come, when he could tell the truth that would help the child. It rose up in him, made his head light, his chest heavy, and walked into his throat. Then he pushed it down, snuffed it, snipped it up until his heart blistered and it was small enough to hide.

He crossed the pavement and bent down near the window. He noticed Jan's face, smooth like a child's skin; the pimples and the spots they'd left were gone. He'd bet she didn't even have to smear pee 'cross it either. "Let's go get us a good eat." She was looking like Jessie used to, back in the times when he'd thought he'd met an angel. A beautiful face now, but soon it would start to wear from the life it was leading. More and more like Jessie, he thought, and turned away.

Jan got out of the car and followed Charles through the garage, slowing behind him. His knees sagged without straightening in between steps, his back tilted forward, and what was once an effortless gait were steps that seemed to cost much more. When they entered the kitchen, her mother had a plate of food on the table. The cake on the counter had been iced completely. "Want me to fix you something too, Jan?"

"No thanks, Mama. I'm so tired, I'm going to bed for a while. I'll eat something later. Thanks for changing my oil, Daddy." Jan walked down the hall, each step a regression in time, ending when she flopped down on the bed, next to her duffel and a set of towels. If it weren't for the items on the bed reminding her that she was a visitor, she would have sworn she was nine, ten, maybe thirteen, and living in a small corner of a town she'd tried so hard to get away from, only to be sucked back into its vacuum. Jessie's and Charles' voices were strained in the kitchen, each trying to keep its timbre safe. Jan swallowed a big gulp of air. *What could you believe? Who could you believe?* She remembered how Ada always said everybody had their own version of the truth. Jan got out of the bed and walked down the hall.

"You know what y'all could get?" Jan asked.

Jessie turned from the stove and Charles stopped chewing a piece of chocolate cake. I waited but the child's lips closed and only her inner voice spoke. *How about a daddy that stops cheating on the woman who used to do the Alabama walk and a mama that stops taking his shit?*

When Jan opened her mouth, silence came. I massaged her throat as she went back to the room that overlooked the garden, closed the door, and fought the silence by turning on the radio.

Sounds of Clay

"*H*ey, babe, tried to reach you over the weekend. Night and day. I know I couldn't have met you before someone else had, but that's cool. I'm here when you want me."

Jan smiled, stood, and peeped over her cubicle. The office was full even though the day had just started. "It's not a problem, I think we can work that out."

"I see, you can't talk."

"Of course, I'd be happy to take care of that for you."

"I gotcha, babe. You get an hour for lunch?"

"Yes, that's correct."

"Why don't I pick you up for a quick meal, babe?"

"That'll be fine."

"I know the building. I'll be waiting downstairs at noon."

Don was double-parked in a large red van. Jan climbed in. Behind her, several busts of women were secured in slatted crates against the walls. "Hey, D.J. I got us some fast food. Figured we could go back to the studio and talk."

"Sounds good." Jan smelled the fried shrimp, picked up the brown bag, and grabbed a few fries. Don took a fry before it reached her mouth.

"So who was feeding you this weekend?"

"I fed myself. What about you?"

"I worked as hard as I did this morning. Some banks and office buildings pay me to set up shows in their lobbies. I just finished breaking down an exhibit, so I'm taking the girls home."

Jan glanced at the crates behind them. Don turned down Superior and searched for a parking space. "Babe, with you working and going to school and me putting in every hour I can get at the studio, then being out there in the street with my work, we're going to have to talk things out, figure out when we can see each other." He pulled into a space near the studio, reached over, and traced her profile with his finger. "I guess we've got to get to know each other a li'l bit better than Saturday."

When they reached the building, Don led the way into the stairwell.

"Home sweet home," Don announced, opening the studio door.

Jan saw a box of cereal on the counter. Maybe he did live in the studio. She slipped her arms around his waist from behind.

"So my girl was away for the weekend."

"I'm here now." She whispered the words in short kisses across his back. Lunchtime was usually eating with or without Sarah. Sometimes, to vary the days, they walked along the river. Now, she imagined being in Don's studio; him missing her and admitting it; the way he relaxed to the touch of her lips and her breath on his back.

"Mmmmm." He turned around and moaned into her throat. "I thought about you all weekend and it's cool, babe. I don't want to know where you've been. I'm not trying to compete with the college boys."

Don stroked her shoulders, easing his face along the side of her neck. "Let me slow it down," his voice a staccato between kisses. Stooping, he opened her blouse, then continued to lower himself until he circled her navel with his tongue. "When you come to me, I want to slow your world down. Slow mine down, too. Take us to the same place. Go with you. Make sure you get there."

They lay close to each other, inhaling the short breaths between them.

Don added words to break the silence interrupted by soft spurts of air. "Babe, we've got to be realistic about who we are and what we believe." Jan rested against him, feeling the boomerang of her own breath, her face almost smothered in his chest. His arms met around her lower back, making the pallet on the floor bearable with the cushion of his body.

"I don't care how different we are. We're artists. I have my music, you have your sculpture." She liked the sound of her voice, assuming it was older, more mature.

It was a new voice, but I knew it was not the right one.

"It's not only the art, babe. I live with a woman." His words sliced the tenderness left hanging in the air into tiny shards. She felt his body retract. His arms still held her, her breasts still rested against his torso, but the best part of him was gone. Intangible and disappeared.

"We've lived together for a while," he continued as if she wanted to hear about a woman who held the place she thought might belong to her. "No marriage, babe, and there's not going to be one. We have separate lives but we respect each other. My days and my art belong to me. I spend my nights there."

Where is there? Jan asked herself, knowing it was someplace off-limits, her body still pulsing with the inner beats left behind from the sex that had flowed between them like water. She didn't want to share any of it.

"What happened in your classroom when you put on your show and what we have now is real. I'll always respect that. I'll always respect the time we spend and give you any freedom you need."

It sounded like a bad campaign speech, designed to cause her to accept him or move on. The child had never started a relationship knowing a man belonged to someone else, and was lying there thinking, it was obvious he wanted to be with her now. He couldn't be too content with the other woman. Besides, most men were attached to another woman when they met someone new. The difference was they lied about it. At least Don was being honest. He even thought she had someone else and that didn't bother him.

She looked at the women on the wall and wondered who they really were. Did they represent real women like the *Lips* bust would represent her when it was completed? The sculptures stared back. She remembered the way the others looked in the van. Parts of their faces peered through the slatted crates like prisoners in cells.

I saw the knife meet flesh and separate it from the first layer of her spirit. Competing voices rose and fell until their sounds collapsed into one another. Specks of colors seemed to surround them and dance in the light that entered the studio. She was sleepy and it all felt like a dream with the busts on the shelves moving toward her, then further away.

"So, D.J., what'll it be? You and me for the time we have or a wonderful morning and afternoon we'll both remember?"

Autumn Heat

*S*ummer ended; sap withdrew from the leaves of the oak trees in the courtyard outside Jan's apartment. I watched trees pull their food down into the roots until leaves traded verdant greens for ripe lemon yellow, red, rust, then folded into an autumn brown and fell from the oaks. Sometimes trees had to sacrifice limbs to feed the roots through winter, knowing they could start over in spring, when branches got so full they hung weighted in cypress, cucumber, and emerald green leaves by summer. In the dreams I explained this to Jan. It took a year, the child's color deepening, changing, falling, feeding, growing, and coming back again stronger. I waited, since time was the gift I could give most free.

Jan stirred the package of cream into her coffee and wished she could ignore the phone lines that blinked in front of her. She reminded herself that her classes were going well and she only had one more year to answer customer complaints before a college degree would propel her, at best, to a radio station; and at the least, somewhere beyond what she thought were mindless days.

Listening to an exasperated woman on the line, she filled out the standard form and decided not to tell the woman that if she'd simply moved the vacuum cleaner cord from under the motor, she would've saved them both time and bother.

Jan worked through the first hour of the morning, cast

the necessary smiles at her supervisor, and rolled her eyes in agreement with the isn't-this-a-dumb-job looks of her peers. When she stood to freshen her cooled coffee, the last line on the phone rang. Jan was relieved. It wouldn't be another customer. It would be an in-house call or Don.

"I'm showing an exhibit in a bank on the South Side, but I started to think about you." No salutation, Don. Jan sat down and began to write on the message pad, hoping no one around her would realize this was the type of call that usually preceded her rushing off to lunch and sometimes returning later than she was supposed to.

"I started to want you and I couldn't control that." She underlined the words: *lover, listener, good advice,* then circled *why share?*

"I want to pick you up for lunch." Don's voice always directed every syllable toward her alone. She wrote *VOICE* in capital letters. Then, as she had done once or twice a week for more than a year, with very few exceptions, she gave him another variation of yes.

"That'll be fine."

"Mmmm, huh. It'll be more than fine. A good lunch, sweetie. I'll pick you up at noon. Won't be a minute late. Thank you."

Jan called Sarah to cancel their lunch.

"Sorry. I just got the information." She continued to speak in the code devised to keep the workers around her from knowing about her "lunch" plans.

"Knock yourself out," Sarah returned.

Jan tore the piece of paper into small pieces and put it in the basket under her desk.

A few minutes before noon, she crossed the shade of the building, walking into the sunlight toward the van where Don was waiting. When he saw her, he leaned over and pushed the door open. "Hey, babe."

"I'm hungry. I didn't bring lunch and you're going to have to feed me today," Jan said, climbing into the van. Oil spots were already seeping through a brown bag on the seat next to her. Don grinned. Jan opened the bag and unwrapped an Italian beef, a crusty Italian roll moistened with the beef's juices and topped with crunchy light-green peppers, marinated carrots, and cubes of celery.

Several clay faces wrapped in sheets of plastic and secured in their slots around the wall of the van offered muted stares. As Don pulled into traffic, he teased, "I told you it would be a good lunch, babe. Hurry up and eat."

Jan bit into the sandwich.

"You come to me sometimes, no matter where I am." He reached across the seat and swiped a pepper off her sandwich. "How's my D.J.'s classes?"

"I'm doing well. Three A's," Jan said, her mouth full. "I told you that last week."

"I know," he lied. "I like to hear it. Smart, fine, and at least I got a part of it."

"I'm a person, Don." Jan wiped her mouth with the napkin. "Not a fraction." She watched the people walking along the river.

"When we're together, you get all my attention, babe." Don touched her cheek. "You seen your folks lately?"

"I'm going this weekend."

"What about your aunt?"

"I called her last night."

"Did she tell you to cancel the ol' artist yet?"

"Not yet." Jan knew what I knew. Ada wasn't going to offer advice that wasn't asked for, especially when the person who needed to ask already knew the answer.

"Good," Don said, parking in front of the loft.

When Jan rolled over and looked at her watch, it was barely twelve-thirty P.M. What used to take a full hour during the week and all afternoon on Saturdays had been reduced to an exhausting thirty minutes. The child groped with sleepy fingers around the pallet in search of her panties and pants. Don was already standing by the window and called for her to join him. Through dingy panes, the barely traveled street rested below. A man carried boxes from the trunk of his car to an open doorway; a woman who seemed to belong somewhere more exotic crossed the street.

"See the woman walking this way?" Jan guessed the stranger was in her mid-thirties. She nodded and waited for Don's usual commentary. Something would be said about the eyes, the bone structure, or another feature. She was more interested in the woman's African attire: a printed tunic-style dress with pants to match. Jan admired the neat rows of braids that ended somewhere down the woman's back. When she turned her attention to Don, he was unusually quiet. He hadn't begun to talk about the placement of the woman's eyes, or what cheekbones that pulled away from the face instead of pulling toward the nose and eyes meant to a sculptor.

"That's the woman I live with," Don announced. Jan stepped back from the window and walked over to the pallet on the floor. When she bent down to pick up her purse, she could still smell the scent from their being together, sour, sweet.

"Don, what are you trying to prove?" Jan didn't wait for an answer. Don picked up his pace behind her and followed her to the door. The faint spirits against the wall began to snicker, hollow tee-hees from nervous memories. I joined Jan. Don slowed her departure by turning her toward him.

"I don't have anything to prove. She knows to buzz." He kissed Jan and opened the door. "Thanks. I'm glad we got together, babe. Take the stairs. Everything'll be cool."

Motherfucker! Jan screamed in her mind. There was no time to scream at Don. *Stairs! Sharing was one thing, confrontation another. And thanks for what? The possibility that I could be in the middle of a hair-yanking fistfight?* Jan took a few hurried steps away from the door as it closed behind her, but was mesmerized into a standstill when she heard Don answer the buzzer.

"Hey, babe." He'd used the same chords when he'd spoken to her less than an hour ago.

"It's me," the woman said, a lightness that lived next to laughter dancing in her voice.

"So what else is new, babe. It's always you. Come on up."

The buzzer sounded. Jan didn't move. Her color raged, anger swirling around her like flies. Maybe she'd walk up to the woman and tell her, *Hello, my name is Jan and I've been sleeping with Don for a year. How about you? How long have you been with him? Could we trade, I take nights for a year? You could have lunchtime, a weeknight once a month, and every other weekend.* That was foolish, she decided. She didn't need a confrontation, or Don with her every night. Jan's mind and body finally began to work together. She started for the stairs. Creaks that sounded the opening of the elevator began. Jan tiptoed over to the stairwell and pushed the door open as softly as she could. Slipping into the dim stairwell, she clutched the edge of the door to keep it from clapping shut. Creating a wedge with her fingertips, she could see a profile of the woman's smooth nutmeg complexion, framed by the peeling gray paint around her. A face without any makeup, one clear brown eye, and two half lips much slimmer than her own. When it was safe to close the door and walk down the stairs, Jan could still hear the flap-clack of the woman's ankle-strapped sandals. It sounded like her heart.

Outside, Jan felt chilled even though the sunlight, humid air, and quickening pace of the city only added heat to a day that had been muggy since morning. Jan glanced at her watch and decided she'd rather be late than take a taxi. She needed the time and the pace of the walk to help her think. If the woman had confronted her, what would she have done? Don must have known his live-in was coming. Why had he been so calm? The answers didn't matter; the worst outcome had happened. She could put a face to the woman whose space she kept nestling into.

I could not calm the child, only watch her color race back to her father, swim around her mother and the young boys and men in her memory.

Jan walked across the bridge over the Chicago River. To the west, the steel-beamed bridges formed intermittent paths over the water until they meandered out of sight. They reminded her of Moleen, a place to get across and out of. Everybody there continually placed one foot in front of the other, leading to more of the same. Then the thought turned and formed a picture before her. The green yards and gardens didn't look any different from the skyscrapers and her studio apartment. She was still living the same life she'd run away from. This time it wasn't a family and a community that she had no control over, it was a man she'd allowed in her life, knowing from the beginning he'd never be what she wanted.

It didn't matter that he listened to her or acted as if he understood her. Don had never fit into her plans. Still, a summer, fall, winter, and spring had passed and he was back again with summer, taking up space while she lived out time, existing like all her former neighbors. Jan crossed into the shade of the office building, grateful for the air-conditioned interior. She needed to visit Ada, sit with her awhile, calm herself, and try to listen to some-one that could help her make sense out of her world.

At the office, she fiddled with some papers, made a few phone calls, and fussed around at her desk long enough to establish her return. Then she called Sarah. They agreed to meet in the bathroom. Sarah was check-ing the stalls when Jan arrived.

"All empty, feel free to chat," Sarah said.

"I have a discovery," Jan said, feigning calm. She re-laxed against the counter.

Sarah waited and I saw her hope building, wanting Jan to be okay, better even. Nerves lit the cigarette, love and hope listened.

Jan told her friend what had happened during lunch, ending with the revelation that she didn't really want Don day and night. All she wanted was a little more time before she moved on.

We heard Sarah's cigarette crackle. Red, then gray ash tapped into the tray.

"What's wrong?"

"Jan." Sarah contemplated the risks of telling the truth, then did what I expected. "I guess this is the part where I have to be honest again."

"Go on."

"I really don't understand this so-called relationship at all."

"Don fills a gap, Sarah. I guess he's comfortable. He doesn't ask for much. He gives me good advice about school and the job. We talk to each other and we listen." Jan's voice trailed off, fading on her own omission.

"Jan, I think I've given you my opinion enough times and you don't get it." Sarah walked away from the counter and stood in front of a stall to face Jan. "I'll be real clear. You're being used for nothing more than 'lunch.' The real deal is this: the man lives with another woman." She exhaled a long funnel of smoke away from them, then folded her arms and waited for Jan's response.

"Sarah, I know that. Aren't you a little late with this 'stick up for the other woman' attitude?"

"Wrong! I told you how I saw it when you called after your so-called interview. The next morning, before we could meet and talk face to face, you'd already slept with an ex-convict who was cheating on his live-in. It was a little after the fact to express myself then, wasn't it? And in case you haven't noticed, I've been sticking up for the real other woman from the beginning." Sarah pointed at Jan.

"I didn't know he was living with another woman before I got involved."

"You found out soon enough. You certainly spent enough time going to 'lunch' to know you were at a dead end." Sarah lowered her voice and stepped closer to Jan. "You spend so much time thinking about how you can change the relationship; what Don should do for you; how are you going to get more time with him. What about your own life? When have you seen your aunt? What's important to you now? Where are all of the things and all the people who used to be important?"

Jan knew it had been months since she'd seen Ada and several weeks since she'd called her parents. "I called my aunt last night and I'm going to see my parents this weekend." Thoughts like she could make Don spend more time with her, and maybe even take him away from the woman if she wanted to, bumped into the words about Ada.

"You keep calling Ada, Jan. But you don't visit. I guess you've got to stay close to your apartment in case Don calls. Who's the convict now? You're about to put yourself in a situation that could place your name in the obituary column and all you can come up with is some lame revelation that you don't really want that much more time. I could've told you that! Jan, you're not even in love. Is that supposed to make it okay? Try telling that to the woman with the braids." Sarah unfolded her arms and walked to the counter to retrieve another cigarette from her purse.

"Look, Sarah," Jan's head ached and her heart fluttered. She couldn't even form a curse word in her mind. *Convict*. She looked at herself in the mirror. "Let's just drop Don from our conversations. We can say it's my business and I'll deal with it."

In a much lower, composed voice, Sarah continued. "Okay, Jan, that's fine. But how 'bout making sure I don't get another call at three A.M., when you've been stood up, you're lonely, and still trying to figure your life out?" She looked directly into Jan's eyes and said, "Since I'm out here on a limb, I might as well finish. Not talking about Don doesn't mean shit. You really need to get it together, Jan."

Jan picked her purse up off the counter and turned to leave. Sarah watched Jan's back slump despite the way she pushed against it. Don was every man Sarah hated; her father for not being stronger than her mother, her ex-husband, and every ex after that.

Sarah decided against another cigarette and clenched her fists against her sides. "Grow up and stop hiding. This relationship is taking all of your time and giving you so little in return. We barely talk about anything else other than Don. I might have a problem or need to talk, too. A man who's good for you doesn't prevent that. But Don's become something more than a man for you, Jan. He's like a contest." Sarah walked back toward the sink. "Before this gets so ugly it screws up our friendship, let me tell you something I've been thinking about for a long time. Just listen."

Jan put her purse down. Sarah leaned against the counter and faced Jan.

"You've always been the positive one. I'm bitter and I know it. I've got a reason. I was in love, so I raced down the aisle right after graduating from high school. David was older, had what I thought was a good job, and Jonathan was on the way. I didn't know what I was doing, but everything started out fine. I lived the suburban life, had a child, cleaned, kept a house, and thought I'd made all the right choices." Sarah massaged her temples with one hand.

"When David stopped talking to me about anything that mattered, I was afraid. Then he stopped eating the food I spent half a day to prepare, ignored Jonathan most of the time, and forgot that his body belonged in our bed. I freaked." Sarah paused, her profile multiplied in the mirrors around them. "Jan, I've got a right to be pissed off and bitchy. I try to control it, but sometimes I can't. My life, Jonathan's life, changed."

Jan watched the tears press against the corners of Sarah's eyes. She'd never remembered Sarah crying in front of anybody; Sarah was always in charge. Jan did remember her inhaling pot like she was trying to sip more life into a space bigger than her lungs, but no outright tears.

"You used to be different. You always had something upbeat to say. Sometimes I thought if there was anybody worth finding, you'd map out a plan. You wanted so much for yourself." Sarah shook her head. "But ever since you've been dealing with Don, I've been put in the position of defending you as the other woman and you've been slipping into your own little world.

"I've tried not to think it, but I really feel that you're no better than the sorry excuses for women that screwed David without the good sense to figure out that he wouldn't do any better by them than he did by me. He was an asshole, but there were women out there hurting me right along with him and they never even knew my name. I hung with that shit for a long time because I was in love and I had a child. Jan, you're not even in love and you know it. So what are you doing with your life?"

Jan was quiet and I saw her colors reach back to Charles again.

"I can't lie about what I'm going to do, but whatever I do in the future, all I can promise is I won't mention Don." Jan picked up her purse. "I'm going back to the grind now and I'll stop by on Saturday."

Sarah followed Jan to the door.

"Jan. I'm sorry. If you considered men and sex sport, that would be one thing. But you're wrapped too tight for that, so you're gonna hurt yourself." Sarah smiled. "Come by on Saturday. Jonathan's been asking about you."

"Good. Tell him I've been thinking about him, too. I'll be by." They hugged and Jan whispered, "Sarah, I promise to have an open ear about your life."

I could have kissed Sarah, hugged her too, but I was busy hanging on to Jan. The child's mind was like an escalator going both ways. Why to hold on, why to let go. But I knew what would happen. She could never finish a thing until it was done.

Perennials

*J*an nestled into the cushions, shifted, then sat up on the sofa bed and pulled the comforter around her until she got it just so. Late autumn had issued cooler days. Her hands, losing the deepened brown of summer, picked up the phone and dialed Ada.

"Mama Ada."

"The cat's got two big eyes."

"I want to know how you're doing."

"I'm the same. Blessed and in high favor. I know Jessie and Charles are good, because I talked to them yesterday and ever since I've been feeling your curiosity. Who is it? You or someone else?"

"It's the artist."

"You and the artist. Ummm."

"Well, it's not working out." Jan was good for an understatement.

"Do you want it to work out?" Ada paused, taking the top off the candy jar near her telephone. We both knew the child was taking too long to answer. "Jan, men and women can love each other, but first they've got to be men and women all by themselves." Jan heard the cellophane crinkle as Ada unwrapped a peppermint, and I listened to them both try to straighten things out with the truth.

"Mama Ada, sometimes I get tired of looking." Jan sat up in bed, leaned forward, and noticed the afternoon sky. It was the kind of day when blue is so beset with the white of clouds, it emits the odor of rain.

"Then stop looking so hard and maybe you'll be able to see." Ada placed the lid back on the jar. "Now, the cat got your tongue?"

"Just thinking."

"Then think, Jan. Pray. Meditate, if that's what you young people are calling it these days. You have all the answers but be careful not to see what you want to see. See the truth."

"Ummm."

"God's got order, Jan. Even if it doesn't look like it. Sometimes a lesson belongs to you until you learn it. And believe me, anything pruned will come back thicker."

They lived in the silence for a few breaths.

"Love you, Jan."

"Love you too, Mama Ada."

Fall fell to winter's first cold winds. When remnants of their gusts whistled through the cracks of the loft windows Don hadn't bothered to patch, Jan sat near the cooling kiln, wrapped in a blanket. "Since we're up front with everything, Don, I thought I should let you know I'm going to be dating other men." His reflection rested on the glass door of the kiln. He hadn't shaved and a tiredness glazed the whites of his eyes. The calm that usually followed their being together didn't change.

"Look, babe, a long time ago, when I told you I'd be your back door nigger, that's what I meant. I don't have all those 'we're going steady' views the college boys have." He worked the clay, kneading, prodding. Grayish white stains spread over his hands. "I'm not sitting at home worried that you might be out with someone, upset because you don't belong only to me. I don't belong to you, either."

Jan envisioned the woman he did belong to, her complexion, the African dress, a cascade of braids.

I don't belong to you, either. The words sounded the way the men she'd met in jazz clubs with Sarah looked. How-many-dates-until-we-go-to-bed was the expression engraved on their faces, and their mouths opened to reveal standard fare, nothing beyond résumé information. Not even the why-you-chose-that-field or what-turned-you-on-to-jazz were mentioned. Different men, same thing. Jan unwrapped the blanket from around her and put her shoes on. She put on her coat and Don reached for his coat and keys.

"I want to walk back, Don, don't bother." She moved quickly to the door. Don began to speak but Jan left anyway, closing the door behind her.

By the time Jan crossed the bridge we both heard what Don said and what he didn't have the courage to utter. No, he did not belong to her, but she could tell he wanted to feel as though he was more than a "back door nigger." I remembered calls in the middle of the day. She remembered many times as they lay on the floor together when her eyes opened before his. The face she saw showed his words to be lies. He'd practically begged her back after she'd seen the woman he lived with. Explanation that he and his live-in had an "open" relationship only challenged the woman-child. I watched stubborn feet walk across the bridge, determined to test her theory. Even if she didn't see anybody else, if he wanted to see her, he'd have to visit her on weekends now. That's what she'd demand and see how far he was willing to go. But stubbornness can't hold a candle to willpower.

A few weeks later Jan was sitting at her desk, thinking that weekends with Don weren't all that satisfying either. She pulled the envelope that held her midterm grades out of her purse. Three A's. After winter break she'd start her final semester. The last line at her desk rang.

"Babe, let's keep celebrating the good news 'bout those A's. I'll pick you up at noon, okay?"

"That's already been taken care of, but thanks for calling."

"That's fine, babe. Whenever you have the time, I'll be here."

The next time she went to the studio, she avoided the pallet on the floor.

"Look, babe, we don't have to make love every time we see each other. It's cool to share your space. Now, what's on your mind?"

"I've started looking for work, Don, sending résumés out to ads in the papers, making calls, going on interviews. It's time for me to change some things about my life."

"Am I included in that change, babe?"

"Eventually."

"Okay, babe."

Jan walked back to the office over slush-covered streets. The morning's white snow had dirtied by early afternoon. Skies more gray than blue created days that ran together. Winter stuttered, reluctant. Snow and biting cold were followed by sixty-degree days, then sleet and more snow. Now, it was thawing again. Jan was perturbed. I watched her face twitch and sensed her frustration. At night I entered her dreams and told her about the beauty of water sinking into the ground to nourish the earth for spring.

A few days later, Jan waited for Don outside the office. That morning she'd watched the snowplows take what was left of the street's snow and ice and dump it on the curb. Now, at noon, it was gone. She spent some good time thinking about how Jessie would be looking out the window and imagining the rows of crops she'd plant not too many weeks from now.

"What's on your mind?"

"Men."

"I didn't know I had so much company." Don grinned and didn't realize the child wanted to slap him. Instead she told a truth followed quickly by a lie.

"You don't yet. Two men asked me out and I don't know if I want to go out with either one of them. I'm tired of your species, Don."

"Go out with both of them. Enjoy life, babe. Keep looking for whatever it is you're trying to find." Don laughed. "Don't think this is good-bye and don't shut me out. Like I said, I'll be your back door nigger." His laugh was full, his sound covering the groan that escaped her lips, but I watched the hurt fall down into her spirit.

"I don't want a nigger and I don't want anybody coming through my back door."

"That's right. When these other niggers complain, say their car is overheating in the summertime. Say it's too cold out in the winter. The brothers complain about how there's too much snow, they don't have four-wheel drive and all that. Call me. I'll climb the telephone pole and scale the wires for you, babe."

"Don, you haven't climbed or scaled a damn thing to get to me."

Don didn't hear Jan. Her voice was too low, and he was still laughing.

We watched spring come in rushes of white-capped water heaving itself against the lakefront. When Jan went running, she pressed away valleys with her feet and took in the sky. She still met Don in the middle of the day and sometimes he came by for a few hours on the weekend. There was nothing real satisfying about that.

They didn't go anywhere, just listened to her music. He brought her lunch. They slept together. We shared these thoughts as Jan became short of breath. Slowing her run, a rhythm moved into her legs. She felt her feet sink into the sand, then lift and sink again. So Don sacrificed a few hours every other weekend. She felt like Sarah's son, Jonathan, waiting for David's visits. Jan slowed to a walk and noticed the tufts of grass sticking up in patches and remembered how Jessie would always talk about the resilience of grass, how it survived hard winters of ice and below-zero cold and at times looked brown and dead, but turned green every year just the same. "It's the roots, Jan. Grass is like people. You can put them through a lot as long as their roots are good." Jan turned and started to run back toward the apartment, thinking about how Charles made sure the grass stayed green through summer's heat. She thought of Jessie's tulips getting ready to bud. She wondered if they would bloom and even die before she was finished with whatever Don meant in her life. She was "lunch" on the weekend or during the week. If Don wanted to screw her she could screw him back. If she didn't want to, she'd watch him, listen to him, talk to him, then return to work or tell him she had to work on an assignment for school or had an errand to run for Sarah, a visit to her parents, any old lie. She ran on the energy from pretending the lack of commitment didn't bother her, then connected it to what happened in the night. It was as if her thoughts formed the recurring dream: she'd be cooking dinner, rubbing a man's back, or feeling him rub her own. Sometimes she'd be underneath this man, and still she couldn't see his face.

The days dragged, then flew together. Time tapped her on the shoulder, then straightened her back, ached her fingers. She itched with spring and found out about the soul's fever. Jan looked out the windows of Don's studio as pellets of rain thrashed against them.

"I keep having the same dream."

"Shoot, babe. What happens?"

"Well, I'm with a man, but I can't see his face."

"That doesn't surprise me."

"Why?"

"You haven't found the one you're looking for."

Jan walked over to Don, who was unwrapping a bust, and turned him around until they faced each other.

"Are you looking for someone?"

"No," he answered. "Confinement is not for people, babe. Animals don't belong in cages."

"I'm not an animal! You're not an animal."

"I'm an animal and so are you."

I watched them play out the habit they had recently formed. Don would talk, steady, quiet, controlled. Jan would get to thinking until she worked herself into an outrage and then the thoughts would come out in anger. Now, in the strange amber light of the studio, she realized she didn't like the way he looked; ill-kept and aging. She didn't like the way he kept calling her "babe" or the way he talked with his back turned to her as he molded the clay. His mouth, even if it burrowed itself into her secret places, had no distinction except that it spoke an honesty to her. Not that it was the honesty she wanted. It was his version of the truth and in it she saw him, an artist growing old, spread thin by greed and selfish living. Don was a man caught with his emotions in too many places for any one woman ever to have enough. She was glad she didn't love him.

Now, and for days after, the thoughts dressed her until her clothes were buttoned and freedom waited for her outside the door. At night, the dreams came more frequently and transformed themselves into nightmares. I danced freely in them now as she opened up and made a space for me. I spiced the thoughts with words that she remembered and they returned to her during the day.

When she was alone, waiting for Don, the words came in whispers, almost audible tones, and lately they were so clear she often wondered if she were awake or asleep. The voices didn't sound like her own. She identified Ada, Jessie, and Sarah, but there were some other women speaking she was sure she didn't know. This made me smile and add my two cents all the more. We spoke in stories and tales about other women or ourselves going back and forth in time. Sometimes the child saw and heard things she knew she'd once witnessed but could only remember parts of.

She saw a young woman with an older man who treated her kindly. The woman was petite, the man tall, and when he touched her you could see their love. She heard the sound of the wind and in it a voice that said, "He's always loved you." Ada's voice repeated the word *inside*. At the end of the dream the visions of different women faded into colors brighter than anything she could recall. Only some of the voices remained and the child thought they seemed to belong to the colors, which brightened when they shouted directives: Stop it. Fight back. Run. Get out. Destroy it. Kill it. Then the colors faded until she wondered if there had ever been such colors, voices, and dreams at all.

Jan crossed off the days leading up to her graduation; twenty-one days left. She decided to call Ada, then visit her parents that weekend to share the news. On Friday, Don picked her up for lunch. As soon as she was settled in his studio, the voices started up again, but she quelled them with a request of her own. "Don, I want to celebrate my graduation with you. You can come to the ceremony and maybe we can go out the night before." She tried to make the request seem natural, as if Don would ever make a public appearance along with her mother and father.

"Graduation ceremonies? Go out?" Don questioned. "That sounds like a date. I thought we got that straight a long time ago. I don't go out."

"Why not? You don't mind cheating on the woman you live with."

"I'm not cheating. We have an understanding." Don stared at the child like she was crazy.

The voices didn't use words this time. Instead, laughter in all different pitches seemed to burst from the cold clay faces of the sculptures all around the walls. The dreams, the voices, the colors, and now daytime thoughts of cackling sculptures reminded her of the spirits Ada saw and talked about. She believed Ada could see things no one else she knew could see and was spoken to as well, but Jan wasn't completely sold on spirits for herself. She didn't believe she'd ever see what Ada could but she was hearing voices and seeing colors. Jan shook her head as if to toss away all these things. Spirits didn't make sense for her. They could belong to Ada and the people from her times, but not a college graduate. It was nonsense, she decided, but the thought of the laughter made her groan.

"Are you okay, babe?" Don enclosed the sides of her face in his hands. "I'm proud of you graduating, so don't think I'm not. I don't do the public thing, that's all. But if you want to stay in the night before graduation, then I think I can pull some strings and stay in with you."

"That'll be fine, Don." Let the woman with the braids spend a night alone, she thought, and closed her eyes, leaning into him. The colors behind her lids danced.

"It's finally going to happen." Jessie smiled over a row of collards, their young, slick, green sprouts a few inches above the ground.

"Yes, Mama. I'll be finished with school in three weeks. I've had a lot of job interviews and I've got a few second round interviews already." Jan realized that the woman on her hands and knees in the garden was more familiar with the collards than any interviewing process. She looked past Jessie and over as much of the town as the garden view allowed, then interrupted the earth-toiling sounds of her mother with a voice unable to hide its owner's relief. "I guess I'm on my way."

Jessie stopped planting seeds long enough to rub her lower back and draw the apology that followed out of Jan's eyes.

"My daddy would be proud of you," Jessie said, freeing a clump of dirt from her hands. "He would've come to your graduation in a big hat and a new pair of shoes." She laughed and turned her attention back to the soil.

"Will you and Daddy come?" Jan asked, doubting they would since Jessie had barely gone beyond her garden and house in well over a year now and was more given to recalling the past than addressing the present.

Waiting on her answer, Jan felt her gym shoes receive a fresh smattering of dirt. When she looked in the direction of her mother's hands, she saw a garden snake a few inches away from her mother's knees. Whispering, she alerted her mother.

"Shh." Her mother's voice was barely audible as she hushed Jan and mouthed, "That's my snake."

Jan wanted to ask, *What do you mean, your snake?* But in the sunlight that poured over the garden and cast shadows of an older woman on her knees and one younger, still, silent, and fearful of a snake no more than a foot long, Jan took her mother's advice. Temporarily mute, her sense of hearing increased until she could hear birds rifling through the trees across the street, a child's frustrated cry in the distance, and the soft brush of a slight summer wind making its way through the willow branches behind her. The snake sucked water from a pan near a row of onions, then headed back the way it had come.

After its disappearance, Jessie's voice ebbed softly over the row of collards. "You may think it's crazy, but that snake comes here every day and does the same thing. I leave the water for him. It's something my daddy used to do." Jessie took a rag out of her duster pocket and wiped her face, dug a hole with her index and third fingers, then inserted a seed from the pouch.

"In the Bottom, believe it or not, we had a nice place. Mulberry trees and white oaks with trunks so wide it would take me and two of my older sisters holding hands to circle one of them. One year when I couldn't have been more than ten or so, a king snake found its way into our house. We heard it move behind the walls at night. My daddy got quiet and prayed about it, but it scared us girls something awful. When he finished praying, my daddy told us the snake would be kind, wouldn't hurt us, would kill mice and protect us from all other snakes. He said that's why they called the snake a king snake. We had to trust our father. I did. Not Sadie, my oldest sister. Sadie swore if Daddy died before she did, she'd kill that snake."

Jessie opened another packet of seeds, amused by the squirms and shudders of her daughter. The older woman's laughter caused Jan to wonder if her mother was on the road to insanity or senility, finding such a cogent joy in the memory of a forty-year-old story about a snake when the real topic was her graduation.

"My father kept a pan of water outside for the snake." Jessie continued the recollection. "In the South you learned to live with the high and the low. You lived off the land and your success or failure was between you and God. Every now and then, you had to judge a thing and make a decision that you felt was right without rhyme or reason to anybody else.

"When my father worked his garden or cooked in the yard during the day, the snake would come out from under the house and drink his fill of water, then go back. My daddy told us the snake wouldn't hurt us, but when my daddy died, my sister waited for that snake to come to the water pan and she killed that king snake with a hatchet."

Watching the ground carefully, Jan walked over to the fence and leaned against it, finding some comfort in the shade. Jessie's voice traveled across the neat rows of onions, tomatoes, and mustard, collard, turnip, and spinach greens.

"We hung that snake on a tree, head up, tail down, so it would rain. It did, though I'd be the first to say rain clouds had been gathering all day. When it rained, we didn't have to go out to the field. Nobody did. People heard about our snake and we had a funeral."

Jessie grinned. "I know you think I don't have the sense of this dirt I'm kneeling in, but I do. That's how it was back then. It was strange how we lived and got by. We could tell the time by shadows, by who and what lived, died, and was buried, what we learned to live with and live without. We loved the dirt, the land, the rain, the trees, the grass, and the snakes. If God made it, we accepted it, sometimes to no good end, but you couldn't accuse us of ill will. That snake was longer than I was tall. We all knew what to do for a snakebite, so if you had faith, you lost fear and lived." Jessie wiped her face again. "Seems like that's what you gonna do, Jan, lose your fear and live. I'm glad you graduating." The older woman's voice drifted off and returned with less confidence. "I don't know if I can come. It's a far piece away and I don't have the fancy things I used to have." Jan felt the metal against her back and braced herself, but the thoughts fighting in her mind couldn't be held back. In a month the fence would be covered with bean vines. *If this garden has a right to be tended to, so do I,* Jan thought silently, then spoke aloud. "I don't care what you wear. I want you and Daddy to come, Mama. Tell Daddy that when he gets home from work."

Jan stood in the shade, glaring at Jessie's arms browning in the sun. When Jessie looked up, their eyes met for a moment and in that sliver of time Jan saw her childhood. She'd regretted having a mother so much older than the mothers of her peers. She'd been embarrassed by Jessie's southern ways, so out of touch with anything in the present except this garden. The only pieces of her mother and father she could find that she understood were the dust-covered albums in the basement. The music represented times worth living, not all happy, but not all somber, either. A mixture of emotions were locked in vinyl discs that didn't banish Jessie to the garden or force Charles into his daydreams. Jan had played their albums, listening to every word of Bessie Smith, Billie Holiday, Dinah Washington, Carmen McRae, Joe Williams, and the rest until she felt the chords, chortles, and chimes of their voices enter her. The music had taken care of her then and she had unknowingly trusted it for her future, molding it into a college degree, and now she was determined to shape it into a career.

The sky reminded her of a day when she'd witnessed a similar cloudless perfection. Then she'd asked for a chip to be placed on her shoulder, a kind of divining rod to help her find a path out of Moleen. Still, the house, her mother, her father, the very ground she was standing on, pulled her back.

Jessie's body returned to its curve as she dug and planted. The thought of begging for what care was left after an old woman finished immortalizing this small patch of land and making friends with a snake seemed silly to her. "I want both you and Daddy to come!" Jan was letting out rage all over the place. "Tell him that when he gets home! It doesn't matter what either of you wear, tell Daddy."

Jessie, having dropped her handkerchief in the dirt and forgotten to pick it up some words ago, tasted the sweat, planted another seed hill, and mumbled, "We'll try."

Jan stared at the small yellow flowers that would fall off in a few weeks, making way for squash, and remembered an old adage Ada always used, *If you try, you can do.* The child followed it with an unvoiced proclamation of her own. *If you're not careful, all that passion you're putting in the dirt is going to pull you right down with it.* To keep from saying what she thought, Jan thrust her hand deep into her purse, searching for keys, her mind still tilling the soil she grew up in. *They can expect me to live a better life than they did, educate myself beyond them, wish me well, but not come to celebrate their efforts or my own.* Then the child got to spinning with how they'd never even seen her apartment with its view of the lake. What made her think they would come to her graduation? How did you care for and raise someone as a child without any curiosity about their life as an adult? Disgusted, she spit the questions out in silence until her mother interrupted with another canting of the past.

"Jan, I never got bit by a snake, at least not the kind I grew up around, but the pains of love and life are like a snakebite. My daddy used to say, if a snake bite you, don't run. Suck the poison out. If you can't suck it out, call for help. Get somebody to fetch some blue stone, beat it in a rag, put it on the bite, and cover it with fat meat and a penny. Tie a string from a flour sack at the top of the bite and another at the bottom. Draw that poison out till that penny turns green as grass. Don't run. Some things you gotta get out as soon as they get in. If you don't, they'll travel through you with every step, until you full of poison and got no choice but to die, even if you look like you living.

"Life is like that, Jan. Most people don't stop and draw the poison out. Most of us run, living with poison in our veins. And some of us just learn to live with a snake."

Jan strode across the rows until she stood over Jessie. "Mama, Daddy's not a snake. All his life he talked to me, maybe he didn't listen, but he talked. I'm over twenty-two years old and you just decided to open your mouth and speak to me. Now you want me to feel sorry for you. Well, I don't. When I was growing up you felt so sorry for yourself, you were sorry enough for both of us. You didn't need to talk about it or listen to anybody else." Jan tried to stop the thoughts from tumbling through her lips, but she couldn't. "So maybe you're as much a snake as you think Daddy is."

Jessie watched Jan push her foot underneath an onion plant and uproot it, then arch her foot, point her toe, and go after another one.

"I didn't come out here to talk about snakes, I came out here to invite you and Daddy to my graduation. I'm going to graduate and get comfortable with my life and if I don't I won't blame anybody but me."

Jessie's tears were falling on the dirt, but Jan turned and walked through the open gate. Jessie's voice followed her. "Time will slow walk you. You hear me? Keep living and you'll get you some understanding. You think I'm laid low," Jessie cried. "You think I ain't got no fight. Keep living. Keep on breathing and you'll find out."

When Jan placed the key in the ignition her hand shook, but the eyes that checked the rearview mirror didn't cry.

* * *

Two nights before graduation the dream changed. All the colors of her mother's garden, greens, ashen like the collards and deep like the spinach; bursts of sweet william with vibrant pinks laced in white; tomato reds. From the soil rose the palette of colors Don used to paint his sculptures' skins, black, browns, blues, purples, and ambers, all changing into a range of nutmegs and coppers. They joined the shades of the garden. Out of these luminous hues Jan appeared and watched herself run along the lakefront until the sand changed into red dirt and she was surrounded by a forest of dense trees. As she continued to run, the trees grew moss that dripped from the branches like fish netting. Before the moss reached her, the forest changed into a field with rows of corn so high the stalks towered over her. Finally, she reached a clearing encircled by trees and rested. In the distance she saw a woman stirring clothes in a kettle over a fire. Behind the woman were lakefront high-rises. Her own apartment building appeared. Before she could walk toward her building, the high-rises turned to housing projects with people littered around outdoor landings. The woman and the wash kettle vanished. In her place a house appeared. As Jan walked, a garden grew around her footsteps and vegetables bent toward her. She picked the ripe tomatoes and placed them in a basket that grew from a bracelet on her arm. Squash, with its rich yellow, and tender leaves of spinach filled the basket to its rim. Jan entered the house and began to prepare dinner for a man whose face she couldn't see.

Morning found her sleepy hands reaching for the phone and dialing Ada.

"Heh, li'l bit a much," Uncle Albert answered.

"Hi, Uncle Al. How's my favorites?"

"I guess we fine, baby." His tease and play was missing.

"Something wrong?" Jan asked.

"Well, you ain't gon' be too happy. We won't make it to the graduation. Ada had to go into the hospital for what they call routine tests. Couldn't talk the doctor out of waiting a few more days. You know them doctors pretty busy in the summer, vacations and all."

"Uncle Al. Where's Mama Ada and how long is she supposed to be at the hospital?" Jan squeezed the receiver, holding on to the arm of the sofa, then slowly sitting.

"Now hold on, Li'l Bit. Ada told me to tell you not to worry, said you can come see her after your graduation. You know how headstrong she is, got her mind and Jesus and don't need the rest of us, seem like, anyway. She told me she ain't 'cepting no visitors till Saturday anyhow."

"Where is she?"

"Over at Washington Memorial, and you gon' have to wait till Saturday, just like me."

"Hmm." Jan reached for a pen and pad, and started writing down information and filling in what was unspoken. Albert was right, Ada was headstrong and if she couldn't convince doctors to wait until after her graduation, then something was wrong. When Jan got off the phone, she called the hospital and was given the same information. No visitors. When she called the nurse's station to try and find out more, a message had been left for her: "Come visit after graduation. I'm proud of you."

Jan hung up the phone and moved to the window. She didn't care about tests, or illnesses. The woman who always opened her arms had to be well. The first tears were for Ada and against whatever was wrong, then tears came for herself, drops of fear. If something happened to Ada, she thought, who in the whole damn world would she be able to count on?

To see and not be seen does not limit my love. I could

have told her how sickness was nothing but going through, how weakness made you stronger and how debts paid made you richer, and I did. But the girl couldn't even see me and was barely able to pick out the voice in her dreams that held a curiosity.

Jan washed her face and dressed in her running clothes, but the tears came again. Heaves and sighs threatened to leave her sunken in the swivel chair facing the lake. Finally, we left the apartment. Jan walked to the lakefront, then ran alongside its waters. With wide mouths and open love, we took in the air. Tear-eyed and puff-faced, she reasoned her way through thoughts of the day and the graduation ceremony, deciding her parents only had the illness of their unhappiness to keep them from celebrating her happiness. Don would come tonight. Jan wiped her face on the bottom of her T-shirt. Sarah and Jonathan would be the only people noticing her name on the program tomorrow and Sarah and Jonathan were wonderful friends, but not family.

Ada's voice came back to her again. *Go inside, deeper,* it whispered. Jan ran faster, until the sweat from her armpits met her wrists. She wiped her face on her shirt and ran some more, asking herself what to do and listening to the air that passed her ears, the sounds of the lake and her feet. It didn't tell her anything, but she made some decisions. If the worst happened and Ada died, life had to be more than bones and flesh carted away. Life had to be everybody in it. Whoever crossed your path, what they said, what they did. She'd ask herself and everyone around her who they really were. She knew what Ada meant to her, but she was tired of wondering about Don. He had to be more than "lunch." She'd find out tonight.

That afternoon Jan surveyed her apartment. Matching towels were in the bathroom, soft champagne-colored satin sheets were on the sofa bed, and she'd mopped and waxed the floors. She'd splurged on dinner. Cornish hens split, then broiled. New potatoes, boiled then tossed in sour cream and dill. A salad of Bibb and Boston lettuce with watercress and a few slices of red pepper for color. The last of her olive oil had been mixed with lemon juice, Dijon mustard, and a palmful of crushed walnuts for dressing. The food was kept warm on the stove and her best plates and place mats were on the table.

Billie and Ella didn't seem right for the evening; she was not sad, pleasantly blue, or healed. But she was feeling stronger, like Dinah, Earl "Fatha" Hines, Betty Carter. Busy with her music, she forgot about the time.

"You look very nice, Don."

That's what she said, but we were thinking the same thing.

The man's shoes were so highly glossed, Jan wondered if they were plastic. His suit jacket was tweed and matched neither his shirt nor his pants, but he looked proud and yet too intimidated to acknowledge the compliment. Instead, he made his way to the Pullman kitchen and viewed the dinner.

Jan saw his face in the fluorescent light over the sink and realized her apartment was too nice for him. It wasn't as large and sprawling as his studio, but her tapes, books, her hodgepodge of furniture, even the meal she enjoyed preparing, captured her and who she was becoming.

"You didn't have to do all this," Don said, looking through the clear glass tops of pots and pans on the stove.

"Well, I wanted to make us both a nice dinner." It was true, even though she knew the consequences would be eating tuna at least three times the following week. Jan began to serve the plates.

I watched Don. He sat down and poked at the food

with his fork. The salad was too light, no eggs or cheese. The Cornish hen was awkward to eat, but good. As his eyes traveled around the apartment, he thought about the one he'd left.

Halfway through the meal, Jan said, "You know, in the dream I walk past all these vegetables and walk into a house and prepare a dinner like this."

"Jan, women are always dreaming."

"Why do you think we dream?"

"Because you want things you don't have, so you create a world in your mind."

She stopped eating her Cornish hen.

"You want to share something that other people don't want to give you. Like this." Don gestured to include the table. From the small corner window, night fell quietly onto the lake. Now the women's radio show they'd created for her class played on the tape deck.

"What is wrong with this?"

"Jan." Don cleaned his plate. "What would you do if I left the woman I lived with and moved in with you?"

"I guess"—Jan paused and almost stuttered—"well . . ."

"Just what I thought. You don't really want me, but you want me to want you. Dinner was good, babe." Don stood to take the dishes to the sink. "Real nice."

"Maybe I don't know how I would feel about living with you, but I don't think it's a serious offer anyway." Jan pushed back from the table.

"No," he said, putting one hand on her shoulder, pressing her back into the chair. "Let me do something. I wasn't serious, but then you aren't, either. You used to be serious, babe. You knew what you wanted even if it didn't include me." He picked up her plate, and with a plate in each hand he bent down and kissed her forehead. "Don't do this again."

Don opened the bottom cabinet and emptied the remnants of their plates into the trash.

"How can you tell me what to do? What about what I want? I like to cook and eat like this. I have a right to celebrate what I've done any way I want to."

"Jan, you can get rid of me when you want. You walked into my life and you can walk out, but don't walk out angry like I lied, told you I was something that I wasn't. I was up-front with you. Straight. I'm asking you not to play games with me, either. Accept what we have. Use me until you get something better, if that's the plan, but don't try to mess up my life to fix yours."

Jan stood up. "Shit."

"Me too, babe. But it's your party."

"Then make me a cup of tea." Jan sat down in the swivel chair and tucked the thoughts of Ada into herself.

"Not a problem." Don turned the fire on under the kettle, took a cup and saucer off the shelf, and found the tea bags.

Jan turned from the lake to the kitchen and back again.

"At first, I thought you could belong to me, even with whatever her name is. Then I knew you couldn't. You don't even belong to her. But I need more time. This is the way I want to spend evenings. Not like us."

Rise like a tree, child. In the spring not all the trees are full with green leaves. Remember the pale yellow of the willows, the white of the flowering ash, the dogwood's red berries, or the deep crimson of the Japanese maple. Move in closer, I told the child, knowing that the sound of the tea kettle was louder than my own.

Water was poured, tea steeped with curls of steam. Don washed then dried the plates.

Walking over to the corner window, Jan pulled the shade. From the albums on the étagère, she found Keith Jarrett's piano concert from Köln, Germany. "I'm going back to instrumentals again."

"What's that supposed to mean?"

"Sometimes I don't want to hear anybody else's words. I used to play instrumentals when I was a little girl. I guess it was for the same reason."

Don brought Jan the cup of tea and sat down on the floor, his head between her legs, the way she used to sit when Ada did her hair. "So you graduate tomorrow. You want me to matriculate with the rest of it, babe?"

"I don't know." Jan stroked Don's bald spot and thought of Keith's fingers raising gospel music to meet jazz and classical, then mixing them with his spirit until low moans left his heart and entered onto the recording. The keys tickled, pummeled, then spoke slow, even words. Without voices the sounds were still full of everything he believed.

"Why did you stop that day at the fair?" Don asked.

"Curious."

"What made you stay so long?"

"I guess it was that line about being an artist."

"That one only works half the time." Don laughed.

Jan pushed Don's head forward, playfully. "My aunt says sometimes before you can get rid of someone you have to find out who they really are and what lesson they were meant to teach you."

"Is that right?"

"Who are you, Don, and why are you here?" Jan massaged Don's scalp with her fingertips.

"It's a long story."

"We've got all night."

Nothing Concrete

Jan turned the album over and let the needle down gently.

"Where do you want me to start?" Don asked, scooting backward until he was comfortable between Jan's thighs. He rested his arms on her knees.

"I've told you about my mother and my father. But I've never heard about yours. Why don't we start there? Tell me about your mother."

"The Grand Ma-Ma," Don leaned farther back into the warm crevice. "You hit the jackpot, babe. The way I remember my mama ties right in to the day I found out I was a sculptor."

Don gazed up and out the window, the sky reminiscent of the time between twilight and dawn more than twenty years ago. As he closed his eyes and remembered how he'd sat by another window and felt the calm of early morning so long ago, I went, too. I lit the words brightly enough to tell a story Jan would not only hear, but also see. Even the streets had finally created a quiet space between dusk and dawn. Police cars passed in silence as street lamps cast a blue haze against a sky whose stars failed to outshine the city lights.

Now Don was soothed by the slow motion of Jan's thumbs making gentle circles around the backs of his ears. Then, he had ached to be touched. Sweat had poured down his back as the summer of his fifteenth year confronted him. In a few hours he would try to go to school again. He needed the summer class to start high school in the fall. The year before, the class of '55 had crossed the stage without him. And now, if he didn't graduate this year . . . his thoughts made leaps from the past to the present and back again.

"I never graduated from eighth grade. I got up one night to see if there was any way to do it. Something told me I needed at least that, and I was trying to figure it out." He'd sat in the window hoping for a breeze. But by the time the wind drifted in from the lakefront, its coolness had departed. Once again, it seemed as if comfort had been given to the rich people who lived on the Gold Coast, their apartments facing Lake Michigan. Puffs of air made their way past expensive shops, restaurants, and grocery stores and crossed LaSalle Street. By then, what should have been a breeze fell weakly, like the last breath of a dying man, against the concrete of the housing project where he lived.

"From the tenth floor I could see junkies that had stumbled into the shelters of alleys and doorways trying to get away from the light that would be coming in a few hours. Dealers had already booked. They were back to their own neighborhoods, dirty money fresh in their pockets. The project's number one moneymakers had turned their last tricks and were probably catching a nap before morning rush hour."

Behind his eyelids the young girls with babies on their hips and little ones holding their hands swayed into the darkness. They too had put their kids to bed. For half an hour, maybe an hour or so, there would be quiet.

Jan's fingers moved over Don's neck, then kneaded the tops of his shoulders. She remembered Charles talking about how he and Jessie had moved to the projects after they'd gotten married. It hadn't taken long for him to see the wrong die was being cast, so he'd saved and did a few shady things to make more money. He'd "flat out refused" to raise a family there.

"I tried to catch a breeze in that window, but God gave it, and everything else that mattered, to the folks on the Gold Coast. For me there was an hour of quiet and a room with a mattress on the floor. I kept my clothes in two separate corners. One for dirty, one for clean."

Don remembered the lone lightbulb that hung down on a cord from the middle of the ceiling. Light green paint peeled down the walls, leaving chips on the gray concrete floor. Its cracks branched across the room, housing roaches and their brown egg pockets.

"Earlier that day, I'd made it past the dealers."

"Made it past them?" Jan asked. "Did they try to force you to take drugs?"

"Babe, it ain't ever about force, it's about choice. They tried to sell, like any other salesman." He mimicked their voices. " 'Don, baby, got something for you.' 'Got your homework all ready in a nice plastic bag, unless you want a li'l piece of foil so you can sniff or cook that sho nuff painkiller.' 'Don, baby, what's your pleasure, school man? When you gonna come 'round, unass some of that cash? Unass it and relax, man, with your summer-school-toting-a-book ass. Too damn much school ain't happening, my man. You got to chill.' That kinda sell. But I kept going like I did every day. Two junkies in the crib woulda been too many. Mama used enough heroin for both of us."

Jan's fingers paused. She leaned forward and kissed Don's head, then rested her face. It touched the smooth bald spot and the short sparse hairs. She thought about Jessie eating, hiding food, and eating as if hiding it would keep it from pouring out into flesh. But Don's mother shot heroin in her veins. Jan worked Don's shoulders deep, then down his spine, and between the blades.

"I made it past the dealers, but mama's shooting partners hung out by the elevator. Jasmine was one." Always, words that meant nothing had dribbled from her lips. "Hey baby. You the man, li'l man. Mama's love." When she'd turned her face toward him, her eyelids shivered from the combination of drugs and sun. "Tell ya mama, I got something for her baby."

The small woman's ragged clothes, nappy hair, drowsy eyes, and blotched skin had tempted him to spit in her face.

"Under the short sleeves of her dirty T-shirt, Jasmine's ashy arms wore needle marks like jewelry. She looked and smelled like a heap of garbage." He'd wondered if she'd ever been attractive. "When the elevator door opened, Charmane was getting out." A cigarette hung from her mouth. She wore a purple halter top, which strained under the weight of her breasts, and tight red shorts with her signature orange spike heels. Charmane stepped back and whistled.

" 'My man. Don, baby. Baby Don. Look at you now. Boy, you put a li'l money together, Charmane may help you grow up.' That was her sell."

Don felt Jan's strokes against his neck change. "Jan, she wasn't serious. It was after noon and she'd been with too many men to spare the time or give a freebie to a fifteen-year-old with no cash. Charmane looked out for me and Mama."

He recalled the way she'd answered the question marks in his eyes. " 'You be sweet and keep coming straight on home from school. Now move, li'l man, so I can get to work. It's plenty money out here.' She'd always say that, pointing to the street. 'And I gots to get me some.' " He laughed now. Then, he'd dodged a pool of urine in the elevator and listened to the music of her heels as the door closed.

"I was on my way home that day, babe. I wanted to

tell my mama what I'd found out. Now, I couldn't read well, couldn't write much, knew enough math to count my money, carried a sorry-ass tune, and didn't give a damn about football, basketball, or baseball. But I could work with clay. When I showed up for summer school, they put me in a special program for students who might not graduate on time. At first, I thought it was a program for the dummies. But after I made the face of a woman and sculpted in her eyes, nose, and mouth, I couldn't think of nothing else."

Jan felt Don's shoulders rise and moved her hands to meet them. Wide circles, followed by smaller ones. Time was tossed between them. I lingered in its spaces, sifting out things meant for dreams.

"Mr. Barclay patted me on the back. 'Finish this, Don, and I think you'll find out you're on to something.' Just like that. My first pat on the back by a man." Don inhaled and silence filtered around them.

"Go on, Don." Jan bent down and kissed the crown of his head again. "Please."

Don remembered barely being able to sit on the sculpting stool. He'd looked at the eyes of the sculpture and tried to believe that if he stared hard enough they just might tell him how to keep that feeling: the touch of a man's hand firmly resting on his back and words that made him equal. All afternoon he'd thought he could be a smart, schooled, cool man, just like Barclay.

"It kept me going that day, babe." He'd walked past the dealers and taken the elevator to his apartment. Jasmine had brushed some of his hope away, but Charmane had put it back. Now, it was his mother's turn. He'd gotten off the elevator on his floor, the heat and sun following him as he ran down the concrete to his apartment.

"When I got home the door was part open. I tried not to panic. I pushed it open, and stood back. It was too quiet, but I walked in." His eyes had darted across concrete, two milk crates, two beanbag chairs. "I saw a package of ground beef covered with roaches, babe. Stepped over that and found milk, broken eggs, and a box of cornflakes. A trail of groceries leading to the bathroom.

"Mama sat on the stool, the rubber loose from her arm, needle on the floor." He opened his eyes to try and stop the vision of her eyes rolling in the slowest motion, through slits barely wide enough to show pupils covered in a glassy film. Her mouth hung open. He'd screamed, "Mama!" and tried to figure out what to do. What could he do? When she looked up, the beige whites of her eyes were sandwiched between fluttering lids. He closed his eyes again. The vision hung in the air and stole the oxygen until his shoulders fell.

"Don, I'm sorry to make you bring this up," Jan whispered. Jessie and Charles' lack of love for each other hadn't taken everything from her childhood. But drugs bought, owned, then destroyed what was left of Don's family. "You want to sleep now?"

"Naw, babe. It's cool. You asked and so you gonna get a day in the life of Don with Mama." He continued, mimicking his mother's voice.

" 'Baby, that you? Don, baby? Let Mama see, now.' " He could still hear her, see the pupils disappear in her head. "I told her, 'You just high, Mama.'

" 'Oh yeah. I'm good and high, Donny, baby. Gonna fix you some dinner, too. Gonna make some hamburger up and some gravy too, baby.' She'd say shit like that."

He'd turned away, his tears watering the concrete as he began to gather the groceries. Cockroaches were all over the food. Some leapt boldly from each crevice of the floor. Stomping his feet, he'd scattered the bugs, then picked up the food. Part of a childhood rhyme went through his mind then and now. "Roaches on the wall, learning how to crawl. Sound off, one-two. Sound off, three-four. Bring it on down now, one-two-three-four, one-two, three-four."

Roaches ran wildly over the room. He moved the food to the bare kitchen table. Still, bugs teemed from the sides of the box of corn flakes, slipped in the broken eggs, and slithered all over the package of ground meat. In the bathroom doorway, he'd watched his mother try to stand. She'd mumbled, "Donny, baby. Gonna get you some . . . nice dinner, babe," then flopped back on the toilet seat. He'd wanted to pick up what was left of her, skeletal bones covered with thin, hard, rough, dry-ass skin, and shake her, smash the drawn face into the rotting meat and scream every name he could think of. But when he opened his mouth, it only caught his tears. He groped for the food, stuffed it into the torn grocery bag, and threw it out the open window.

"My memories of Mama ain't none of that Donna Reed shit. I sat up at night trying to think of something more than my life, something different. It was like my whole life was rising up from my toes." He remembered water in the dingy, cracked face bowl and imagined it stopping at the base of his neck, threatening to choke him. Why would people want to live, walking past dealers, talking to whores, coming home to a bare group of walls and a mother who was a drug addict? Where were the Barclays? Who was he going to be like?

"Don." Jan remembered Jessie in the pictures with the gloves with no fingers. "Do you ever remember a time when your mother wasn't an addict?"

"Okay. Lemme see." Don sat up, then stood and stretched. "Before you were thought of and I was in first, maybe second grade, my mama sang to me and read them crazy animal books and shit. I liked them." He grinned, facing Jan. "Books with people in 'em like the ones on television. When we'd visit someone's house with a TV Mama's eyes would get all big, watching the people who dressed in clothes from the downtown store windows. She'd check them out, living in houses with a lot of furniture and eating at fine wooden dinner tables with lots of food on everybody's plate, and bowls and platters for when that ran out."

"I remember that." Jan stood and began to take the pillows off the sofa sleeper. "The women wore pastel cotton dresses even when they did their housework and they had waists so tiny the men could put their hands around them and almost have their fingers touch."

"Yep, them the ones." Don pulled the mattress out.

Jan changed the tape, more instrumentals.

"I had friends to play with, then. We lived in the nice projects. Neat little row houses without elevators and gangsters. The dealers and prostitutes only came there for a visit. That's where I had my first girlfriends. Two sisters a few doors down pulled dandelion petals in my honor." Don laughed. "You know, all that stuff about he loves me, he loves me not?"

Jan remembered doing the same thing as she opened the window facing the lake and the one above the stereo, hoping for a cross breeze. Don joined her. They looked out the window, seeing nothing, hearing the lake.

"I didn't even like girls back then." But, he'd liked the way they made him feel and recalled the constant atten-tion. He'd loved his school and, unlike the school he would soon attend, his first school didn't have bars on the windows.

"My daddy used to come around then, spend the night, and leave big envelopes full of money on the table. When Pops stopped coming around Mama tried welfare, liquor, reefer, LSD, and finally a needle found its place." Don imagined the needle lodging neatly in her arms. Over and over, she'd shot the dope until she was no longer a mother, a woman, or anything but a thrill seeker for the dirty powder she cooked to enter her veins. Watching her left him without the taste for any of her ills.

They took the pillows from behind the sofa. Don sprawled across the sheets. I sat in the window seeing through the darkness and hearing more than the sound of waves.

"That's why I could walk past the dealers. I knew what they took from me. When I found out I could sculpt, I decided to make my own women."

Jan thought about the women on the shelves at the loft and turned his face toward hers. "Are they real people, Don?"

"Babe," Don said, turning uncomfortably, "I could slip off these sheets."

"Or, away from my question." Jan pulled Don's arm until he faced her.

"Okay, so most of them came from somewhere, babe, but not all of them. A few are what you could call a mixed bag. This one's eyes, that one's chin. So now you know about the women."

"I suppose I'd thought about them like that anyway. It's kind of slimy, Don."

"Slimy." Don considered the word and laughed. "So when did I tell you I wasn't slimy?" He grabbed her and pulled her to his chest.

Jan pulled back. It was almost too playful for Don.

"Okay, nosy, what else do you want to know?"

"Why did you start to steal? And, I don't mean just because you were poor." Jan pulled herself up on her elbows and looked at Don. "My father was poor, I was poor. But what made you take things from other people?"

"So, whenever you pull these sheets out you got to know everything from when a man cut his eyetooth?"

"Just want to know what I'm asking, Don." Jan

buried her hand inside the space between his neck and collarbone, then pulled in closer to listen.

"Okay, nosy. At first it was to eat and then, for Mama. I knew I wasn't going to make it through high school. Somewhere in the world, people my age were getting ready to go to college. I'd heard about that, but it wasn't on my agenda. I chose the streets and stealing came along with it. I was tired of being alone, walking past everyone and not fitting nowhere. I guess with no mama and daddy, I wanted some friends."

"Nothing's wrong with wanting friends, Don."

"Yeah, but the kind I got had both feet in the wrong direction." Don turned Jan away from him, then snuggled up close to her back. "A typical day with my buddies, or let's say my indoctrination to the boys, went kinda like this." Don pulled the sheet up around them and spoke for his former friends.

"'We can go up to Rush Street.' Spider always led the group.

"'I know this two-flat on Seneca where they don't even lock the back door and this man never locks his car.' That would be Ray.

"'We won't even have to break the glass.' Bobby, Spider's brother, was the funny man. We'd all bust up when he got started.

"'I've been casing it. I watch this fine babe leave in them high heels and bend down, slipping a key under the mat.' Bobby tiptoed, then acted like he was pulling a skirt down. He showed us how the woman hid the key. 'Check this out. About an hour later, this old, worn-down black bitch comes dragging her fat ass up to the back gate.'"

He felt Jan's body tighten. "That's how it went down, babe.

"'Going to clean for the massah.' Spider would stick out his hand to get five.

"And Bobby would map it all out. 'Heh, we just get in there right in between big tit Raquel and Aunt Jemima, fill our pockets up, sell it, and chill.'

"When Spider gave the deal the thumbs up, it became the plan.

"'Hey, man, we may have time to watch "Leave It to Beaver."' Bobby would co-sign Spider." Don laughed. "And the dude was still a thumb sucker. Once I went down to his apartment and saw Bobby lying on the sofa watching TV with his thumb in his mouth.

"Spider would grab his stuff and say if we ever found a woman inside he could get a little beaver. Bobby would say something like, 'Yeah, I'd be riding that ass at about forty miles an hour.'"

Jan shook. "That's how raw it was, babe. He meant what he said. By then Bobby had raped a woman and he always talked about how he wanted to do it again."

Jan stared into the darkness, trying to see. Boys who raped and stole over and over again were not really boys.

"The first time we pulled a job it was easy. Just like Spider said. I never knew a home could smell rich. Real flowers stood in tall vases of water. Your feet could get lost in the carpet. Perfumes and colognes in the air, sculptures in the hallway, and a cat who only looked at us, purred, and walked away. That's when my palms began to sweat." Jan remembered the way Don's hands always felt moist.

"I wasn't no fool. I knew I wasn't supposed to sneak into other people's homes. It wasn't the same as taking a bag of cookies or a package of ground beef in my army jacket 'cause I was hungry.

"But I'd joined the club. Bobby and Spider ran upstairs, talking about jewelry. I went to the refrigerator and stuffed my coat with meat from the freezer. Picked up a toaster and threw it down. I didn't know what to do. By the time I ran to the staircase everybody else was on their way down the stairs, carrying jewelry boxes, a small TV, a radio, and flashing cash money.

"'Guess this was for the cleaning lady,' Bobby yelled, waving some bills.

"They asked me what I got and I played it off, too shamed to say I ran without nothing but meat in my pockets. Next time, I went straight for the jewelry and hit the freezer on my way out. For a year, the burglaries cashed in better than the welfare check me and Mama shared."

"Weren't you afraid you'd get caught?"

"Yeah. But when you don't get caught, you think it might not happen."

"But it did."

"I stood in front of a judge twice, but at first I was a minor and when I was caught, I wasn't inside someone else's crib. So I played dumb."

"Don." Jan pushed her body back into his. "Didn't anyone ever try to tell you to stop?"

Don closed his eyes again and saw Charmane. "When I tried to sell a TV to Charmane, she said, 'Don, you'd better stop that bullshit. I thought you was gonna be some damn body,' stuff like that. She even got me a part-time job bagging, stocking, and cleaning up at some little grocery store."

"I guess she did look out for you." Jan thought about the people that had looked out for her other than her parents. Mrs. Mont T, the women, Ada.

"I took my first check to Charmane. Tried to buy a piece of that love, babe. At first she turned me down. Then I told her I had cash and I'd just spend it on the competition. So she told me to put my money in my pocket and laid down with me for free. She kept telling me to go to work. But every day I handled all that good food and watched registers total up—$47.92, $68.91—

while all I could do was bag a bunch of cans, fish, and meat. A lot of people pulled twenties, even fifties out of their wallets. They paid for the food in cash, not food stamps."

"It sounds like a good job, not a career, but grocery stores used to pay."

"The money was cool, but it wasn't enough. When I started to hate the customers' faces and dream of robbing them or killing them at night, I walked out on a break one day and never went back.

"Charmane told me to 'hang tough and be a man.' So I got a job at a car wash, but the same thing happened. The shine I buffed on the Cadillacs, Lincolns, and Deuce and a Quarters made me want to bash in their windows, rip out the stereos, and attach the quarters in the tip box onto my knuckles and beat the drivers until my fists stopped."

"Do you know why you were so angry?"

"Yep. I guess if I had sense I would've just beat my mama and found my father, kicked his ass too, but I just got back in tight with Spider. By then, Spider had graduated, street-style. When he'd do a break-in he wouldn't steal anything first. He'd look for spare keys to the family car. Sometimes we'd steal, load a car, take a joy ride, and sell the goods before the sun went down. The fourth time I stood in front of a judge it was for car theft."

Don shifted in the bed.

"What's wrong?"

"Babe, I can barely stay on this bed, you got me sliding."

"I thought you'd like the sheets." Jan allowed her voice to drift.

"That's all right, babe. Been on a few, but that's later in the story."

This wasn't the evening she had planned and I could not tell her that plans made by earth folks are never more than an outline. At best they are sketches without color and subject to change.

Don pulled Jan under his arm. "I noticed a familiar face in the back of the courtroom that last time. At first, I bought a fantasy. Thought my father had finally found me. Like he was looking.

"The man in the back row was my ol' art teacher from sculpting. A few more pounds, a few more years, but it was Barclay. The old man must have read the papers, or maybe Charmane found him.

"Charmane and my moms was in the front row. Mama had tried to clean herself up, but all she could do was shake and cry. I couldn't tell if she understood what was going on, or just needed a fix. Charmane must have thought that bringing a junkie in the courtroom would help.

"The prosecution presented the evidence; keys to a stolen car and two steaks found in my coat pockets." Don remembered the way the police laughed when they pulled the meat out and said, "No matter what they get, a nigger always wants to eat.

"When they searched my crib, they found televisions, jewelry, and a microwave I'd been trying to fence. My mother begged the police not to take me from the projects. All they said was, 'Why not? Afraid we got your drug ticket, junkie?'"

Don turned and sat up. The room wasn't completely dark; with the shades up and the windows open you could see out into the courtyard. Jan pulled herself up next to Don.

"Right after I heard the click of the handcuffs around my wrists I heard my mama making noise, talking smack. 'You nineteen now, Don, baby. This ain't no game you playin'. I'ma get Charmane to try and help you, boy, but you done did it this time.' Her simple ass had just got good and high off of that money, but she was backstepping when my back got even with the wall.

"I didn't name anyone else, babe, didn't contest. Prison was looking better than the streets. I'd have two years where I wouldn't have to steal food, look at a junkie mama, or think about how I failed that man in the back row.

"I was wrong. Prison was much more than a pan of slop three times a day. It had as many junkies as the projects, a bunch of homos, and there were no women, only men who tried their best to look like women." Don stopped staring around the room and closed his eyes, re-membering his prison bed. At night his dick would get so hard he thought it would fall off. It throbbed until his head ached. He had dreams of fucking Charmane and even of raping his mother while she lay back in a nod with the belt around her arm. But there were no women, not even a wasted junkie. If it gets too hard, too bad, let the quiet one put it in his mouth and don't look, but don't let them fuck you in the ass, he'd told himself. You'll drown if they push it in your ass. He kept repeat-ing the command to himself as he became sick inside. He was thinking thoughts from a street he'd never crossed before. He was a man in neck-high dirty water and he knew it was going to cover him, he was going to drown. How could he get out? *Get out and stay out.* He played the tune in his head. *Get out and stay out. Get out and stay out.* Do everything they tell you, work hard, don't talk back, don't look up. Eat alone. Keep your eyes down. Work hard. Don't talk back. Don't look up. Eat alone.

The white trim of windows across the courtyard were highlighted by the moon. Jan thought about being trapped in Moleen, but it didn't compare to prison. She knew she could find a way out of Moleen, had known it all her life. Bide time during the school year and there would be Ada's every summer. Make grades and she'd get to college, get to college and she'd really escape. "You must have been afraid," Jan said.

"If you keep living, twenty-four-seven, weeks turn into months, months into a year, babe. Seasons didn't really matter. I knew time was passing and when I had a little more than one more year to go, I worked in the prison yard. I was shoveling dirt that would be free sooner than me. The yards had rich black soil, we shoveled it, other prisoners bagged it, and then the dirt was on its way, stacked in a store, put in somebody's garden. That dirt had freedom. I didn't hate it, just wanted to be like it." The guards had teased him about his concentration: "Lighten up, bro," "It ain't nothing but dirt," "Don't be dumb as this shit you shoveling." He'd decided then that dirt had an intelligence of its own.

Jan was thinking about Don's daily visits to the railroad tracks to shovel piles of dirt, his version of a health club. It made more sense now.

"One afternoon, during exercise time, I moved away from the other guys, got off to myself to think, and noticed how much the ground was different from the work field. I took off my shoe and dug and hit clay. The prison guards let me keep some. It wasn't the store-bought, ready-to-work stuff, but it was clay." He'd kneaded it with all his strength, sitting at the table near the exercise yard trying to sculpt while other prisoners played ball. The clay wasn't right for sculpting. All his efforts seemed to be wasted, but he continued each day, adding water, experimenting with salt when he could get it. While the rest of the men exercised, he molded the clay. When they came off the exercise yard, slapping him on the back, they teased him and nicknamed him Clay Man.

"Hey, Clay Man, make a bitch for me," Smirts shouted.

"Yeah, stop making them faces and put a pussy on her." Dan D Lion stood and pumped his stomach, grabbing himself. "Clay Man, what you do with all them falling-apart-ass women at night?"

"I made some crumbling-up women out of that clay." Don laughed. "You shoulda seen 'em. But figure this, a newspaper reporter came to the prison, saw my ladies, asked me a few questions, and took some pictures. Man made an article out of that, then a TV station saw the article and came out and taped me talking about it. But you read all this, babe. It was a trip."

"I didn't read about this, Don, some of this isn't in any of the articles."

"Nobody ever asked. They didn't want my eyetooth, they was after what they called the sound bite. I guess my life was too full a plate. But those bites helped where it counted at the time." The inmates' faces co-signed the announcement and their words proved his work was no longer a joke. "Inside, the news spread. My cellmates said I was 'the most macked-out famous motherfucker in the joint.'

"Barclay came to see me. He was the closest thing to a daddy I had.

"'You're on your way out now,' Barclay told me. I didn't believe him at first. 'Be careful. Don't mess up. Keep straight. I knew you could sculpt eight years ago. You got to believe in yourself. If only I could have taken you home. My wife, Barbara . . . well, anyway, keep your nose clean, you'll be out soon.' Barclay got all excited, talked about how he wanted to bring me home, years ago.

"After that press, the warden let me go to the gate to pick up the mail. That may not sound like much to you, but it was the best job in the joint. I could almost taste the outside. That's when I believed Barclay.

"Three women from the Museum of Art's educational

committee came to see me, saying stuff like 'Art makes a difference.' 'Your talent is more than any crimes you've committed.' 'You can stay straight.' 'We believe in you.' Told me I might get some grants and a scholarship to study when I got out. Brought me gifts, books, real clay, and sculpting tools. They started talkin' to the warden, suggesting I finish my G.E.D. 'A little more English, a bit less shop.'" Don mocked the women's voices, but the change in his tone was one of gratitude that branched into desire. They attracted him and made him nervous when he waited for them.

They were white women, dressed from the pages of expensive magazines. High heels clicking across the concrete with skirts that clung to their bodies, ushered in and leaving a scent of flowers, slender, curved vases wrapped in crisp hundred-dollar bills. Their hair fell onto lean shoulders, caressed the sides of their faces, and moved each time they turned their heads. Their lips were too small, but painted in lovely pinks, faint oranges, and the red of watermelon, rubies, raspberries, apples, red lights, and blood. They changed the color of their lips with each visit.

When he'd tried to avoid their eyes, he saw their hands, fingers decked with rings like ones he'd stolen. The nails painted peach, fiery red, or clear, and shaped in perfect half-moons. They encouraged him to talk and listened to every word he said. If they caught his eyes they smiled and he lowered his own, only to find himself eye level with the puff of soft cotton sweaters or slippery, smooth silk blouses that clung to their breasts like fingers. Their stomachs were flat, surrounded by hips that made shallow hills. He dreamed about them at night, he smelled them in the clay, and he thought that they were angels who would come one day and take him to school.

He was going to have another chance. If he could just

look down, do what they told him, act appreciative, stay out of trouble. His hands began to moisten then, the way they had when he'd run jobs with Spider, but this time they had been kissed by a dampness that would not go away.

"When summer came 'round I made parole and the babes made me a student at the Museum of Art's Program for Advanced Education. They put me up in one of the museum's corporate apartments for visiting curators, exhibitors, speakers, big shots like that.

"You shoulda seen my digs. I'd only seen fine apartments like that when I was running through them trying to get out." Now, the sheets beneath him reminded him of how he hadn't been able to get comfortable on the stiff laundered sheets, sit quietly and watch the large color television with its steady pictures, or take food out of a refrigerator and freezer filled with some things he'd never bagged in the grocery store. He became as nervous as he'd been at the sound of the prison cell locking behind him.

"Did you ever go back to the projects?"

"I was afraid to go. Afraid everything would disappear if I went back. But, I got up one night and walked to the old neighborhood. Didn't hardly take fifteen minutes to get there. I stood across the street from the projects and thought about my mama. By then she was dead, buried somewhere in a potter's field." Standing there, he'd tried to forgive her and when he couldn't, he thought about Charmane. "I wanted to check on Charmane. Her letters had stopped coming soon after I made my first anniversary in the joint. Word was she was getting old on the streets and had to take on a pimp who kicked her ass daily. I knew I couldn't get involved. It wasn't my place no more, so I walked back to the other side of town."

Jan got up and changed the music. "I know you didn't

want to be in prison, but I'm glad you got out of the projects." Stars hovered over the lake. "Come look out the window with me," Jan whispered over her shoulder, and soon Don was there with his arms around her. We looked into the night.

"So is all this storytelling my good-bye gift to you?"

"It's a gift, Don. You tell me about you and it answers questions I didn't know I was asking."

"Guess your life don't seem so bad, huh? Wanna trade mamas or daddies?" Don's laughter was weak.

"No, but I didn't live your life and I think I've got to live mine more. You know, focus on my career, turn one of those interviews into a job, make sure I can stay on my own. I guess it doesn't sound so tough now."

"Just don't get scared, babe. Once you get started things will happen, stuff falls in place. When the babes got me my first one-man show, they sold raffles, 'chances,' they called them. They even had auctions of my work and they sold some of that crumbling clay from the prison yard. I couldn't believe it. The same reporter that had written about me when I was in the joint came back and national TV got in on the party. The warden spoke, Barclay spoke. That's how I got my loft. Once I had junkies and prostitutes for neighbors, then inmates, then academics, then artists." Don shook his head.

"Do you have what you want now? Or are you still looking?" Jan asked.

"Don't you know?" Don rested his chin on the top of her head.

Staring out into the darkness, Jan thought about the woman with the braids. "I think I know, but I want you to tell me."

"The graduate gets what she wants," Don said, leading Jan back to the open sofa sleeper. "It started back from since I could remember. My mama had something

I wanted. I knew that much. I'd figured out that, whatever it was, she wouldn't or couldn't give it to me. Then I found out women had something they could give me, so I started to take it." Don sat down on the bed and pulled Jan on top of him. She rolled off and settled underneath his arm. "I didn't know it would be so easy. Even after the joint."

"The three babes from the Museum of Art visited my loft. First they offered advice on marketing my work at banks, corporate functions, and charities. Two of them began to offer me more than advice and sculpting tools."

"You slept with the women who got you out?"

"They slept with me, babe, and I was surprised every time. Barclay wasn't. When the one-man shows got harder to come by, Barclay told me interest in my work was slowing down. He helped me manage my dough and warned me to be careful. I wanted to keep my freedom, stay in the loft. The women, with their bodies and their money, made it happen. What was I supposed to say, 'Put your clothes back on?'"

He'd never felt breasts so firm yet soft or parted hair so fine. He'd thought their skin must have been massaged daily. He couldn't find pimples or scars on any inch of the perfect bodies. Sometimes the women laughed as he took his time, gasped when he entered them and dug their manicured nails into the skin of his behind. When it was over, they trembled and held on to him. He told them how beautiful their bodies were and whispered "thank you" before they left his arms.

"I knew it couldn't last, but I didn't know what else to do. I started to sculpt black women only. I'd learned to sculpt white women in the museum's program and the babes had posed for me, but I began to sculpt black women, with full lips and noses that could fit next to mine. I put together parts of women I knew, Jasmine, Charmane, my mama." He remembered wanting them to come alive. He'd imagined telling them why he needed them. But he was uncomfortable around real women, especially black women. The only black women he cared to think about were his mother before the drugs and the prostitute he'd spent the nights with who had become his friend and, reluctantly, his lover. He wondered about Charmane, but he didn't want to go near the old life.

"Barclay told me. 'A relationship. That's what you're looking for, D, a relationship. If you want a woman, you got to get past Michigan Avenue's high society.' So, he'd known all along. Told me he knew it was good stuff. Said the women would come around for a while, but they had husbands with big cash, other lovers, and other charity cases to tend to. He told me most of the black women coming my way would have another set of problems, babies. That meant they needed a meal ticket and a bill payer. In short, a little sex, a lot of cash. Barclay told me to find a young woman, no babies, no street smarts. Told me to join a health club, stop going over to the train tracks shoveling dirt every morning. Go to a disco, a movie, pizza, places like that."

"Did you do it?" Jan tried to imagine Don dating.

"It didn't work." Taking women to the movies, discos, or to dinner only etched an anger into him. The confines of the tables, the way a fork had to be here and a knife there, the darkening of theaters where you sat next to strangers, only put him in a cage. "I had to tell Barclay I couldn't go to those places. So, he said when the young women come to the shows, when they stopped by the festivals, start looking up. I'd learned to look down in the joint. 'Now you're out. You've got to look up to find a woman. But you've got to be careful.' *Careful* was Barclay's theme."

Clay, drying white, traced the brown of his hands and Barclay sat across from him on a stool, married, an art instructor, going home to his wife every night, living in a house with a two-car garage on the South Side and growing fat around the middle. Don considered him a man with everything, even time to spare for an ex-con sculptor in a worn studio loft with a second chance at life. Was that the plan? How did some people find it and some people exist every day only to get a peek at it? Was life two brown thighs parting with a moaning voice telling you not to ever stop? A woman waiting for you to come home at night, preparing dinner and putting it on the table in a dress that fit tight at the waist, pressed hair, a short Afro, or long braids leading to a nice ass? Did he want that? Don quizzed himself and decided, if he lived Barclay's life, he would have to play Barclay's theme, and he didn't want a careful life, didn't know if he was capable of living it, or if he would ever get the chance.

The only chances he could think of were his second chance at life after prison and what the white women sold at shows and events. "Take a chance. Chances here, fifty dollars. Someone's going to win a sculpture by Don Obatunde, an original oil by Vanessa Reeves, a dramatic pencil drawing of the Old Water Tower by José Ementes. Chances. Chances." Their voices clear, urgent, and sweetened to sell something they had only touched, not made.

Don began to lift his head and see women. His mind blended the range of their skin tones and read their emotions through their eyes. He tried to think like a man who held his head up. "I entered more shows and fairs. Barclay helped me put together some press packets from the television release, newspaper clips, and show brochures. The press kits said the things I didn't want to talk about and the women came."

They came from the long lines at bank windows, to the shows, the jazz festivals. They came out of galleries

in Old Town and in New Town. He'd learned to speak
to them and when he did, he found most women to be
just as hungry for attention as his craving for the opportunity. For a while they thought he was someone special,
different. Some were older, a few his age. Some bought
the magic he served up with jive talk and penetrating
eyes. Some didn't. Then there were the young girls longing to become women. Their youth whet his appetite
and he brought them to his studio. He showed them his
work and they took him to their apartments and visited
his loft. He got all the taste of home he needed from
those visits, but he settled with a woman more his age.
She had a good clerical job and a mind open enough to
let him come and go as he pleased, as long as he spent
his nights there.

He continued to bait and catch the young girls and
they reminded him of the even younger ones who pulled
yellow petals of flowers in his honor. That's what he
missed most, a combination of innocence, hunger, and
satisfaction with the little he offered. He wanted women
who sacrificed tender pieces of their lives for his, offered
him freedom, another place to go when the studio and
one woman's home began to feel like a cell.

Don listened to Jan's breathing, more even now as she
drifted in and out of a light sleep. He tried to think of a
woman he'd loved and pictured the figures that lined his
studio walls. Not one fully came together. There were
eyes, lips, cheekbones, many where he'd blended one's
features with another's. He'd captured older women
who had tried to be kind to him, the whole of his
mother, her face when she was younger, older, the way
he imagined it at the end.

He'd sculpted the young women that fell into his
magic. Their best features were brought to life, mixed
with those that belonged to another, burned in the kiln,
placed on the wall, then moved into the van. When he

sold them, he listened to people tell him that the sculpture reminded them of someone and he wondered if they knew.

Now, his finger traced Jan's sleeping lips and his mother, Charmane, and the white women seemed to settle around him. Women kept making a pit stop in his life with another destination a few months, or if he was lucky a few years, down the road. Going. Going. Gone. Maybe he could learn to love the woman he lived with, he thought as his fingers rested on the lips of a woman he would soon have to live without.

Barclay had told him to go slow with each woman. "I'm sorry, man. If you want to play by the rules, it's going to take a while to hide the salami. But in the end you need to look for a woman to share your life. Take your time and you'll be able to put it all together. You don't want to be alone. Man, if it wasn't for Barbara . . . well, that's another story."

"Don." Jan's sleepy voice called him.

"You've been sleeping, babe. Go on and get them z's."

"I heard you, I was listening."

"So, now do you know who I am, babe?"

"Yes, Don," Jan answered, waking for a moment.

"Then, that's your graduation present." Don considered the darkness, quiet around him, and the gift he hadn't given to anyone else.

Under Don's arm, his body turning then curving around her from behind, Jan dreamed the dream again. This time it started with a man who waved at her from the distance. There was no house, just an open field. She squinted and held her hand across her eyes. She stood on her toes and tried to make out his face. His frame began to fade away. It was large, not very tall, and from far away, he reminded her of Charles.

Divine

The receptionist behind the counter checked the list again. "She's in for some routine tests," Jan said, holding on to and peering across the cool marble counter.

"Hmm, let me check another listing. Fields, Ada." The young woman's pencil glided down several pages. "Here it is, oncology. Take the elevator to the ninth floor, make two rights, and sign in at the nurse's station."

"Oncology. Are you sure?"

We watched the receptionist's professionalism turn into a weary compassion. She bobbed her head up and down. Jan walked toward the elevator, her mind tumbling. Cancer. Parts of articles and news broadcasts she'd hardly listened to resurfaced. Mutation of the cells, no cure, remission, tumors, malignant, chemotherapy, weakness. Jan pushed the button for the ninth floor and leaned against the back rail of the elevator. It smelled like coffee and some type of disinfectant. When the bell for the ninth floor sounded, Jan wondered how she was going to help someone who had always been the helper.

Over Jan's shoulders, I saw Ada's colors draw nearer to me then pull away. Knowing that the Spirit's joys can be earth's sorrow, I banked my fire under the day the child would come to know her name. I felt both my girls. Ada struggling for the child and so many others. The child never having considered Ada not being. Time tested. People failed. Earth folks assumed time was running out, when time can only pass from one place to another, from the place where eyes see and clocks tick to the place where years, centuries, and millenniums crisscross the ages.

"Excuse me."

A short, stout, blond nurse stood and walked over to the desk.

"I'm Ada Fields' niece. I'm here to see my aunt."

"Certainly." The nurse extended her hand. "Congratulations. Mrs. Fields is one of our model patients. And, she told us that a beautiful young lady who just graduated from Chatham University would be coming to visit her."

Jan signed the clipboard. When her mouth only half turned up at the corners, the nurse placed her fingers on Jan's forearm. "She's handling everything very well."

The hallways gleamed their whiteness until Jan stood outside the doorway to Ada's room. Ada lay in bed, eyes closed, silver hair matted against the pillow. Some routine check-up, Jan thought, and slipped into the chair beside the bed. A curtain separated them from another patient. Ada opened her eyes and saw us both.

"My graduate is here," Ada managed, becoming stronger. Jan reached for Ada's hand to stroke, but when she saw how the peanut-colored skin had stretched and swollen until it was nearly limpid, her fingers formed a fist. Ada lifted her left arm and offered the other hand instead. Jan held it. So did I.

"Mama Ada," she whispered, "why did you say it was a routine check-up? If I knew, I would have tried to get here."

"And what, not known what to do, worried, and graduated with the wrong thing in your heart and on your face? I'm fine, Jan. I've been lying here thinking that cancer in your body may be something to heal your mind." Ada squeezed her niece's hand and cleared her throat.

"But that's about all of that. It's good to have so grand a visitor. Come here and kiss your old auntie."

Jan's lips met Ada's cheeks. When their bodies came closer together, Jan only felt the comfort of one breast. Looking down, next to the one ample breast, she saw the way the covers sank into a flattened space in Ada's gown.

"Ada?" Jan tried to keep her voice steady.

"Breast cancer, Jan. One breast gone. But the old woman is so much more than a breast. Now, get my Madam Walker. If I had two good arms and my hot irons, I'd make a fortune in this place. Negro women lying in a pool of naps around here." Jan almost laughed, ungluing her eyes from the dent in the covers.

"Now tell me all about the big day I missed."

Jan straightened herself and got that almost-grown look. What she had successfully hidden from her eyes, trickled down the back of her throat until we found the tears in her voice. "I want to help you, Mama Ada. What can I do?"

"You can tell me about the big day I missed and give me my beauty treatment."

Ada pushed a button and the back of the bed began to lift her into a seated position. The whirring of the motor mixed with Ada's hums. Mahalia. Jan adjusted the pillows, put a dollop of Madam Walker on the back of her hand, and began to part Ada's hair. Jan scratched the scalp gently with the comb, then dabbed the tip of her index finger in oil and smoothed it across the scalp, trying to keep her eyes away from the well in the covers.

"Mmmm. That's good," Ada sighed. "I knew I'd get the best from my girl. A big graduate with enough sense to visit an old woman who got cheated out of grade school." Ada patted the side of the bed with her strong arm. "You know, I'm like the cat that swallowed the canary, full, pleased, and proud. What did Charles and Jessie say about that little piece of paper?"

"Nothing yet."

Ada's movement almost upset the dollop of Madam Walker.

"They didn't come, Mama Ada."

I sent my calm to Ada and watched her cast it aside and drop Mahalia like a bad tenor. Our spiritual eyes met and I told her the child was doing fine. Then I had to repeat myself and Ada knew what that meant. I was hardly one for saying a thing twice when I was on earth. I didn't have a foolish repetition in me now. Jan was fine. Pain is something that often helps more than it hurts and I had given her a verse to hold on to. "Faith is the substance of things hoped for, the evidence of things not yet seen."

"Well, looks like my brother is not as smart as I hoped he would be. That's one reason I can feel the worst part of his blue hanging like leftovers from your best day." Ada turned her head to see a strained profile of Jan's face.

"That's the adult version of that same look you'd give me when I'd served you the last of my mashed apples with butter, a pinch of cinnamon, and too much brown sugar according to folks these days. You used to hit your little fists on the table and puff your jaws out until you looked like Satchmo.

"Jan." Ada reached up to rub the child's fingers. "When a man rules a house, a woman does what the man says do. That only works when his tone is filled with love. That way the house is ruled together. Everybody is the ruler and teacher of what they know best.

"I suspect your mother would have come, Jan, but

your father was afraid of a place that represented something so big it would make him feel small."

Jan rubbed oil along a part, thinking Ada's health was more important than her parents' helplessness.

"It doesn't mean they don't love you, Jan, it means sometimes they just don't know how. If you want to know what to do, I can tell you. But I'm not sure you want to know."

"At first, I wanted to talk all about it, Mama Ada. But I don't feel much like complaining about anything now." Jan avoided glancing over Ada's shoulder.

"It's not my missing breast that's got your tongue. If you hurt, you hurt. It don't have a thing to do with me and I asked, so tell it."

We waited.

"I'm angry, Mama Ada." Jan parted another section of hair. "I'm going out to see Mama and Daddy after my job interview tomorrow, but I'm angry."

"Forgive them." Ada waited two full parts to mend the silence. "If you forgive them, then when I have my brassiere stuffed fat and I'm looking like I used to, you'll find yourself forgetting what you saw today and remember something more important. Let go of things you can't change. People are God's business. You don't own anybody."

Ada took a small blue ball from underneath the covers, placed it in her right hand, and began to squeeze. "People make mistakes as long as they're living, but people who forgive other people open themselves up to a place they would never get to if they wallowed around in blame and anger. If you forgive them, then when you're riding out to see Charles and Jessie or sitting by yourself and thinking about them, it won't hurt half as much.

"My girl is awful quiet. Quiet can be good. Just think

about what I said." Ada reached up and stroked Jan's fingertips. "Think about it."

Jan made another part.

"Now what else is on your heart, filling up this room with all your papa's blues."

Jan thought about the Michigan Avenue lakefront buildings she'd passed on the way to the hospital and the people represented, then frowned and questioned God. All people were in some phase of dying and if so many were simply here to die, how did you figure out who and what was worth living for? "Ada, I'm still seeing the artist."

"Umm, huh. And I still don't hear any desire in your voice."

"It's gone."

"Well, if you're just filling space and biding time with your life, you'll never get what you want. But nothing is a waste of time. There's something you need to do before you can put this man behind you."

Jan thought of Jessie saying, "If you can't see it, I can't see it for you." The child tried Ada anyway. "Like what?"

"Sometimes things and people keep walking through your life. Same thing, different shape. Until you face that part of yourself, ask the right questions, and be honest, you won't find the answers. Ask Jessie about that, Jan. That's something the two of you can talk about."

"Half the time, she only wants to talk about her garden."

"Then listen. She's a farmer, Jan. Ask her about the laws of the harvest, how life is laid out like so many acres. Ask her that." Ada let the ball rest and relaxed underneath the movement of the comb.

A few minutes passed in silence broken by their even breaths. I draped truth across the air between them and sat underneath it.

"Ada, can the spirits, the ones you sometimes talk about, come like little specks of colored light and voices?"

Ada closed her eyes, thanked God and me. I kissed the air around them. The spirits were trying. Jan was seeing some of the things Ada and I saw. Soon she could be close enough to touch.

Jan, having finished oiling Ada's scalp, began a slow massage with her fingertips. "I guess I sound silly, huh?"

"No, you don't." Ada tugged on Jan's arm until the younger stood and came around the bed to sit in front of her. "When I was young, I never thought a woman could have anything but small breasts or big breasts. Now I've found out about one breast and no breasts. Life moves, taking people with it, showing us something else when we thought we knew everything about a thing. Like my breasts and your degree. Now that you've got that, you got a whole other set of things to learn and they start on the inside." I felt Ada's color wane. She was tired.

I sent up prayers of restoration and spread out my deep auburn hue.

Jan remembered the specks of light in Don's studio, the way they made her feel open to something more than the things around her. She felt the same sense now, but didn't see the lights. She found her comfort in Ada's voice.

"Yes, the spirits come in flecks of colored light. Voices? Yes. Loud, low, wise and otherwise. Any way you call them, any way they can get here. The good trying to help, the evil trying to hinder. When you know yourself, you can find out what spirits are speaking and choose which one to listen to. Your spirit is your light, Jan, it guides you. You remember, 'a lamp unto your feet, a light unto your pathway.' Use the light, but don't forget you have a knife. Cut out what you don't need, what hinders. But look closely and cut deep, get it all out when it's time, or it will just come back again.

"People are in your life for a reason. Find out who this man is, figure out what he is to you, and then you can figure out what to do with him."

Ada's voice returned in an exhausted whisper. "Now go get ready for your big interview and let your old auntie get her beauty rest." Ada managed a wink. Behind Jan, the same nurse who had been at the front desk stood by the doorway; she held a small cup of water and another smaller cup.

"She's right. My best patient has to get her rest. Although it can't be for beauty. She doesn't need any more of that."

The nurse brought the medicine to Ada. Jan brushed Ada's hair back and pinned it.

"When you go see your folks, remember what I said. And I'm sure you'll get that job tomorrow. How could they not hire my girl?"

Jan waited for Ada to take the pills. Then we kissed her good-bye.

Lamps and Knives

*J*an stuffed two hours' worth of coins into the meter and fell in step with the noonday crowds heading toward Michigan Avenue. We joined heels that clicked against concrete and heard snatches of other folks' conversations. The voices of men and women stirred with a humid wind. Jan looked present, as much in the moment as the next person. But instead of lunchtime aromas, from grilled fish to charred steaks, she recalled the odor of coffee and disinfectant. Evans' display of mink coats in the summertime didn't turn her head, furniture cleverly arranged appeared as slabs of wood, jewelry like useless baubles. But it was the way the female mannequins in Frederick's of Hollywood's windows displayed hard, plastic, nippleless breasts through thin chiffon nightwear that pressed her legs back and stilled her feet. There was no inviting lust or lure, just an involuntary hand reaching for her left breast. Jan stood across from her reflection. She wanted to reach her arms out to Ada the way her aunt had taken her hand and led her mind away from the slow, tree-lined streets of Moleen.

When we began to move again, Jan looked at the women of Michigan Avenue. They didn't remind her of anyone she knew, but all the men made her think of Don. She stopped at the corner, bought a lemonade from a street vendor, then stood near Walgreens watching the crowd. *Push,* I told her, but she didn't hear me. *Press,* I whispered, but she sucked on a straw, staring at her feet. I held my post and prayed for her feet to move, until she looked at the two black pumps and pictured them walking into the Water Tower, finding The Fishery, and leaving it with a job.

A breeze brought warm, sticky salutations from the lake. Jan felt her underarms moisten and Don's smells raced up toward her nostrils like steam. He had called last night. "Come see me after the interview Monday," he'd said. "Remember, it's your second interview. That means they want you. Negotiate the money, babe. Then come to me and we'll celebrate."

Turning into Water Tower Place, Jan knew she had enough mettle to think about negotiating a salary without being told. She scanned the directory. The Fishery was on the mezzanine level. She took the escalators, ignoring the store windows and the crowds.

"I'm meeting Raye Gasby," she told the maître d'.

"She's been here all morning," the young man quipped, picking up a menu. "Holding court, eating toast. Not ordering a good meal," he complained, voice only half under his breath.

Raye was Jan's height, with a tawny complexion, and wore her hair in a closely cropped Afro. She stood and shook Jan's hand. "Good to meet you."

"Thank you. It's nice to meet you, too."

Jan sat down. Raye pulled out a folder.

"Please order. You're my last interview, so I'm going to have something myself. I hear the trout and the whitefish are excellent." The waiter smiled.

Jan had the trout encrusted with pecans, pureed carrots, and saffron rice, talking her way across Donald Byrd, Bobbi Humphrey, and their contemporaries. Then she turned the conversation to Ella, Dinah, Miles, and Coltrane.

"I've got to agree with Tonya; you are the best candidate for the job. The position involves a lot of grunt work, but it can lead to interviewing and eventually deejaying in a smaller market. If that's what you want. What I'll need more than anything are your creative ideas and full production of the overnight show. Out of all the proposals, I liked your concept of theme shows the best. But I want to know if we can get twenty-two solid themes produced for the balance of this production year."

Jan explained that the themes would be set by the artists themselves. Rather than playing the same song by Ella, Sarah, Billie, then Carmen, the themes would surround stories the artists told. Dinah's "A Man Only Does What a Woman Makes Him Do" could be followed by Billie's "Ain't Nobody's Business If I Do," then Joe Williams' "All Right, Okay, You Win."

"Hmmm." Raye relaxed but still questioned, "What about instrumentals?"

"We could create a theme around weather, for instance. Say Wes Montgomery does 'Baby It's Cold Outside,' and we follow with Herbie Hancock's 'Sun Touch.'"

Raye added, "Or mix it up with Charles Lloyd's 'East of the Sun.' Stan Getz's 'Rainy Day.' I think it will work. You could develop a list, I'd check it, you'd mix it, record my intros, and drop the spots in. Let's try it. I'd like to offer you the job at two hundred dollars a week, and I need you to start on Monday."

My girl didn't miss a beat. "I can start on Monday, but I need more than two hundred a week. I'm willing to work all the extra hours needed to get up to speed, but I was looking for two hundred and fifty dollars a week."

"Jan, that's twenty-five percent more salary than I offered." Raye's lips dropped into a straight line.

"I really want the job, Raye, and I really need the money."

"If you take the job at two-twenty-five a week, I'll see what I can do in three months instead of six. Deal?" Raye handed Jan the manila folder. "And I want you to update and expand that Women in Jazz series."

"Thank you." Jan accepted the folder and glided out of Water Tower Place, busy figuring out when she could see Ada and how much to pinch off of her vacation check, then manage on the two weeks' pay held back from the Harper Group until she received the first check from WJZZ. Graduated and employed. She walked toward her car. Jessie and Charles would be the first to get the news.

But instead of getting in the car, she put two more dimes in the meter and started swinging her spindly hips toward the artists' district. Young girls who want to be women often forget what their hips are made for. Some don't have the slightest idea when the destination should be a foreign place, new territory. I hoped the woman in her would begin to rise like the trunk of palm trees in Puerto Rico, reaching through earth toward tropical breezes, slanting out of the dirt in the swell of mature hips, held not by a girl or child, but a woman. I moved the strains of sun-stained hairs above her ear and whispered, hoping the moisture of my breath, now gone, would take form and put the fire out. Then I forgot myself and spat.

Jan entered Don's dark gray building and boarded the freight elevator. Paint peeled from the dingy walls of its insides. The screech of the cables ended at the second floor. Don opened the door of the studio and stepped back to let her enter. "So, you got the job, babe."

"Yes," she said with enough bite in her voice that he realized it had been her news, not his. Jan walked into the studio. The pallet was not in the corner this time, but in the middle of the room and covered with a blanket. Track lights were focused to its center. "Don, is this my celebration? Sex in the middle of the floor, not the corner?"

"Stand here," Don commanded. "And stop minimizing what we have. I don't want you to lie down, just stand. Step out of the pants." Jan turned around, folding her arms, while Don walked around the room, turning on more lights and focusing them on her. "I should sculpt your body," he announced, and walked toward her, then pulled her against himself. She stepped back, but his hands were warm from being washed and slicked with oil after working the clay. He put them around her waist, gently tugging her pants down as he kneeled. The lights were hot and Jan found herself responding to his touch, the thin layer of water between his hands and her body.

"You're graduating in more ways than we talked about the other night." Don's voice began to fade. He parted her legs with his hands. "A graduate the other night, a job today. You're on the move, babe."

Left. Circles pressured left. Jan felt her body become too weak to stand, but Don held on firmly. Left. When she closed her eyes, it seemed as if hundreds of lights penetrated her lids. So much more left than anything right. She was aware of her body convulsing under the pressure of his tongue, so delicate in kisses only a few nights ago. Increasingly left. Now it was strong, more like a weapon, taming her. Left.

I retreated and sat among leftover pieces of women who sensed me, continued to observe Don and Jan, shivered, shriveled up, and tried once again to die. Jan heard her voice, the sound of a distant oboe. Wind instruments.

I have understood passion and known lust, but if I

were human I would have slapped them both. She was weak, flowing downward with flashes of heat from her toes into the inside of her knee and through her thighs, unsteady, falling, crumpling, meshing down toward the pallet. I shook off the dust of the shelves and danced, sending up praises, claiming for her what she could not claim for herself.

Don cradled Jan, then pulled the covers over her. The lights retracted slowly. Jan swept in and out of consciousness. Lights became dimmer, bleeding beige-yellow spots under her lids until they led into a darkness where colors peeled their outer layers and soaked up the dark around them.

When the dream came again, she was in a bedroom. She could see herself asleep, her arms circled around the waist of a man. Awake now, she spoke to him. "How long have I been asleep?"

But it was Don's voice that replied. "Little more than an hour." Disappointed, she opened her eyes as Don walked toward her, wiping his hands. He stooped, pulled back the covers, stretched alongside her, then pulled the covers around them both. "What will you do now?"

"Go visit my parents, then get ready for next week," Jan answered as she curled her body away from his. Still wrestling with complete consciousness and the last moments of the dream, she smelled the thick, damp, moldy odor of clay. When she focused more clearly she found herself facing the women. The busts glared back at her, funeralized on shelves along the wall.

"How much longer can you stay?"

Jan read her watch. "It's two-thirty. I want to be at my parents' by four." She turned over and saw the same expression that had drawn her toward him ever since the art festival. "I parked at a meter. I'm going to have a ticket if I don't hurry. It was a four-hour meter and I didn't have enough dimes." She pulled her clothes on underneath the covers, feeling Don's eyes as she dressed. Lights, unnecessary in the early afternoon sun, fought with the faces on the shelves, casting their images on the floor.

She imagined them speaking, perhaps laughing through their mute forms, older voices with sage sounds. "They're pretending." "There's no celebration here." "This is just more of the same." Soulless gasps, squeaky cackles, and the low hum of smothered grins bounced off the walls. The elevator's creaks entered from the hallway. Squeals from its lazy descent barged through the studio walls. Car horns outside made her wish she were driving away.

"Don, I have to go," she mumbled, looking at the bust of her lips. It had been finished for some time, but never sold. If it had a voice, it didn't sound like any of those around her. Still, sounds gathered like a chorus in her head. She walked past the bathroom door, careful to avoid Don's eyes and that grin. *Can this be the last time I come here?* she asked herself, and turned to leave. The clay women's open mouths, closed smirks, and big lips seemed to be laughing again. Ventriloquists, she thought, spurting snips of stories she remembered women whispering in her mother's kitchen or underneath Ada's curling irons. "To that fool, something was better than nothing." "Woman lived by the creed, 'a half a man beats no man at all.'" "Well, it comes easy when you ain't busy no way." "Hainty fool." "Chil' ain't got nothing but feet that run toward evil."

"I'll call you tonight, babe." Don's promise followed her into the hallway. "Thank you." His last words fell against her back like knives. The hall was dim in the daylight and the elevator's groans let her know it was on its way to another floor. Jan fought back tears as she headed for the stairwell. Without turning around she tossed mumbled excuses over her shoulder, "My meter . . . a ticket." In her mind she screamed, *Fuck you and all those decapitated women on your walls!*

But she did not say it. Once the child got her full voice back, I was going to work on cleaning it up. At least the girl was hearing and trying to speak. I never understood that "cat got your tongue" saying. In this realm, felines were never made to speak. People have an obligation.

Graduation

Jan didn't notice lazy blue waves humming against the lakeshore. She ignored the kaleidoscope of people, shops, cars, and the shimmer of Michigan Avenue. She just drove down Ontario until it merged onto 94 East. Our destination was different, a place where neither time nor events upset rituals. Jan imagined Jessie in the garden and Charles at the mills. The thought worked her nerves.

Jan exited the highway and began to snake through the small towns that led to Moleen, remembering Ada's words, "Forgive them." She had no intention of forgiving anybody. But words have a power of their own and once loosed can resurrect entire conversations. "I'm so much more than a breast." Jan remembered Ada's voice, strong in its weakness, but she didn't want to think about that either. I left the child's shoulders and sat in the passenger seat. A forgiving spirit can be knocked down by a combination of shame, anger, and fear. These are the worst of company and deposited Jan in front of a question I couldn't answer. *Is my aunt going to die?*

I've seen those spirits and their reflections in a Mississippi window's dingy pane and watched their flicker break the room's dark at night. I've bosomed fear, shame, anger, then fought, observed, and reluctantly become prey. But neither humans nor those spirits ever hold the keys to death and Jan's question was not one I could answer. So, I got back on the child's shoulder and apologized for spitting in her ear. I whispered love stories, perhaps in vain, or maybe in the hope of adding to the dream. Each truth ended with love's power to cast a death key into flattened metal and turn a waning heartbeat into life itself.

Jan opened the vent under the dashboard. Her legs began to cool. Driving with one hand now, she held on to the frame of the window with the other, passing a collection of weeds that fought their way through the concrete of dilapidated sidewalks. She dismissed the hand-painted business signs. Red lights flashed ahead. "Always a train," she sighed, turning her head away from the large peeling sign with its missing letter, WE COME TO MOLEEN.

The stir in the air was such that I went ahead. Low at first and under the train, then high over housetops until I found Jessie admiring the marigolds that laced their way around the vegetable garden. Bursts of yellow, spun into the center of their tightly sewn petals, spread a bouquet of watchful eyes around the garden. The flowers reminded Jessie of life in the Bottom when she'd realized that chickens loved the sweet taste of marigolds as much as she savored their meal to the eye. Aged from memories, Jessie dabbed at the sweat on her forehead. Then, tucking the handkerchief in her duster pocket, she gathered tools and propped them against the side of the garage. Afternoon was fading.

"No chickens to shoo here," she mumbled, speaking to the absence of livestock. Examining the marigolds, neat rows of collards, green onions, peppers, tomatoes, cabbage, and pole beans that climbed the fence, she inhaled a sense of accomplishment. It was not the Bottom, but it was a garden that could hold its own. Jessie stood with her back against the garage in the cool of its shade. Being in the garden all morning had calmed her jitters, but now they returned.

Nothing should have kept her from being front row center at her only child's graduation. She touched her thinning hair, enacting the feel of her father's hand. He would gently massage the crown of her head, letting her know when she'd done well in her studies.

She could touch Jan now. It wouldn't right everything wrong between them. But a good hug never hurt no-body. It had been a long time since her hands—gnarled, wrinkled, arthritic, and dirt-loved from the garden—had given a tender touch. Jessie caught a sliding shovel and propped it up beside the garage, wondering what it would be like to lean on the man in the house. "Nice to get some love." She let the thought slip from her mouth like too many seeds scattered from a hasty palm in late spring. No way to collect a broadcasting of seeds. You just have to let them grow and thin out the planting the best you can, she told herself, wrapping her body in the memory of the only man other than her father who'd loved her. Then she lamented that it was not the same one that lived in the house.

A bee climbed into the bud of a withering rose a few feet away. As it made its way to the next flower, Jessie considered the roses lying limp in the shade. They'd never made it to Jan's graduation. Jessie fingered the address and directions written on paper, still stashed in her duster pocket. She knew when she cut the roses and wrote the directions down so carefully that she would never get in the car and try to find her way to the address on the piece of paper. Charles hadn't offered any help.

"No suit, and I ain't got no shoes. I'm a working man," he'd hissed when she asked him to get ready. Lying. His shoes weren't much to speak about, but she'd seen the secondhand suit in the back of the closet for just as many months as she'd heard his coughing. Sputtering, spitting, and sitting up until all hours had made him afraid.

Courage should have forced her to get in the car, follow the directions, and sit front row center at her daughter's graduation, even if she had to do it alone. She'd pictured it: her large frame still snazzy in her black and white pantsuit with a splash of red in a scarf around her neck. She would have walked to the end of the stage and offered the loveliest of roses to Jan; three red, three salmon, three pink, and three ripened-banana yellow, as bright as the eyes of her marigolds.

In the front yard, Charles listened to the sound of the water sprinkler and witnessed the leaves of aging trees. With every breeze they entangled one another. Turning his back toward the Indiana-bound east where the promise of steel mills seemed invented to make him sweat, he decided his idea of heaven was a day off. For five, six, and sometimes seven days a week, 3 to 11, 11 to 7, and often both, he poured a part of himself out along with the molten steel the machines carried.

If that wasn't enough, he took the shit of the white man. He placed the sprinkler down firmly in its new location. Whether they knew more or less about his job, it didn't matter, he had to work for them. When they looked at him, or more accurately, *through* him, he could see that whether his family ate or not, had a roof over their heads, or whether his daughter got a decent education was further away from their minds than the scraps of metal underfoot.

When he forced his mind past their faces, he could look and not see them as well. But it ached to pay back hate for hate and was no way to treat or be treated by a man. Dr. King had got that much straight, he conceded. Hate was a choice that boomeranged its owner. So he'd promised himself that whites would mean no more than a paycheck to him. But if he could have his way, he wished black skin on their backs. Be black for a while, he thought, then remembered Jan.

When his dreams had folded up as neatly as the undershirts in the chifforobe, stained no matter how much bleach was poured into the wash, there'd been nothing left to do but live for her. Now, Jan was grown up, a city girl with a graduation that caused Jessie to raise Cain. He couldn't go. No need to take a day off for all that traveling when he couldn't sit still for more than an hour with all the trouble of holding his water lately.

Sprinkler in place, Charles paused to follow the slow arcs of water across the lawn. He returned to his seat on the porch, remembering when Jan and her friends ran underneath the sprinkler, trying, or so they claimed, not to get wet. Now, Jan came around with talk of things like running on the lakefront. He shook his head. Frankly, he saw no reason for it, running to run.

Shifting, he settled into a familiar indentation in the concrete, so slight it would be imperceptible to anyone else. Time had melted like butter in hot syrup. You couldn't see it anymore, just hoped you'd added enough richness to sweet, since soon it would be gone. Days had passed into weeks, months, years. Years rose into teens, then tens. The concrete under his bottom felt cool and hard. He tried to recollect when the tree-lined street had become like a painting for him. When they'd moved from the city to the suburbs, homes in Moleen were just being built. It had been hard to buy a tree after spending so much for four walls being put together. But each family had bought one or two trees for their front yard.

Now maple and elm branches met in the streets, their leaves seeming to play with one another, a replacement for the children who'd supped on their air, then scampered like fools to Chicago. Hightailing it to the very place the generation that birthed them had fled. Charles lowered his eyes from the quiver of leaves to the rows of houses. Most of his neighbors had come from the South, the majority from Mississippi, only to find their salvation did not rest in city life. With what hope remained, they'd ambled out to the suburbs, patching together a life that could in no way rival the best parts of their southern home. There, simple sharecroppers and farmers, down-home country folks used to sitting on the porch with their shoes off, enjoyed the slim lives that lay full around him. Those were the folks that made his cup of tea. He liked the way he'd twisted the properness of having a cup of tea, a thing of city folks, to mix with a tale about himself and his neighbors. He fused rough-edged memories of city life with imaginings of Jan negotiating a similar territory, and wiped the last seam of humor from his lips. Chicago could take the might out of a man and do double duty to a woman, not to mention a young girl who couldn't yet write the *w* in woman.

City life bled you. The plain old work of living was never done. There was no time to sit with your shoes off. Three-flats and six-flats had more people to a room than southern shanties. Negro men had conks that needed to be processed. Women tried to cover runs in their stockings when greased bare legs used to be enough. Poor was something to be ashamed of. In the red hills dotted white with cotton, being poor meant you had done the best you could for the year. Often, it put you in right good company. A walk in the fields made everybody equal. God had made the land and in the end, the land, if it chose to, would protect you. Night or day, miles of sky loosed you into dreams of what the next crop might bring. Chicago had to be reckoned with every hour. Take a bus, ride the train, walk past people you didn't know, Negroes nodding their heads but forgetting to smile, then forgetting to nod. To hell with Chicago, he thought, getting up to move the sprinkler again. He wanted to see Jan run back and forth under its waters, abandon her search for something so much better. And stop chasing men. He'd heard Jessie mention them from time to time. One called himself a deejay, like any man worth his sense and salt would go around playing records for a living and being called by the initials of some fancy name for the thing he did. He wasn't fooled. *Deejay* was another name for a clerk, a damn paper-pushing ladies' man, probably as weak in the knees as he'd be in the pocket. And lately, for too long, there was some drivel about an artist. What the Sam Hill was that? Grabbing the base of the sprinkler, he walked a few feet and set it down again.

He wished Jan would come to her senses about the city and jack-legged men. He aimed to tell her so, reckoned she'd made it through her graduation. Now, all she had to do was come on home, let the men with worth and the job she was hunting follow her. Things ought to go her way now, 'specially since she'd gotten that piece of paper she was after. Jan's life could be taking a nice shape now. He'd tell her that and offer a rent-free place to stay. All she had to do was to leave that city and come on home. "Damn Chicago." He gave the thought voice. A small suburb wasn't Mississippi, but it did him and could do his daughter mighty fine.

I stroked his forehead and kissed the dimple where love welled his concerns. The blue of his light glowed across the goodness deepening in him. I knew it would allow me to go further inside. As a child, he went to anyone, wandered anyplace, as if the world would open up and take care of him. He never understood that the earth was peopled with those who would not treat him fairly just because. Manhood became a hard lesson. Now, he wanted to do what was not done to him and could not rightly be done for any other. The girl had to become a woman on her own.

Journeys Home

When the car door slammed, Charles was in the kitchen soothing his throat with a tall glass of buttermilk and reaching for his second piece of crackling bread. He waited in the cool of the kitchen, expecting Jan to come in like she always did, a flurry entering the side door of the house, streaming through the kitchen and going straight to her room, putting her things down like she was coming from the school bus not that many years ago. He dipped the corner of his bread in the buttermilk, took a big bite, and waited. He'd tell her a few things about city life and welcome her to come back home. Rest up. Give her pocket and her mind a break, look for one of them fancy jobs she was wantin', and save her dollars until things came to be.

Outside, Jan dodged the water from the sprinkler and was about to open the side door when she saw her mother stooped in the backyard. She dropped her albums and her overnight bag in front of the door and walked toward the garage. "Mama!"

"Hey, Jan." Jessie looked up from fidgeting with her tools. "You going to stay the night?"

Jan didn't return the nervous smile. "All the way out here, I've been thinking about you and Daddy." Jan glared at the garden, then Jessie. "I've been thinking

about everything. You both missed my graduation yesterday. You didn't even call. Nothing!"

Jessie considered Jan. The hoe and hand shovel lined
neatly against the garage began to slip.

"What did you do all day?" Jan placed one hand on a
thin hip and pointed around the garden with the other.
"Bet you were out here listening to your vegetables
grow. Or did these flowers win some award yesterday?"

Jan stepped forward past the wilting roses. "Were you
putting the finishing touches on this heap of shit and
praising yourself for your green ass thumb?" An accus-
ing finger snipped through the air. Even Jan didn't quite
believe the cursing or the anger, but loosed, it grew hungry. "No show. That's what you are, that's what Daddy
was, and that's what Don was. I guess it's Sarah, or is it
Ada, that's supposed to be my mother, father, and all my
family now?"

Jan stamped a few feet into the garden. Stepping on a
marigold, she pushed the toe of her shoe under a matur-
ing onion and uprooted it.

Jessie sturdied the hoe and shovel and turned to see
the pearl white roots resting on top of the dirt. Jan's foot
burrowed down again.

"What were you doing that was so important yesterday?" Jan demanded. "Trying to rebuild that damn
'Bottom' you always talking about? What?"

Jessie walked out of the shadows of the garage into
the full sun.

"I'm glad you graduated and I'm sorry I didn't come."
Jan's foot kept working the dirt until Jessie's voice
gained an anger of its own. "But don't you curse me and
kick my labor around." Jessie grabbed Jan by her upper
arms. The child felt her mother's hands close like fists.

"I planted more than these seeds when I had you,
Jan." Whispers seeped through her teeth. "I may not
have made it yesterday, but I made it when you couldn't

see what was behind you, in front of you either." Jessie pulled her hands back and held them out to Jan.

Jan rubbed her upper arms, trying to catch the anger that drank up the air around them. Her face was heat, even if her tongue was quiet.

"You don't know my days." Jessie moved in closer. "Some sunrises the only thing I could do was to come out here and get on my knees and plant another seed, pull a tomato, or wait for winter to be done so that I could get something in this ground.

"I did more than plant a garden. You standing there in a huff at me, you may have yourself a case, but I got one, too. Gave you more than you know I gave and if I missed a beat, didn't miss many. Wanna huff 'bout what I didn't do? What about what I did?

"Your father in there now, putting buttermilk and crackling bread down his throat. Humph! There were days when, I have the Lord as my witness, I'd've cleaved his head off his shoulders while he slept if it weren't for you. When I was young, fresh, styled up, and prettier than any showgirl at the Savoy, I wanted a baby and a life with a man so bad I swallowed when I should've spoke my piece and stood my stand. Waited in a train station in Chicago for the man that knew how to rub my shoulders, kiss my neck." Jessie's eyes blared in response to Jan's posture of disbelief. She straightened herself, pushing her neck up from the collar of the duster. "Umm, huh. I had one of them kind too, cared about what I thought and felt. Has that ever come your way, Jan? I'll bet my fall planting it ain't. I been loved, 'cause I knew how love looked. Seen it every day when I was growing up. When it came time for me to get a love of my own I got scared and ran. You wasn't an egg meeting a sperm back then, but I was smart and I was wanted.

"Time ain't changed that much. You done felt it too, when a man want the part of you that can help him out of his mess and you know it's the same part of you that can make your dreams. Missed my chance. Waited till I thought I couldn't wait no mo'. Then, settled for your father." Jessie's voice fell against the collards. "Damn foolish, I guess." Hard and low, each word slapped the peas. "Planned my salvation, then turned around and snatched it up."

Jan saw what I saw, annuals and perennials nourished and grown each year by secrets. Curiosity welled up in her hands. She rubbed each upper arm again. Four finger marks and a thumb print began to fade.

Jessie reached for Jan, but the child flinched. "Did you really want me there?" Jessie asked, afraid to wait for an answer. "Did you know I used to dance night into morning, clap my hands just high enough so that everyone at the table would notice that my gloves didn't have fingertips?"

Jessie reached for Jan again.

"Just wanted to touch you, that's all." Jan allowed her mother's hands to fall near her arms. Hesitantly at first, then fully, Jessie stroked both of Jan's arms with her hands.

Jan's tears slid onto her mother's shoulders. The meeting of the two bodies was not fluid, bearing jerks and spasms, then folding into cushions and enclaves.

"I named you Patience 'cause I didn't have enough," Jessie whispered, soft enough to caress the petunias.

When Charles walked into Jan's old bedroom, eased toward the window, curious to see what was keeping Jan from coming inside, and peeped at the two women hugging each other, their tenderness caused him to step backward and turn away. Rubbing his own arms, he wandered through the bedroom, then down the hall. The kitchen seemed too dark, empty. He started toward the porch, trying to remember the last hug that gave him comfort. When the memory would not come, he reached the front door, opened it, and met a brisk wind. He searched his insides and fell backward into the years. What was school like? What did people do when they thought you had done a good thing? He assumed Jessie had given Jan some heap of praise to have them clutching each other so. Before he could bend down and grasp the sprinkler, gusts of wind grew strong enough to carry his mind to a Mississippi forest.

Packed tightly, tall trees grew out of red dirt, far behind the red plank house. It was a day just past his eleventh year. He'd gone out into the thicket in spite of Ada's warnings—"Charlie, you better not be goin' so far deep in them woods." But at play, he'd seen a squirrel and began to chase it. Once inside the thicket, he found the squirrel again, high up in a tree. He threw rocks after it and watched the squirrel scurry from one branch to another. "Swing like a monkey!" he called, proud he'd learned what a monkey was. He'd listened at school, held the picture book tight when it came his way, and knew every crinkle in its yellowing pages, memorized words and pictures until he could draw them in the dirt.

A possum scampered for cover. He tailed the animal to a brook, then recalled a possum's disposition, stopped the chase, threw stones in the brook, and felt the power of having moved water by launching something from his hands. Peering over a fallen tree, he met his reflection, a face with looks older than eleven and black waves that curled about his shoulders. The hair made him feel a tinge of hatred for me since I wouldn't cut it until he talked plainly. He hated the long curly hair, said it looked like a girl's, and told how the young'uns teased him at school, even though he didn't go anymore.

Sitting down on a fallen tree, he grew aware of the thistles and brambles on his clothes and in his hair. For almost a month he had headed for the fields. When the teacher sent word that the bus would no longer ride down Greenville Road, he pruned his desires. He'd wanted to be a schoolboy, soaking up learning like dry ground did rain. But he didn't understand most of what the teacher was saying and he already had to walk a far piece to get to the bus at Greenville Road. Dust rose through his toes and around his feet as he shuffled them near the water. He could handle a four-mile walk, but with the bus stop moving, his walk would double. Eight miles to a bus you'd better not be late for, then eight miles back, rain or shine, with or without shoes. It was plain too much.

The school bus changing its route was unfair and Charles talked his plainest to tell me so. I'd told him not to worry but we knew the ill in my body was causing my fight to dwindle along with my flesh. On his first day in the field, he worked without complaint. By the end of the week he made sure he picked more cotton than some grown men. But on that day in the woods, amidst an audience of trees, water, and animals camouflaged around him, he was simply a child running along the brook. Branches crackled underneath his feet, his voice calling out all the words passing through his mind.

"Soap. Purple. Fire. Cotton. Chalk. Squirrel. Verga. Shoes. Trees. Spiders. Monkey. Red. Summer. Ants. June. March. Maple. Sap. Songs. Words. I talk. I'm talk'n' soundin' fine. Plain and fine talk'n' what I does."

Charles leaned against a poplar to catch his breath. The sun told him it was time to head back. Retracing his steps, he relaxed. Just before he reached the clearing, he tripped over a fallen branch thick enough to smart his ankle. Sitting up, he wished the soreness away, but the ache only met fear. He felt more twigs in his hair and began to pull them out. When the sun disappeared and returned, it did not warm him.

Amidst bugs, reeds, brambles, ants, pines, poplar twigs, and the ache of his spirit, every sense shouted what everyone tried to keep a secret. His mother was dying. They made excuses for Ada doing everything. Ada, Ada, Ada, he pulsed. Whose mama was she? He'd heard some say she'd never even get a baby, much less the fun to go along with it, her being so self-righteous and all. Who gave a milk curd or a cow's tit? His sisters thought they had a secret. But nothing had been hidden from him so well he couldn't find it.

I watched his knowledge spread in red smudges of wiped dirt moistened with tears across his face. It flowed along the brook, seeking a level to match the truth. It danced in the clearing with intermittent clouds and trysts of sunshine. But he saw death creep across the clearing and knew it would soon meet him at home. Underneath the heat, he knew the house bore a chill no matter how hot the day. Rooms once filled with women's talk held whispers now, bosoms rising and falling like a bad cake. Whispers and bosoms.

Underneath the smell of bread, collards, okra, and fried corn, a stench of medicines and another odor he'd not known before lingered. It increased after the food smells were gone. He blinked, wanting to see the thick braid swing in the sunshine, not tangled hair moist with sweat covering a head that seemed to shrink into the potato sack pillow, or eyes no longer clear as creek-dipped water, but shiny with a yellow hint and focused too far away to hold a boy's heart. Instead, the gaze engulfed his insides and tore them slowly. He could not find the face all women used to want for themselves.

Now, together, we traveled time back to the days when I was barely alive and my son was fighting for both of our breaths. We watched the strange medley. A coughing spell came over my body. Spiny hands grabbed hold of the bed's side and everybody took silent, pretending they had minds and sights on other places. But Charles could not look away, only track the pain that seemed to strut across my face. He remembered when the coughs were passing sputters and Paps spent all day and night in our room, only coming out to work and eat. But pleurisy required ten to twelve raw eggs a day, and when there were no more eggs in the henhouse he woke early to see what Paps would do. Paps started to town, dressed in his Sunday clothes mid-week, coming back with a basket of eggs, then only a few, then returning a day or two later, filthy as sin and smelling like moonshine. That's when Charles began to take to the woods.

"Charlie Guss." He called his name aloud. "What I gonna do?" He whispered to the trees, pushing himself backward until he was supported by a large oak. His ankle stung and throbbed, but worse, he knew there would be the telling of how he'd gotten his hurt. He tried to smooth his hair and moaned as he felt more twigs. His clothes all but matched the red dusty ground where he sat.

I was sick, near dead, Paps was looking like the next town drunk, and Charles knew as soon as he got home, he'd be considered a limping piece of trouble. "Where I gonna be?" He asked the sun shining in the clearing. "Who I be with no mama? Who I gonna be? Where I be without my mama?" He rolled each word off his tongue fast-like. So seldom did he speak aloud in the red plank house that his voice fell strangely against the barks of trees.

He questioned my love, but not my provisions, and wondered who would make his provisions now. He knew Ada would boss him, and chose Verga. Even if she was only three years older than him, he reasoned that she looked more than that and recalled old folks saying she was on her second round of life. Verga had been talking about making the days on her own since crop time two crops ago. It was settled. He'd live with the person he loved the most, the one that talked with him as if his words were smooth and clear as any schoolhouse teacher's.

Temporary comfort followed the sun behind the clouds, allowing a sobering cool inside the clearing. Living with Verga was a start, but not a finish. When the sun returned he would ask. He limped to the middle of the clearing and fell to his knees, taking silent. He clutched handfuls of dirt because it seemed too much like a simple to talk to the sun even if the sun reminded him there was a God. He believed my saying so and thought anything you could feel every day but never touch had to house the ears of God.

"Who I be?" He heard his voice, low and ashamed. When no answer came, he asked again with increasing power, taking care to make each word proper-like. "Who I be?" He cried out louder yet and held his breath. The sun bathed the clearing with its strong yellow light and his first thought was that he would be a father.

"A father." He'd said it slow, liking the way the *f* bumped into the *th* sound and it all rolled over the *er*. Father. That was enough. He promised to do it better than it was being done to him these days. He stood and turned his back on the shadows cast by the sun. There is a God and *I will be a father,* he told himself.

Feeling a cool spray of water stroke the side of his face, the image of a little boy with long hair limping from a clearing faded into the thickets. The child stepped jerkily forward, then was lost in the greens of the trees and Charles returned to the sun of this day.

I kissed his face and wiped my tears across his loneliness. *You are loved,* I whispered, knowing he could not hear me. I placed the coolness of my tears across his lips and watched them drip down to the deep place to bathe his heart.

Charles, feeling the brittleness of his bones, bent down, careful this time not to be caught by the water. He moved the sprinkler and returned to the concrete steps. Instead of sitting there, he chose the flower box and hoisted himself up with the last of the child left in him, then dangled his legs over its side.

The trees had grown over the years and he had been a father. Maybe not the best, but better than he'd had a blueprint for. He'd try to be even better. There was still time, he consoled himself, then puffed up with a swell of pride. He'd raised him a college-graduated daughter. He wondered what it would have been like if he had talked to God more often over the years, but decided he hadn't quite known what to say. When Jan was young he found out all he needed to know about church in one visit. It was too fancy a place, women in hats, men in suits, and children with enough grease on their legs to fry a chicken. When everybody opened the Bible, he did good not to have it upside down. Turning to all those books and chapters inside one book, that was another thing. And what the Sam Hill was all them crazy names, "begets," "thees," "thous," and "therefores" about? Church wasn't a place to go, didn't teach you nothing, just expected you to know everything. School was better.

"A man ought to be able to talk to God fair and square," Charles said to no one in particular. He was supposed to be a father and that was that. He thought about what Ada always said, if you hadn't talked to God or if you asked God a question and couldn't hear an answer, just keep doing the last thing you heard. Maybe she had that much right. He'd tell Jan what he saw in her life. She may have graduated from college but she still had a heap of learning to do. Running to the city as soon as she got the chance and now, according to what he could glean from Jessie, seems like she'd taken up with some artist. As if that was anything stable, or different than every other tale they'd grasped about Jan's men from the bits and pieces of information she'd leave like hanging dust in a wind. He'd bet a dollar to a doughnut that this latest one, the so-called artist, was less than cow shit. He made up his mind to tell Jan that as soon as he could get a moment with her away from Jessie and all their goings on. If he couldn't feel the closeness he'd seen between them, he'd help the best he could. He was a father and the least he could do was figure a way to tell his daughter she was wasting her time on the sorry approach she had to men. He focused once more on the tree-lined street. Charles witnessed branches nearly a block away swaying, then sat motionless and took the breeze.

Jan placed her albums on top of the box beneath the windows, laid her books on the edge of the bed, and peered out into the backyard. For the first time since she'd moved to Chicago she found herself in this room and this house because she wanted to be here. Now it ripened around her. Jan walked down the hall to the kitchen and uncovered a pot on the stove. Young mustard leaves with bits of salt pork were bobbing in pot liquor. She spooned several pieces of the meat on top of her greens and sat down.

Jessie came in the side door.

"Big-time college girl finds a job, goes home, and eats a plate of greens." Jessie laughed. "That may not be on the ten o'clock news, but that's good news to me." Color rose into her cheeks, even if she cut her eyes away from Jan before too much gratefulness broke free.

Jan's mouth was full, her heart busy measuring the beginning of this new camaraderie. Parts of her heart ached, and there were too many things unexplained.

"Mama," Jan said, holding up a forkful of greens.

Jessie turned, fidgeting with the paper in her duster pocket, not sure that it made sense to tell Jan that she'd really tried to come to the graduation. "Who was the man who loved you?"

Jessie moved to the stove, grabbed a fork, and stirred the pot of greens too fast. Outside the kitchen window, the willow danced.

"When I met your father, he could pick me up and toss me between his legs." Jessie walked over to the table. She saw Charles out in the yard and pulled a chair up close to Jan. "We Charlestoned and jitterbugged till daylight then. Your daddy courted me away from a house I couldn't stand.

"See, my daddy and mama had died. I was living with Daddy's brother and his wife. Uncle Will wasn't half the man my father was. His wife ran that house with a hatred she'd cooked down to a low gravy. I don't know what made her so evil, but I know she didn't want no parts of me. I thought it was 'cause I was southern, young, and yella. Aunt Nell was quick to say a drop of blood didn't make nobody black when they was so light you could see veins of blood showing through their skin, and that that much white could never be trusted."

Jan added some chopped onions to the greens, realizing that only her father's side of the family had welcomed her.

"Truth is, I went out with your daddy to get out of that house. Aunt Nell took to him for some reason. She never cared for Bobby D. His full name was Robert Dawkins. Bobby D was what I called him. We courted and when he went away to the service, we wrote each other and made big plans. But a letter ain't much to hold on to when you're hating every day. I saw my uncle growing smaller and the evil in Aunt Nell was bigger than the good in him." Jessie pushed the Tabasco sauce toward Jan. "I wanted to leave my aunt's house so bad, some days I had to walk into that place and hold my breath."

Empathy slid across Jan's face.

"I called myself using your daddy, Jan. But a trick was played on me." Jessie laughed the old way. Jan cringed but kept silent. Jessie folded her arms, moved in closer to the table, and lowered her voice. "See, everybody knew Bobby D was coming back to town. By then your daddy had proposed and Aunt Nell was egging me on. I was trying everything I could to keep the news about Charles and me from getting to Bobby D. Your father played doorknob dumb.

"The day I was supposed to meet Bobby D at the train station, he wasn't there. I knew that the letter said it was the right day. I'd found it in Aunt Nell's room and read it till I could recite it right now. But Bobby D never made that train. He left me standing on the platform of the train station to receive a note instead. One of the other servicemen walked up to me and handed me a big typed letter. It said Bobby D knew what I was up to and wasn't interested in coming back for spoiled goods.

"When I read it, I walked all around that station, that block, until I couldn't walk no more. When I got home, your father was sitting out in front in a shiny new Cadillac. He had a ring in his pocket and an offer of going to the Justice of the Peace.

"Fool that I was, I took him up on it, cried all night, and woke up the next day as Jessie Campbell. Stomped proud into Aunt Nell's house, packed up, and left. She wasn't angry at all. You'd have thought she would've waited up for me that night and beat me like I'd stole something for staying out until well past daylight, but she didn't. She welcomed your daddy in the house like he was king of something. That heifer all but helped me pack."

"What happened to Bobby D?" Jan asked, raking her

fork back and forth in the plate stained green from pot liquor.

"I didn't forget Bobby D, but he made it his business to forget me. When I saw him, he'd eyeball me, cross the street, leave Club DeLisa, or walk past like I was a statue. He was tall with hazel eyes and he was a gentleman. First one I'd met besides my daddy, opened your door, walked on the proper side of the street, and listened to you as much as he talked." Jessie stood and walked over to the kitchen sink. She dipped Jan's empty plate into the tepid water, scrubbed, and swayed with the willow.

"I haven't told that story in what seems like a year of Sundays." Jessie rinsed the plate and put it in the rack to dry. "I was gonna run off with Robert, get married, make us a home, and have plenty babies."

Jessie tucked the rest of the story safely into her memory. She didn't tell Jan that once she started courting, Aunt Nell waited up every night until she got home and made Jessie squat and pee in a bucket. It had been a long time before Jessie figured out Nell's reasoning. Whenever Jessie questioned the old woman, she pointed a skin-covered bone in her direction and said, "Your pee is my business, long as you staying here. Checking it is my means to an end, and be lucky I ain't found it yet."

At first, there was no need with Robert. He'd promised to wait until they were married. But when he moved away from the boarding home and got his own place, she'd found out what Aunt Nell was looking for. Before her aunt could find the telltale clot, Jessie made a point to pee before she went home.

Jessie wiped her hands on her duster and walked over to Jan. "If you think I'm old, dumb, silly, and selfish, that may be true, but back then I wanted a baby so bad. I guess I thought I could make Crawfordsville all over again. Your father didn't see things the same way. He'd had a harder life and less love than I'd figured on.

"I thought a house and a baby was all it took. Don't make that same mistake. I never loved your father."

Jan heard the words and knew that she'd believed them all along. It was a part of what was wrong in the house, in the town, in her life.

"Just wanted to settle," Jessie said wearily. "Too tired of my life to keep trying to make a way. But settling is coming up short and knowing it.

"I can't say I don't care what you think of me. There was a time when I lived only for you. But you gone. Was goin' ever since you came here. Over to Ada's in those first months, walking early, talking early, bound to leave. I couldn't live for you no more than I could make a man into someone he never was."

Jessie unfolded her arms and offered one last piece of the puzzle, reaching a timid hand toward Jan. Jan held her mother's hand and as it led to her face she remembered Ada's arm, swollen, en route to a missing breast, and wondered if anything in life was really complete.

"I never loved your father and Bobby D never typed up that note. It was a trick played well enough to change the life I wanted into this thing I live. I got my house and I got my daughter. But it's funny. Today, telling a truth I'd been saving, is the fullest day I've had in so many years. You holding my hand, listening to me. I sure hope you don't put all my foolishness against me, but life ain't what you think it is, it's what it is. No matter what you do, you sho 'nough planting seeds and you'll have to reap that harvest."

"Mama, is that part of what Aunt Ada calls some type of laws of life or something?"

"Unh, unh, unh." Jessie loosened her hand from her daughter's. "Me and your aunt took to each other from the start. She knew your father was a full henhouse so she sat me down and told me the laws of the harvest way back then. Been a time since I thought about it.

"Every farmer knows, they don't even have to stop to think about it, and it works whether you're a farmer or not. You know that saying 'you reap what you sow'?" Jessie asked. Jan answered with a nod.

"Well, farming is like life. You born in the spring. Nothing much you can do then but wait for the ground to get warm enough to plant. Grow up a little bit, get educated, soak up the water from somebody else's winter, people that done gone on before you.

"Late spring and early summer you plant your seeds. You can plant a few in early fall. But spring-summer is your real planting time. You old enough then to know what you doing and time don't wait on no man, woman either.

"Well, you plant your seeds and sure as you planting, the first law is you going to reap what you sow, but that ain't all. Second law is you reap more than you sow. Whatever you plant, good or evil, each little seed will search for water tucked deep in the soil. Mixed with dirt, that seed will find everything it needs to grow into a plant much bigger than any seed. Set out tomato seed, then eat fifteen to twenty tomatoes from that one seed. Now, fancy people not believing in God. Set out evil, lies, mischief, and jealousy, it'll grow up just as strong.

Jan smoothed her hair back and crossed her legs, trying to imagine Ada, younger, talking girl-like to her mother.

"Third law is, you reap later than you sow. People forget about that. Act like they never heard that third one. Most of 'em skipped over it in the Bible, just fixed on 'Lest there be a mockery of God, you'll reap what you sow right here on earth.' It's all your good deeds and your bad that amount to a harvest come reaping time. If you ain't planted much, that's what you'll get. If you planted a heap of evil, it's coming for you, and if you plant good, it'll find its way back, too.

"In the fall of your days." Jessie sat back. "Fall is where I am now. Your body may get tired, but you got to gather that harvest even if you don't want it. I know, 'cause I've seen people plant, pick, and eat evil. Had a few bites myself.

"Whatever your harvest, you got to depend on it for winter, when the ground ain't growing nothing but holding on to what's beneath it and getting ready to pull you in. Tell your aunt I told you." Jessie reached for Jan's hands again, shaking away the conviction of her own words the best she could.

"I bet your aunt wore a special dress and one of them southern hats to your graduation." Jessie tried to stave off the jealousy of her sister-in-law being in a place where she wasn't.

"She didn't come, Mama. Didn't you know she was in the hospital?" Jan asked.

Jessie sat back heavily in the chair, glancing in the direction of the front porch. "I didn't hear nothing about Ada being in the hospital, and I don't think your father did either."

"Mama, she's got breast cancer." The words left Jan's mouth dry.

Jessie's voice wavered. "God knows his business, but Ada ailing don't seem right. Ever since I knew your aunt she's been a good woman." Jessie sensed Jan's fears. "I know it hurts you. I know what she's been to you. But don't worry, Ada's got God and Jesus if anybody does."

On the porch, Charles felt the winds rising and for the first time that day he wondered if it would rain, after he'd spent all day watering the grass. "Goes to show you," he mumbled, and stood. He walked around to the side of the house to turn the water off, passed the side door and, after a few more feet, bent underneath the kitchen window to turn the water off.

". . . It may not seem right to you, but loving ain't always a reason for staying and not loving ain't always a reason for leaving. It's true I never loved your father. And I don't expect I love him now, but I didn't leave once I had you. I stayed because of you. I knew full well raising you alone wouldn't be right. But I fixed it so I wouldn't have no more children. And now that you grown up and living on your own, it ain't no reason for me to stay."

Charles listened. Not one word was a surprise, but hearing it out loud as easily said as "good morning" made his mouth sour with the sting that comes before vomit. He forced the bile down and listened.

"What I got left? Another ten, maybe fifteen years in this body. I figure now, I'll die here, just like your father. One of us got to go first. All we owe each other now is to be decent. You never know who's gonna have to mop your mouth before you leave this world. After a time, a body is like an old tree, best stay where it's planted."

Jan folded her arms on the table.

"Get up and go on to sleep now, Jan. Get a nap. You tired and probably want to spend some time thinking. Can't say I blame you. I know I've spilled more than an earful today," Jessie said, eyes on the willows. "And don't you worry about your aunt. Cancer coming to her, don't mean she got to go to it."

Charles rubbed his left arm with his right hand. It was numb and tingling more than ever now. He cursed arthritis and rubbed as if he were trying to erase Jessie's words. Each syllable danced on the sound of the rising wind, then settled deeper than his ears. "I never loved your father." He mixed the words with the news of his sick sister and imagined Verga, leaving as she had years ago, a spirit on a gust of wind.

Parting Clouds

*T*he spirits of Jessie, Charles, Bobby D, Ada, and Aunt Nell had robbed night's restful hours. In the early morning, Jan dressed, wrote a note, and left out the side door before sunrise. Moleen clocks were approaching five A.M. when we crossed the railroad tracks on our way to the city. Now, as her thoughts turned to Don, I traveled ahead and got there first.

In his loft, Don languished on the last moments of a dream where Jan was cooking on a stovetop. Pots simmered, sautéed, stewed, and nearly bubbled over. Music from speakers near the ceiling trilled throughout the studio, reels of tapes were shelved across from the women.

He moved and felt the pallet on the floor, dampened by his sweat. As his eyes adjusted to the semi-darkness of the loft, he was amazed at how often he spent nights away from his woman now. Sitting up, Don pulled on his pants. A chant from the happiest days of his childhood rested on the last fringes of what had been a pleasant dream. "She loves me, she loves me not," his mind hummed, his arms entering the sleeves of the same checkered shirt he'd worn the day before. Jan was slipping away.

When he stood near the phone, he wanted to call her. *Babe, now that you gigging downtown, a straight shot over from me, maybe we ought to loft together.* He practiced the invitation and heard the impotence of his words, rubbed his hand over his face, then roughly in the corners of his eyes, and moved toward the bathroom. Besides his woman, the first problem, how could he ask Jan to move into a loft with no tub, no shower, only a sink and a toilet? An outline of his reflection in the aged tint of the mirror above the sink convinced him that he could make a kitchen and set up Jan's recording equipment in the east corner. Through the doorway and into the last ebbs of darkness he tried to envision Jan cutting tapes before she left for work. Filling his mouth with water, he scooped a fingerful of soda out of the Arm & Hammer box on top of the commode, scrubbed the powder against his teeth with his index finger, gargled, and spat. She could live near her job and in the middle of his. He cupped his hand, filled it with water, and rinsed his mouth again. He peed and washed his hands. Who was he kidding? Slivers of light entered the studio. Moving closer to the mirror, Don considered the gray hair he ignored most days. The cotton shirt worn thin at the shoulders echoed the same reply. When he looked past the mirror and into the depth of his own face, he knew that all he was, is, and would be were not what Jan wanted.

Don moved methodically through the disappearing darkness. *Bitches,* he thought, passing the busts' glaring faces. He reached for the shovel behind the door, walked briskly down the hall to the rear, and took two steps at a time down the staircase. On the ground, his pace quickened. He felt sweat trickle down his back, meeting more perspiration on his tailbone, slipping slowly between the crease in his behind.

He wanted to fuck her, not make love or whisper a tender word, but ram her, bite at her nipples, and watch her fear turn into greed. Didn't he make her leave her desk and walk straight to him like she was hypnotized? The sun, rising on his back, began to eat through his shirt as he half-walked, half-trotted, toward the tracks. With one hand he opened several buttons on his shirt, letting that hand fall and stroke his penis. He cupped himself, and when his hand returned to his side his penis was throbbing, hard and as angry as his heart.

Reflections on the railroad tracks a few hundred feet ahead caused him to squint. He slowed to a swift walk near the tracks, until he reached the pile of dirt he'd shoveled yesterday. It was darkened by moisture wetter than dew. Sometime during the night it had rained. He dropped the shovel, unbuttoned his shirt, peeled it off. Sweat shined his torso. He threw the checkered material across the top of the high grass. Now, with green seeded blades peering through the shirt he often wore without thinking about its worth, it appeared to him more like rags than clothing. His hand brushed the grass. It looked dry, but when the blades met his fingers he felt the dampness.

"Sneaky-ass rain," he scolded. *Wake up one morning everything looks fine. Then just when you thought it was time to get cozy between two breasts near your earlobes, thighs that hugged you, get used to warm breath singing against your neck, nipples on your back, soft hair against your ass, kisses, a bunch of fucking rain.*

He picked up the shovel and it eased into the ground. Before he knew what women were he was empty. Dirt fell against a pile that almost met his waist. Then, no matter how many thighs he parted, he was still empty. Another shovelful of dirt splayed through the air. Now, the hollowness was like a cave.

"Love me." The words passed between his lips, and he imagined them turning to liquid, soaking the pile of earth more than any rain, creating mud, then a rush of water. He sunk his shovel in the ground, loosening, pushing. By the end of the morning, the pile would reach his shoulders, the newest in a chain that ran the length of the railroad track as far as he could see until it lost it-self around the bend. A man's workout, he told himself, digging.

"I can lift more dirt than any Michigan Avenue man lifting weights in a health club." His voice was louder now. He heard the whistles and glimpsed a flicker of light as the train came around the bend. "I don't drink, don't give a fuck what wines to order. Restaurants ain't shit. Love me," he said, squeezing the command out until it joined the dirt flying through the air. The whistle sounded as the train began to pass. Dirt rained. The ground trembled under Don's feet, his thighs stiffened.

"Why the fuck doesn't somebody love me?" Don shouted, but his voice was drowned by the sounds of the train.

I left his spirit and traveled over the piles of dirt. For more than two miles, with only a few yards between them, cone-shaped hills dotted the bend. In the earth, tossed over his shoulder and liberated through his sweat, I saw the color of his soul, yellow, thinning, and growing pale in the coming day's light.

Jazz

Jan sat on the 151 express bus, staring at the sky's blue. I could have told her it was preparing for heat. Only sparse clouds, dissipating, drifted high above the water. Earlier, as she'd run by, Lake Michigan had called for her attention with a gentle knock against its shores. Now the lake view offered itself to replace apartment fire escapes, clothes hanging limp or stiff on lines, and flashes of sparked light against dim walls in the underground terminal. A train ride on an elevated track to a job that tallied complaints had been traded for a new route to the beginning of a career. The lake was bound to show off its waves, whitecaps and froth outlined against the sand. Jan acknowledged the new path, too. That's why the phone message Don left made her imagine him whispering in the receiver late at night while his woman slept. It tapped weariness into her shoulders. *First day! Studio at noon.* She crumpled the piece of paper and stuffed it in her purse.

The bus slowed, stopping on almost every corner. Jan read the address of WJZZ from Raye's business card. Six twenty-five North Michigan stood on the southeast corner of Michigan Avenue and Ohio. She crossed the street and continued toward the building, its numbers cast in bronze against pebbled concrete. On the plaza level, waiters at a café were already snapping linen tablecloths against the air in anticipation of lunchtime crowds. Inside the building, Jan stepped easily over the taupe marble floor with its swirls of maroon.

When the elevator stopped on eleven, a tall, blond, blue-eyed man was coming through glass double doors. His tan implied days spent someplace more exotic than Rush Street's beach. Jan's curiosity was quickly captured by the man behind him. Slightly taller, she noted his skin was the color of Ada's iced tea, clear, strong, translucent, lightened with lemon. The crisp white shirt and brown pin-striped trousers fell around him like the silk handkerchief poised in the breast pocket of his navy blue blazer. He held the blazer in one hand, draped over his shoulder. With the other hand he held the door open, nodded, and said, "Good morning."

"Morning," Jan returned. "Thank you." She caught the door and a backward glance of him putting his arms into the blazer then following his colleague onto the elevator.

In front of her, the receptionist spoke over headphones. "May I help you?"

"Yes, I'm Jan Campbell." Before the child could tell who she was here to see, the young woman responded.

"Ms. Gasby is expecting you." She held an index finger in the air signaling Jan to wait, then mouthed an apology and waved her over to a row of maroon chairs. Black-and-white photographs of the station's personalities in 36-by-24-inch frames lined one wall. Black leather scoop chairs surrounded a red and gray marble table on the wall facing the skyline. On the remaining wall, city scenes bordered the station's call letters: WJZZ stood out in granite.

After a few minutes, Raye appeared, motioning for Jan to follow. "C'mon back and let me get you started. I've just snagged an interview with one of your favorites, Bobbi Humphrey, and I'm on in less than half an hour." Jan imagined the speaking voice of the flutist live in her earphone while her hands potted up the sound. *Power the board, mike check, punch up the utility line.* She followed Raye through a maze of cubicles enclosed by offices with full glass windows. They zigzagged through its center and reached a large studio to the rear of the office space. Inside, she was immediately under the impression that her college studio had been an antiquated play toy.

"Listen and watch. You'll catch on." Raye read Jan's expression.

It was noon before they left the studio. Raye showed Jan back through the maze to a cubicle near the front office. "This is your home outside of the studio," she said. "Get settled. I've got an appointment. I'll finish going over some things with you after lunch."

I kissed "be anxious for nothing" into her spirit while she put her purse in a drawer and placed writing pads, one containing edit notes from the interview, on her desk. A half-hour later, she was scrounging under the desk, hunting for an outlet for her tape recorder. Looking up, she noticed the man who'd held the door open for her that morning. His office was right across from her cubicle. Smiling, he gestured and ran his hands under the desk. Jan copied his movements and found the power strip, wondering how long he'd been watching her. Face flushed, she sat at the desk, remembered Don's offer, picked up the phone, and dialed.

"So how's the first day?" Don asked when he heard her voice.

"Busy."

"Listen, babe, you know your shit. What you don't know, you'll learn. Been waiting for you to call. I'm on my way to pick up some shrimp and fries. Start walking. You're closer to me now. By the time you get here, we can 'surrey and picnic,' babe."

"On my way." Jan hung up, but her lips didn't curl into a smile. She took her purse out of the drawer and stood to leave. The man who'd transformed the maze into a fishbowl was coming toward her, his hand extended.

"Hi. I'm Phillip Thomas." He wore glasses and his hand, nails manicured, palm soft, swallowed hers. "Finding things okay?" He smiled.

"Yes. Thanks for playing charades. I'm getting there. It's been busy already."

"That's the way it is around here and believe me, busy is good. I'm the sales director, so I'm not really involved in production. But if I can ever offer any help, well, you know where I am."

"Thank you," Jan said, wishing his office were farther away.

He looked at her purse. "Are you on your way to lunch?"

"Yes. As a matter of fact—"

He interrupted. "Well, I'm just going downstairs to The Bistro. If you're interested in a little history on this place, we could grab a bite together."

"That would be nice, but I'm meeting a friend for lunch," Jan replied.

"Well, we'll do it another time, then." Phillip smiled, a little less teeth this time, and walked toward the reception area.

Jan waited by her desk. She could have called Don and canceled, but she just waited. A few minutes later she was on her way, walking west until restaurants and shops began to disappear. A part of her faded as the shops turned older, some abandoned, less of everything. She searched for a phone booth and a dime.

"Sarah."

"Hey! How's it going, girl?"

"I'm a mess."

"Jan, A students just apply what they learned. You are not a mess."

"Sarah, I'm on my way to Don's studio."

"Shit, Jan. Screw that lunchtime shit and get a new routine. . . . Are you there?"

"Yeah."

"Where are you, exactly?"

"Ohio and State."

"Don't go. Just turn your ass around and don't fucking go." Sarah was louder than she needed to be at work. "Girl, these nuts are listening to me. Turn around," she whispered.

"Sorry. You're right. I don't know what I'm thinking about. One of the guys in the office wanted to go to lunch. Anything would have been better than this, shoot! I don't know."

"I can't talk, but I can say this, turn around and don't go. If I'm sick of this shit, Jan, you got to be sick of it, too. Damn."

"I'll call you tonight. I'm going back to the office."

"Please."

Only a few people entered the eastern edge of the artists' district. Two women, one with waist-length hair, the other with bare legs and clogs. They turned toward Hubbard. A man clad in jeans and a T-shirt rolled up at the arms had a pack of Kools in one cuff. His other arm, tattooed to the wrist, clutched a large portfolio. Mechanically, Jan tried the coin return, stuck her fingers in the slot, nothing. To the east, people became groups, crowds again. She smoothed her skirt, one of five skirts Sarah was making as her "girl, got you a new job" gift. She secured her purse over her shoulder, walked toward Michigan Avenue, looking for a sandwich shop. The need to go see Don fell with every step. Jan thought Sarah was right. I did, too.

Now, Jan could no more feel my arms tightened into a

hug around her neck than she could my face getting lost in her hair as it fell around her collarbone. So I knew she didn't hear me carrying on about how the brown strands reminded me of my own, more rich mud than black, still just as thick. Sometimes a deaf ear is filled with life, so I kept going on with how we had good heads atop majestic shoulders with outstretched necks and feet that would find a straight path. I cursed the niggling feeling that came across her belly that this was the beginning of the end and not the end. It did not matter. Rejoice in the smallest victories, I shouted. Since the tree goes the way of the branch, I told the child we were moving in the right direction.

The rest of the week, Jan lived, for the most part, in the studio or sequestered in her cubicle. It quickly filled with tapes, transcriptions, notes, and day-old cups of coffee. At home, when she wanted to talk, she called Sarah, Ada, and her mother. When they wanted her, she told them to call back after ringing once, twice, or three times depending on the caller and she would return the call. Sarah said that was the "stupidest avoid-the-issue tactic" she had ever heard and that Jan should just tell Don things I'm not likely to repeat. Ada hummed and Jessie grew silent after an attempt to laugh, but followed instructions anyway.

On the days that Jan was near her desk at lunchtime, Phillip was hardly ever in his office. When he was, men and women entered and left all day. The rain check on lunch seemed to have been forgotten. So she focused on what came naturally, putting the music together, creating bridges that talked to one another, jazz that let Joe Williams talk about "Falling in Love with Love," while Carmen McRae declared she was "Too Much in Love to Care." Raye checked Jan's music list, made a few changes, and gave Jan two weeks to work on the show they jokingly called Crazy Love. Late nights and early mornings in her apartment found Jan surrounded by ribbons and reels of tape on her platform. Cleaning the floor would have created a concert.

On Friday, The Bistro was full. "So what did you think of this first week?" Raye lit a cigarette.

"It feels right, a lot different from school, but good."

"Your work will hold, Jan. You're doing well."

Jan sipped the lemonade to keep her smile from spreading. They talked about the interviews, the mounds of tape they'd been through, and jazz concerts that were coming to town.

Raye explained that a group of people "in the business" would be going to a jazz club in the South Loop later on that evening. She invited Jan, then winked. "You can bring a man if you want to. Mine's out of town."

Jan remembered Don for the first time in days. "Mine wouldn't be able to make it on such short notice."

I picked more lint out of the child's hair, amused. Earth folks always talk like people were made to possess.

From the outside, Solomon's white stucco veneer announced itself among rows of dark brick buildings. South State Street had had its day. Jan remembered when Michigan Avenue was off-limits to blacks, made so by sales clerks who would hardly come your way and security guards who followed you to the bathroom. Those were the times when Ada treated her to the dress shops in this section of the loop. The shops were gone now, unable to compete with restaurants, hotels, and office space. She listened to the elevated train a block away, thought about Ada, and assumed the noise from the train alone would disturb any relationship you could hope to have with a piece of music.

"Wait until you're inside," Raye told her, opening the door.

Two steps in, the atmosphere proved perfect for jazz. The walls were the same white stucco as the exterior. Exposed oak beams ran across high ceilings encircled by a balcony. Low lights cast a pale orange tone against the walls, and men and women moved in welcomed slow motion. A trio played in the middle of the room. Jan was trying to place the slow romantic interlude when a man approached them in a camel-colored linen blazer and a white crew neck shell underneath.

"Raye, who's the lovely lady?" he asked.

"Jan Campbell, Roland Gray. Jazz connoisseur and aficionado. Knows his stuff and always gives me the best seats in the house," Raye said.

"Pleased to meet you." Jan shook Roland's hand.

"Just seat us with WJZZ."

"This way." Roland was leading them to the middle of the room. "We reserved six tables for your party right across from the musicians. A few of your friends have arrived." As soon as they were seated, Jan scanned the tables that had been arranged in a rectangle across from the musicians. Candles in bowls of water floated enough light to illuminate the groups of twos and fours. In front of her and to the left, Phillip sat speaking into the ear of a short, wheat-toned woman with a small Afro and large eyes, but Roland temporarily blocked her line of sight.

"The waiter will be over to take your orders in a few moments. We have a complimentary vegetable and hors d'oeuvres bar in the back. Enjoy yourselves. Tonight's trio is Always Summer, the vocalist is Jessica Vinnette. Traditional, Cannonball Adderley–type jazz. The best." He winked. When he left, Jan had an unobstructed view of Phillip.

"So what do you think?" Raye turned to Jan.

"I like every note the trio is playin', but I've never heard of the vocalist."

"I know. She's new in town. *The Defender*'s review gave her high marks. We'll see."

"I can use some of the Bobbi Humphrey, but after logging the tapes, I see where we could use another interview and live piece on that Women in Jazz series. If Jessica Vinnette works, she could offer a local angle."

"I knew you were right for this job."

They talked about upcoming projects. A few more people from WJZZ arrived and Raye suggested she introduce Jan on their way to the hors d'oeuvres. The jazz became heavier with a touch of blues. Jan couldn't help but notice the care Phillip seemed to take of the woman he was with, ordering for her, his hands carefully removing the short black jacket. Occasionally, he would stroke her bare arms and shoulders.

"Everybody's here now. Let me take you around," Raye said, standing. Jan followed Raye as they greeted WJZZ people at each table. Most had guests from advertising agencies, a spouse, a "friend," or someone in the business. Phillip introduced the woman he was with as Felice something. At least the child was polite. Raye led the way to the hors d'oeuvres.

Sipping tonic water, Jan waited impatiently for the vocalist. Raye knew almost everybody that came into the club and there were more introductions when people stopped by their table. Jan relaxed, tuning in more to Raye's chatter and observing Phillip's table less. The house lights dimmed, a spotlight appeared onstage, and a thin woman held the mike. "I'm Jessica Vinnette and I'd like to start you off with what has become a favorite song of mine, because it tells the story of a lady who found her voice when she was four, but had to wait until she was almost twenty to sing this song." Jessica Vinnette's alto dived straight into Nancy Wilson's "Guess

Who I Saw Today." After a few more tunes from Nancy
Wilson's Cannonball Adderley days, Jessica ended the
set with several songs of her own. Raye and Jan hardly
spoke from the first song until the applause at the end.
Jan forgot about Phillip until the house lights went up
and she saw him stand, hold Felice's chair, and help her
into her jacket.

Jan bent across the table. "I guess some of our party is
leaving. Raye, what station does Felice work for?"

"Never seen her before," Raye replied. "But Phillip
did say she was from Philadelphia. He moved here from
several different cities. So he knows a lot of people, been
around the block a few times. You know?"

"Oh." Phillip and Felice walked past them and toward
the door. Another group was leaving and Raye was saying good-byes. Jan was trying to recover and wondering
why it was necessary. Phillip didn't mean anything, he
had only asked her to lunch to be kind on the first day.
What would she have to say to Phillip, anyway? Still, her
mind was going on and on, not listening to Raye.

"Jan. Where are you?"

"Sorry?"

"What did you think of Jessica Vinnette?"

Jan was scrambling to come up with something. I listened and thought about the sayings earth folks had that
fit, some that needed a little twisting, and the way
Charles always tweaked a phrase to suit him. Don't go
in the kitchen if you can't stand the heat. Out of the frying pan and into the skillet. You can't miss what you
don't measure. Then I listened to Jan's thoughts and
split the difference. Even if she was getting ready to put
an iron in the fire or touch the hot stove, I had truths
that were ancient. So I whispered those stories trimmed
in love because facts are misleading. True, a stove, iron,
frying pan, and skillet can be hot, but I have witnessed
days when the heat was taken out of fire.

Joy

On Saturday, the apartment waited like me. We wanted the shades to be pulled up, bath or shower water to fill the tub and steam the mirrors, music to flow, so women could say what they needed and we could hear the men reply. But Jan just wallowed extra in sleep land, stretched and turned over until the sheets looked like chitterlings. Two hours later than she'd gotten up in years, she opened the doors of the Pullman kitchen and outdid herself, found a recipe for eggs Florentine with Mornay sauce and got it right, then packed up, and we shared our morning meal with the sound of waves.

If the tub was lonely, it got its chance to heat porcelain and drip condensation over the side. Jan stayed under bubbles over her shoulders until her hands pruned. Then she rivaled Queen Esther in applying oil and lotion. Cuticles cut, nails filed, toes and fingernails polished, eyebrows plucked, she didn't need a bit of makeup, and when she got in her car, we didn't start for Moleen or the West Side, but drove straight to Sarah's.

We heard the hum of the sewing machine before we could reach the top stairs. Inside, Jonathan lay on the floor watching television.

"Hey, Jon, what's on?" Jan asked, closing the door behind her.

"Cartoons," Jonathan replied, bleary-eyed. "Mom, can I go to the arcade?"

"See what you started?" Sarah pointed at Jan.

"Hey, I just walked in the door."

"Jonathan, Jan just walked in. You could've said hi or something first."

"Hi, Jan."

"Hey, I got a few extra bucks. Want two for the arcade?"

The boy popped up like toast. "Thanks, Jan. Mom?"

Sarah shook her head. "As long as the big spender is here," she said, then turned to Jan. "One dollar is fine. He can play four games with that, and you better put them pennies up until you get a check."

Jan handed the money to Jonathan. "Does she think I'm her kid, too?"

"Yep!" Jonathan laughed, opening the door. Jan followed him out into the hall. "I liked my graduation card," she called after him.

"You sure got a job quick," Jonathan said on his way down the stairs, then to Sarah, "Hey, Mom, tell Jan she smells good and looks pretty."

Jan closed the door, laughing, and sat down.

"He's got a crush on you, you know that, right?"

"He's sweet, Sarah. You've done a good job."

"Thanks." Sarah stood up, bowed, and sat back down to the sewing machine. "He was right too, you were quick on the job thing, Jan. How's your aunt?" Sarah asked, re-threading the bobbin.

"I haven't been by, just calling. She sounds okay and Uncle Albert said she's got more energy. But you can never tell about her, Sarah. She could be really sick, or she could be recovering, I really don't know."

I saw the child push back melancholy and thought about the effort. It was a spiritual act. She was waging war against the blues.

"I've been carrying Mama Ada with me all week, my mother too. It's strange, Sarah. I feel like a part of them wants me to come to see them and a part wants me to stay away, at least for a little while. You know, not check on them every weekend."

Sarah went to the closet to get Jan's latest skirt. "That could be true. You're a daughter to both of them, and I know how it feels to hold a child close and know that you also have to push them away."

Sarah wiped her eyes in the closet before she turned around. When she faced Jan her smile covered all signs of tears.

"Go see her soon, though. You know, tell her about the job. That's the kind of talk that will make her feel better."

Jan cut the TV off. "You're right, I'll probably go over next weekend. I've been trying to keep up. I feel like I'm on skates."

"Girl, you are doing it. Got a job, got rid of a man, and everything. Any sign of Don?"

"Not yet."

"He'll be back."

"Thanks for reminding me."

"Jan, when you get the man thing straightened out, you'll have it down."

"Wanna hear the latest?"

"Shit, Jan, you haven't gotten all the way out of the frying pan yet."

"I didn't do anything."

"What's the latest, Jan?" Sarah threw the skirt across the room. "Try this on and tell me all about what I bet is going to be Phillip at that club last night."

Jan pulled on the navy skirt. It was short and had two pleats in the front. "Gorgeous." She twirled, then plopped down on a beanbag and told Sarah about Phillip and Felice.

Sarah lit a cigarette. "Let's walk down to the arcade. I've got to check on Jonathan. I believe Raye read Phillip for you. Seems like he's been around and whether you know it or not, you all but told him you had someone else by saying you were having lunch with a friend. Now, the boy may have had an attitude. Big man on campus and you, the assistant, turns him down. You don't even know what you did."

"I didn't think about that till later. I was trying to get myself together." Jan walked to the door.

"At least you had some food for thought. . . . Girl, take that skirt off."

"I'm not."

"What's wrong with you? Saturday is for jeans and that skirt is for next week."

"You know I always wear my new stuff as soon as I get it."

"You're so crazy. That's three out of five. Next time I'm going to wait and give you the skirt on a weekday." Sarah laughed.

Jan ran her hand down the banister. Sarah slid down the last one.

"Who's crazy?" Jan asked, trailing the tops of ever-green bushes with her fingers.

I kissed Sarah too, because she found room to be happy for Jan when her own heart was breaking. Like I said, I liked them both and they'd added a new thing, joy. So, we took joy and all its strength with us, them hop-walking and me riding shoulder-high down Belmont, toward the arcade.

Summer's Rain

$\mathcal{F}$riday evenings in Mississippi's foothills never meant much more than other weekdays brought to their natural end. A darkening sky meant time to eat, wash, and sleep, since most sharecroppers had to work on Saturday. Often a sixth day was devoted to the landowner or tending your own crops. Now, two generations later, north of Mississippi, Friday evenings sear the city air. Rumbling gray skies bring a late summer downpour that only adds to the friction. Quietly, their eyes shifting and mouths mumbling about traffic, workers leave the office before five, but few plans are canceled. Many are highlighted, moved up, rearranged, needed.

I had observed these people with their jobs. Some call them careers, and most use that excuse to fill days with labor they take so seriously I supposed it could only lead to nights of hunger. After five days of one-way living, no wonder they seem famished for some life at the weekend. I wanted the child to live every day of the week with purpose. Earth people always thinking they have jobs to make money, like God would put them around other people to waste time and not touch lives, encourage. There is no waste, only opportunities. So I told Jan to look into the dream. Find the sharecroppers that produced bounty from the earth, field Negroes who took in the sun, African griots telling stories that are still repeated, and gardeners who bordered beauty around each footstep in the place where music began. Go back to the fields, the land, break up the fallow ground. Live in the city, but don't let it seep into your bones, I cautioned. You are a spirit, just housed in a body. Remember what you used to know as a child.

But Jan kept working. For at least an hour after the others had left, she'd been alone with headphones, a tape recorder, and a typewriter, logging an interview. If you spend your time on a shoulder, there's no harm in looking over it. So I saw the work. It was everything it needed to be without desire. Jan folded her arms on the desk, cradled her head inside them, and remembered her bus rides. All week, she'd left early enough to get off several blocks before her stop and look in the shop windows. At first, she pulled together fantasies of clothing Sarah could make or jewelry she would one day buy. But passing Saks Fifth Avenue, Brooks Brothers, and Tiffany's, she kept wanting to tell people who didn't care who she was that her aunt had one breast and was lying in bed, squeezing a blue ball; and she was so afraid to go see her, she had to battle fear just to make a phone call. Then there was Jessie, whose mouth reflected hers whenever she opened her compact, her eyes a mirror. More troubling, the same hint of deep disappointment frozen in years across Jessie's face shadowed her own.

She listened to the rain and imagined Jessie crying, even now, about the man she'd wanted and the education she never got. Somehow she was going to have to visit both women this weekend. And then there was Charles. He'd seemed so tired during her last visit. I wanted the child to find out she didn't have to go to be there.

I am waiting for her hips to grow.

Jan opened the drawer, took out her first paycheck and put the envelope in her purse, and began to clean her desk. She heard footsteps, then saw Phillip. He was drenched.

"I came back for my umbrella, saw the lights, and wondered what you were doing here."

"Oh, I needed to finish up an interview."

"It's a monster out there." He pointed to the windows. His inner sleeve was dry, beige toned. The rain had deepened the color of the rest of his overcoat. "How are you planning to get home?"

"I take the 151. It lets me off right in front of my building," Jan explained.

"The buses are backed up from here to the Tribune building. You know what rain does to traffic in Chicago. If you don't want to wait in the rain, you can come with me and I'll give you a lift home. I'm going the same way," Phillip offered. "I take an el, then I've got my car. I'm parked on Clybourn."

Take the el to a car. All of us knew logic had nothing to do with the offer. "Are you sure? I really don't want to inconvenience you," Jan said, watching his hands, remembering them on Felice's arms.

"No inconvenience. You won't have to rush and you won't have to wait in the rain. I'm going back to the bar across the street and have a beer before I go home. When I see you come out of the building, we can leave together or you can catch your bus, if it's out there. Fair enough?" He turned to leave.

"Fair enough," Jan agreed, knowing he had made it fair for himself. Going back to the bar and waiting was the same as protecting himself from no as an answer. Fifteen minutes later, Jan was standing under the awning of the building, trying to save her umbrella from the wind and keep her coat down. Several buses inched past, not one 151. Phillip joined her with his open umbrella and helped her close her own inverted one.

He stuck a hand under her elbow, ushering her toward

State Street. Jan's hair clung to her face. Once they crossed Michigan Avenue she said, "Let's run. I'm getting soaked."

"One, two, three!" Phillip held on to Jan's arm and balanced the umbrella. They hit several puddles before they reached the stairs to the el.

"You're pretty fast."

"I practice every morning."

"You're a runner?" Phillip wiped his face and took off his raincoat, then his suit jacket, and draped the jacket over her shoulders. It was warm and she was shivering. "I'm a runner, too."

On the train, Phillip seated her nearest the window. When the cars began to creep from the underground terminal onto the elevated rails, Phillip reached across to the window and wrote, *Dinner?*

Jan didn't answer immediately. Phillip reached over and wrote, *Please.*

Jan fingered *O.K.*

Ten minutes later, velvet pictures in primary blue, red, yellow, black, and green told stories of Mexico around the walls of Raoul's. Raoul yelled from the kitchen, his wife took the orders and seated the patrons. Their children played with jacks at a table near the kitchen.

"I sell jazz, cook some mean chili, run seven-and-a-half-minute miles, had to move to four cities in six years, and you are?" Phillip's eyebrows almost connected across his forehead. His hair was coffee bean, eyes curious.

"Assistant to the producer, runner, never timed my miles, a good cook even on a bad day . . ."

"Hmmmm."

". . . a deejay in the making, and the only place I've lived outside of this city was a small town where some people would think this"—Jan pointed—"was Mexico."

Phillip laughed. "Sounds like I come from the same place. Raoul would be lucky to get a customer."

Jan slipped her feet out of wet shoes.

Phillip ordered coffee for both of them and handed her a menu.

"When you finish deciding what to eat, tell me why a twentysomething-year-old would like jazz old enough to be her mother."

Jan ordered. "I grew up on the old stuff. It was my mother and father's only music. I guess I didn't have a choice."

"Between the Beatles and James Brown, you had a choice." Phillip played with the sugar packets on the table.

"You want to know a lot for dinner." Jan's foot bumped Phillip's leg underneath the table.

He looked down, then wrinkled his nose. They were laughing when the plates arrived.

"I had to work hard for this."

"For what?" Jan asked.

"*Buen provecho.*" Raoul's wife smiled, sat the plates down, and walked toward the children.

"The privilege to take you out to dinner. You were too busy for lunch. I'm surprised you said yes."

"First-day plans."

"So are you free sometimes on the weekend?"

"Maybe that's a better question for you?"

Phillip spooned jalapeños on his enchilada. "I'm free on the weekends."

Jan spooned fine red peppers in an oily sauce over her tostadas. "Then, so am I."

A Choice of Meals

*E*arth folks think they can manipulate time. So I saw Jan and Phillip attempt to coax and cajole the days, when they could only live them. They measured the weeks by meals. Every two or three evenings, Phillip introduced Jan to a new restaurant. Maxime's, tucked away in the basement of the Astor Towers; Sage's, where there was a new trio and vocalist every week; Sweetwater's, a hub for the Rush Street regulars and tourists. They laughed in The Bakery, with its Hungarian owner who made everything, including his own potato chips; and always, with the remembrance of rain, they drank the darkness of Mexican coffee and absorbed the heat of jalapeño peppers at Raoul's. When they started to repeat their favorites, dinners carried over into evenings that lasted more than the night.

So much for all the plans of sleeping in "their own spaces." I saw mornings when they used each other's toothbrushes, rushed home to change, and began to keep duffel bags underneath their desks void of health club attire, filled instead with the next day's clothes. For a while they were careful to take different trains until they forgot themselves and rode together. Then Jan would linger behind a newspaper at the station until she thought Phillip had made it to Michigan Avenue. When Phillip couldn't wait for dinner, he'd leave Jan a note in her mailbox. Then they would catch separate taxis to someplace far enough away from the office to eat lunch and keep the secret. At the office, even I was tickled to see the way they spoke casual hellos.

Now, I will not say the women of my earth time never heeded a call from across the field. Most field women found the men of their futures smiling across a row. I expect house-slave women looked at the drivers. And I remember working in the field, cotton framing the naked backs of men strengthened by humble spirits. We lifted our eyes across a row, and they saw us, and blinked, becoming the revelations of our dreams. We could not keep the secret. Older women marked our faces, sensed the movement of our hips, and rushed to teach discernment learned from years of experience. Still, we had our nights when a walk under the moon ushered up a feeling that made you wish you'd stayed under the eyes of someone wiser. But we laid down less and were more because of it.

Jan, far from watchful eyes, had mistaken the freedom offered by this pill, that foam, and options not as deadly as the ones I'd witnessed, for safety. But for all her freedom, she lives with a weakened voice. The child all but left her speech down the steps almost ten years ago when I came and I'm still trying to help her restore what she doesn't fully realize has been lost.

The women of my time knew what women have always confessed inside themselves but are afraid to own. When we dusted off the dirt, put our clothes on underneath the burlap, or unpressed our backs from barn and schoolhouse walls, we left a piece of our souls in the place we'd been and with the one we'd been with. We were reluctant to give away so many pieces of what we could not get back.

Now that Phillip was ever present, Jan was answering the phone, which didn't keep Don from calling. Each man touched on different nerves.

"I'm seeing someone."

"Does he wear a three-piece suit?" Don asked.

"Yes," she answered, sucking her teeth and hanging up, dreading the next time the phone would ring.

Sometimes when Phillip called, Jan didn't want to see him either. On those nights she called Sarah or cut a tape and thought about the woman in the black jacket.

The heat of early autumn was finally giving way to cooler days. On a Friday just after noon, the studio was quiet. Jan had finished splicing an interview together according to Raye's notes, and it was lunchtime. She stacked the reels and gathered discarded tape from the floor. She'd saved the best parts, but when she told herself *I am getting better at this,* she wasn't just thinking about segments and shows. It was the way she could feel her arms wrapping themselves around her own body and hearing her voice say no to seeing Phillip, the way she could visit Jessie and Charles, Ada, or Sarah, or do nothing at all, that began to open her vocal cords. It was the way she could meet Phillip for dinner and decide to go home even if her body didn't want to.

Jan ran some afternoons instead of morning, and played music she didn't like just to hear what other folks were listening to. So now, with her work done and her heart content, she picked up the phone and dialed an old familiar number. I heard more than the phone ring. She might not have been speaking her mind entirely, but I believed the child was at least clearing her throat.

"Hello."

"Don."

"Yeah, long lost babe in the woods. The back door nigger keeps his doors open. It's lunchtime, so come on home."

Jan placed the receiver down, walked through the maze, boarded the elevator, continued outdoors and onto the crowded street.

Once she reached Don's building, she frowned at the elevator and took the stairs.

"C'mon in, babe."

"Hello, Don."

"Job must be right for you, you look delicious, babe." Don walked toward Jan, arms outstretched.

She breathed clay, sweat, paint.

He held her hands.

"I came to talk to you." Jan stepped back, putting her hands on bony hips.

"So talk, babe. And in case you didn't notice, people move up when they have something to say, not back."

"Don, I'm not here to start things up again."

"Okay, babe. It's him or me and you chose him. So why come see me?" Don leaned against the table.

"I wanted to tell you that I chose me, Don. Not you or him. Me. What I want, what I need. Not what you want and not what he wants."

"Okay, babe. I always knew my role, but Mr. Sharp doesn't know about your back door nigger? Is that because he doesn't take care of business, or is he taking care of it too well?"

"I came by to let you know I didn't stop seeing you because of somebody else. I left because I wanted to get myself together. He came later. I came by because I'm okay, I did make a choice, and you don't have to keep calling me."

"Let's see, first I listened to the dial tone. Now I'm listening to "the back door nigger is out, the three-piece suit is in." I lost you a little while ago, babe; passed through my fire and accepted it, was losing a little bit of you after the first time we rolled on that pallet on the floor."

She followed his eyes. It made her tired to see the pallet. She was still curious as to its latest smells and who they belonged to, but drained.

I told the child to get her strength up, keep talking, get it straight, get it out. I looked at the lingering spirits on the shelves and they formed a cheering section.

"Sit down." Don pointed to the beanbag chairs on the floor. "You know I'm just an old man artist who has to have his say." Jan kept standing.

"It's been nice, babe. You came in here and filled my space out for a while. I won't say I didn't enjoy your sweetness, living that world of pastels. But, I paint in earth tones. You splashed some of your color around here and I guess we took it as far as it could go." He stood, took one of her hands, and relaxed against the counter, pulling her toward him. Jan freed her hand and let him lean on the counter without her.

"If I were alone, I would have asked you to live with me some time ago. We could have done it together, my art, your music, your interviews. Two black bohemians. We'd have moved to New York maybe, saw some sights. But I'm attached, not married, attached." They drew separate images of the woman in braids.

"I would have shown you Harlem, not midtown Manhattan." Don walked over and grabbed her hands again, his palms sweating in hers. "We would have eaten off the street corners, not the Chez this and Chez thats of the world. But that's not who you want to become. So, I have a question for you. What are you going to do"—he pointed at her heart—"with this?"

Jan was seeing Jessie, grabbing for cookies, still hungry, then Ada, squeezing a blue ball, determined to live until she wanted to die, facing things, pressing against them, fighting back.

"Don, all I know is I have to go on. I have to find something. And I don't know what it is yet. Maybe I want this man. Maybe I don't, but I don't want both of you."

"If you can't handle it, babe, then you can't. I sure

wish you could. And I know your packing up on me is about more than a man. You're a motivator, babe. You gonna motivate this man, but the question you have to ask yourself is, what will he do for you? Will he allow you to go where you need to go inside yourself? Will he help you or get in your way with his stuff? That's what you need to know before you give him all that goodness."

Jan wondered what Jessie could have been if Charles had helped her learn what she wanted to learn. He could have listened to her read, bought her books, or told the truth and let her go. "What did you do with all my goodness?"

Moving closer, Don used his camouflage laugh, the one designed to put some time in between her question and an answer he didn't have prepared. "I'd feel better if you already knew." He stroked her hair and slid his hands from her shoulder down her arms. "Should we share some magic for the last time?"

"No." She wasn't about to fall for the bait in the corner. I felt the war between them. My girl didn't drop her eyes or bat her lashes. "No, Don."

He was quiet.

"Then I'll remember it like it was, made peace with it a while ago. But I know who I am and I've got a feeling of what you'll become." He traced her lips with his finger. When he reached the center Jan didn't have to hold her breath to prevent her lips from parting. They parted when she said, "Good-bye, Don."

"I guess young women do grow up." Don bent toward Jan.

She stepped back, the kiss falling in the air between them.

In the hallway, she heard the elevator coming, but we took the stairs.

*   *   *

On Saturday, ribs of clouds clung low to the horizon. Jan ran along the lakefront and didn't mind the threat of rain. Maybe that's why the raindrops waited patiently until she finished her run. An hour later, Jan drove slowly through the downpour. Jessie was expecting her, the way she did with each visit now, never telling her she missed her or that she was disappointed when the excuses came. Still, the way Jessie prepared the greens or had a bag filled with frozen stew, vegetables, or meats for her to take back to her apartment let her know how much the visits meant.

They sat at the kitchen table listening to Charles taking advantage of what he called "good sleeping weather." Jessie was snapping beans.

"Do you believe in spirits?" Jan asked. Charles snored heavily from the bedroom.

"Yes," Jessie answered, reaching behind Jan and turning up the fire underneath the stew. "Sure do. Why?"

"I know Ada does, but I didn't know if you did."

"Ain't too many Negroes around, at least not my age, that don't believe in the spirits. May not call 'em that, but they believe and Ada got a reason to more than most."

"More than most?" Jan asked.

"First time I met your aunt, she knew what I felt and didn't feel for your father. Ada sidled up to me as soon as the men had gone in the house and left us out walking through some fields not that far from here. This place wasn't built up like it is now.

"'Why?' That was the first thing she said." Jessie stood and filled a bowl with stew. "Her first word, once she got me alone, cut right to the quick of it. 'Why?' She had to reach straight through my spirit to ask me that, and I knew she meant why had I married her brother and why was I moving out here in this house. I didn't say a thing. I was too outdone to speak."

Jan took the bowl of stew. Steam climbed its edges and spiraled above the bowl.

"Your aunt began to hum while we walked, then pointed for me to stay standing where I was. She walked over to a dead tree and reached her arm into its hollow. When Ada brought her arm out of that tree it was covered with bees. I moved slowly, crouching to the ground, then laid out on the dirt. Every country fool knew if you saw a swarm of bees in the field, you laid down. Bees would cover anything moving, but unless they saw you moving fast, they wouldn't go low to the ground. Your aunt put her arm back in that hollow, shook it a little, then walked back to me.

"'It'll be hard for you.' She offered me some of the honey, warm from her fingers. 'If you want honey, you got to go to the right tree.' Called my life as plain as if it were her own. But I didn't have the courage to change my life. You've changed your life already. That's 'cause you were as touched by the spirits as your aunt, a long time ago. You may not know how to use that part of yourself yet, but keep listening."

Jan heard her father cough.

"Who's in there?" Charles called sleepily.

"Me, Daddy."

"Go see your daddy. I'll keep your stew warm. I'm going downstairs to fold the clothes. Your father's been working too hard lately and he keep telling me he wants to talk to you." Jessie started for the steps.

Jan went into Charles' room, trying to remember how long it had been separate from Jessie's.

"Sit down." Charles patted the bed next to him.

Jan couldn't remember the last time Charles took a nap midday. Even if it was "good sleeping weather," it was his time to work on cars, water the grass, sit on the porch, anything but rest.

"I been meaning to talk to you." Charles coughed,

then sat up in the bed. "You been coming out more lately and that's a good thing. You and your mother talking up a blue streak till a man can't get a word in edgewise."

Jan wondered if Charles thought she'd been neglecting him. He held his hand up before she could speak. "It's a right good thing. Your mama is a good woman." Jan was taken aback. Neither one of us could recall Charles giving Jessie a compliment.

"My daddy was a coward and my mother was mostly just evil."

Now, I nearly lost my peace. I knew where Charles' thoughts came from. Sons and daughters are the last to complete the quilt our blood begins. They are too busy trying to understand the beauty of odd colors and patterns to see that stripes and prints, flowers and squares, wide stitches and small meticulous ones are all meant to be sewn together.

"Even if I hurt your feelings, I ain't got an evil bone in me for you and I ain't no coward. Loved you ever since you struggled out of your mama tearing up everything behind you. Saw Verga in you that very day, see her in you now, and so many of the others. So don't get mad. I've lived the life you wading through.

"You have a man problem. I can see it in your walk when you come here. Hear it in what you say and what you don't. I ain't asking for no details, don't need 'em. I been a young man myself. If you could get rid of that thing in a woman that makes her think a man can solve her problems and move on, you'd do well."

Jan was cold-staring Charles. He'd been right to tell her not to get angry. Charles coughed again and cleared his throat.

"You've got that degree, you'll be meeting different people, going different places. Go where you need to go, don't make do, don't live a whole life making do. Most

men using women to get back to the happiest parts of
themselves."

Jan heard the dryer door close and wondered how
much Charles knew about the man in Jessie's life before
him. Did he know what he stole from Jessie, and what
led him to believe he knew anything about the men in
her own life?

"You ain't gonna like me for it, but I gotta tell it,
'cause truth is the best gift I can give you." He sat up
fully in the bed.

"I married your mama on a dare. That's right. Somebody, can't even remember his name now, dared me that
I couldn't get Bobby D's girl. I saw your mama from my
window when I was living with another woman who
wasn't worth sheep shit. Drinker, liar, cheater, loose, and
low. When I saw your mama she was kind looking,
pretty as they come, 'Bama walk, and hair busy calling
for a man's fingers. I waited, watched her, and planned.
Then I found out she belonged to somebody else."

Charles looked at his hands against the blanket. They
were closing down like the mills, not as strong as they
used to be. He felt as small as he had those many years
ago. Out loud, the truth stung his ears as well as Jan's.

Jan saw the strain of his forehead, the way the dimple
worked back and forth. Pinheads of perspiration began
to line his temples. She held her breath and, when
needed, took short sips of air while waiting for the
whole truth.

"I was with a woman who cheated on me and it made
me want your mother even more. It made me stop looking at the kindness in her, 'cause it showed up the hurt in
me. I got your mama, Jan. I ain't gonna even tell you all
the lies I told and things I did to get her. But I got her.
And after I got her, I couldn't treat her no better than I'd
been treated. No better than the lowlife way I got her.
Robbed her from somebody who really loved her and

couldn't love her myself. I couldn't love her 'cause she reminded me about the part of myself I hated the most. The part of myself that walked away in the hard times, the way my daddy did. I lied and cheated the way I was lied to and cheated on."

Charles' voice cracked, but his face stayed the same. Determined. He looked up from his hands and into Jan's eyes. "I promised myself I wouldn't treat my wife or my children the way I was treated. But a lot of us men who had our necks stepped on by the white man, by our mamas and daddies or some women, found out we could step on a woman's neck even harder. Seemed like we couldn't wait to do it. I'm sorry now, but I got to tell you so you'll know. Snagging a man is catching hold of all the stuff he got, and you may not want half of it. You gotta pick careful and not be picked.

"A man ain't laying on top of you trying to think of ways to make your life better."

Charles felt Jan's weight rise from the bed and sit again. Her eyes fell. "A man that lays on top of different women is just trying to find his haystack needle. Just after happy times instead of moving ahead to make his own.

"A cheating man grabs two seconds of the past and is satisfied for a finger snap. Ain't willin' to live up to his own responsibility. Too foolish to make the time around him and the people he sharing it with better, running away from hard work and on to the easiest way a man know to feel good."

Jan stood and walked over to the window. She hated what Charles had done, but couldn't hate him for telling her. She was thinking everything ugly and dark in the house was shrouded by his deceit. Way too late, he was sorry. By the time she was ready to tell him some combination of *thank you, but you don't have to worry about me,* and ask *what are you going to do for my mama now,* she heard his breathing change. The covers were rising and falling, his snores congested.

Jan went back to the kitchen. Jessie was reheating her stew. "You haven't been spending the night much. Something wrong?" Jessie asked.

"No," Jan lied, wondering what her mother knew and didn't. "Everything's fine." The lie rested between them, Jan not sure her mother should know all the truths she'd heard. Jessie placed the warmed-over stew in front of Jan. Jan blew a spoonful until it cooled. It was rich, full of root vegetables from the garden, and slightly sweet.

Southern Suns

*S*easons take their time. The earth has to eat before anything can grow. So I knew it might be years, perhaps decades, before we could talk to each other, if ever. I could wait. But I would tell the child that people had mistaken my sternness for anger and my means for evil. If they knew the half of evil, they could have seen my red had nothing to do with harm and hate. It was no different than the base of blood, human passion, and family love. Charles breathed it when it was fresher than June roses; now it's aged into a potpourri. My time to love was short-lived on earth, but it's stronger now, waiting to be grown, pruned, and nurtured, dead seeds to be watered and tended until life appears. Charles' childish thoughts fermented into questions he could only answer with fear. I am an ancestor that sees and cannot be seen by those who have only earthly eyes, but my love is the opposite of evil, a love that casts only light.

When Jan's feet sprang from the sand of the lakefront, I could tell her heart was opening, her throat was clearing, and soon we would hear her voice. Ada had laid the necessary foundation, and above, spirits were waiting. The child had only to ask for more. Find her tongue, use her voice, and ask. Jessie and Charles had delivered their gifts. But we were still shy of her full attention.

Jan dressed to Betty Carter, Phillip on her mind. As Jan neared the office, I followed her colors. When she

sat at her desk separated by the maze of cubicles from
Phillip's office, I continued to go forward and found
Phillip daydreaming. I traveled from the day of the
dream into his past.

Young, sweating, lips sucked in, mind all aflutter, he dug
away at the dirt under the tree behind Ol' Man
Rutherby's tool house; used his hands to loosen the soil,
then sticks, then his hands again. The more loosely
packed ground he removed, the more excited he became. Before long there was as much dirt on his checkered shirt and blue overalls as there was in the little piles
that surrounded what had become a hole about six
inches deep and almost a foot wide. He seemed to have
forgotten about the sticks or the feel of moistened earth
crowding the space between his fingers and wedging its
way underneath his nails. Instead, he felt the egg-like
mounds beneath the soil. When he'd uncovered his first
treasure he sat it outside of the hole and uncovered three
more.

Phillip shook his hands free of as much dirt as he
could and wiped them on his pants. Picking up one of
the green mounds, he peeled the skin back. Then another. Small flakes of husk that covered the yet un-
ripened pecans compacted the dirt and added a layer of
dark lime residue underneath his nails. Once the green
husks were completely removed, he squeezed two of the
hard brown shells between both of his palms, grunting,
eyes closed, lips pressing against one another. With no
success, he loosened his grasp and smacked the shells
against the tree, then squeezed them in his palms until he
heard the familiar crack. He removed broken nut meats
from the pecan, placing its fragments on his pocket
handkerchief, thinking hard on pecan pies, pecan rolls,
homemade butter pecan ice cream, and piles of pecans.
It didn't seem to matter that just yesterday he'd

climbed the tree, then shaken the premature nuts down and hid them. He saw his wait as having been not twenty-four hours, but two years. And since it was the year for the pecan tree to bear fruit, he wouldn't wait any longer.

A fitful night of sleep, marred by several awakenings before dawn, had found him peering over his siblings' heads and out into the night. Phillip paid no mind that he'd compromised the natural sweetness of the nuts by picking them early. The taste of the long-awaited pecans would be good enough for him, and he excavated each hull, gathering the halves and broken bits and pieces until all the nut meats were ready. He scooped three fingerfuls and placed them on his outstretched tongue, then, reeling them in, he'd planned to chew slowly, but they were bitter. So bitter he spat them out, and spat more. Disappointed, he wiped his hand on his pants and dusted himself off.

Overhead, moss hung from the trees, dripping lazily from one branch to another. The sun promised a day too hot for bother. Phillip began to walk home. He didn't care for summer that much; he'd rather be at school. His mother cleaned and cooked at different homes in the town and his father worked the shipyard on the night shift. His day was filled with chores, errands, and what he determined was too much care given, at times reluctantly, to his three younger sisters and three younger brothers. School was different. In each classroom there were teachers who taught him everything he wanted to learn and only a few things he couldn't care less about.

Mrs. Andrews would set her jaw, and when she opened a book, you'd better not be too long getting on the same page as she was.

"You may have a southern drawl, but you will be speaking the English language without error when I'm through." She'd make the same speech every Monday, adding "*Ain't* does not exist in the dictionary, this class-room, or in the world in which you will become em-ployed. Now, let's start the week off right."

Phillip never said *ain't* in Mrs. Andrews' class or while he was in the school itself, but he sure said it when he left. He and a few of the boys would run the first block past the school in silence, each set of feet out to be faster than the others. As soon as they reached the large oak tree with branches so thick and old that a few lay close to the ground, they'd climb the branches in less time than it took to pass an offering plate on Sunday, and each would claim one for his own. On Mondays, they said as many *ain't*s as they could, dropped every verb they remembered, and mocked Mrs. Andrews correcting them until they laughed themselves limp.

Mrs. Andrews and Mrs. Johnson were two of the best teachers in the school. While Mrs. Andrews was no southern belle, they all agreed Mrs. Johnson was the ugliest. Her face resembled a chocolate chip cookie, deep brown moles dangling from its sides. She taught Latin, and Phillip loved Latin most of all. He derived the words, pronounced them perfectly, and often helped his friends with their homework. Mrs. Johnson was the only teacher to teach Latin and she let the students know they were privileged to enter her room. Latin classes were kept short to accommodate all the students at Winslow Elementary, and there was a lot to be cov-ered. Phillip practiced at home, even if he did say, "Lucas, I ain't gonna laud you no mo'," to his brother from the tree's branches. He guessed if Mrs. Johnson saw him mocking her and heard him talking after school, she'd never give him the extra work she man-aged to slip him each Thursday after class. Although he played along with the rest of his friends, he'd become Mrs. Johnson's prize student.

If there was anything he'd have skipped in his school

day, it was gym class. Physical education was "jokey" to him. Phillip really didn't care to do anything but run. He didn't mind playing with the boys, but basketball and baseball took a lot of unnecessary time and, being team sports, depended on everyone doing his share. He looked forward to fall, when he'd try out for cross-country, and spring, when he'd try out for track. He only wanted to depend on other people when he had the opportunity to be judged on what he did, which would ensure him placement among the best. Stopwatches never lied like boys complaining of a foul or a missed layup. Most important, he could run against himself. When he did, he felt even better than the thrill from his pursuit of one-day-old, early pecans on a hot summer morning.

Phillip looked at the sun and decided not to walk home, heading instead toward the grocery store. Women who didn't work days during the week would be doing their grocery shopping now and he'd help with the bags. Not all the time, but most times when he carried one of the women's bags to the car, they'd put a nickel or a couple of pennies in his palm. You could do a lot with a nickel, and a lot more with a few of them, and that's what he was after. He had plans.

Phillip dusted his pants off again and wished he hadn't been so careless uncovering the nuts. He didn't want the women to figure he might rub against them and muss their dresses with the green husks. He wiped his hands on the back of his pants, then over his face, not knowing the result was a dirt-and-lime-streaked forehead with cheeks to match.

"May I help you with your groceries, ma'am?" Phillip asked a woman with two small children, four bags of groceries in her cart, and a look of frustration on her face.

"Chil', you musta jest been sent from Jesus." The

woman's kind face blushed relief. Phillip wondered what Mrs. Andrews would have said if she heard the woman speak. A corner of her flowered dress was caught in the fist of a little girl. A small boy, sucking on a Tootsie Roll while waving his pacifier, was trying to get her attention as well. "Put 'em right there in that blue Chevy, between that truck and that li'l squishy car. Person must not plan on having no children with a car a nip larger than a Palmetto bug." The woman unloosened her dress from the little girl's balled fist and clasped her hand instead. "Ray Ray, get over here and hold Loretha's hand, now, and stop buzzin' 'round me."

Phillip admired the way the little boy did exactly as he was told. He stocked the car with groceries. When the woman worked her way into her bosom to extract a change purse, he busied himself gathering a few carts from the cars of other people putting their groceries away. He'd learned that if he kept the parking lot clear while he was helping with groceries, the bag boy would come out every so often and look at him with approval. Other boys had been asked to leave before, so he made sure he was helpful. "May I help you, ma'am?" "Can I help you, sir?" "Yes, ma'am," "Yes, sir," "Thank you, ma'am," and "Thank you, sir" were the only phrases he used in the grocery store parking lot. Once, one of the deacons from the church had seen him and given him quite an embarrassment. "See that boy?" The man spoke loudly, pointing at him. His wife nodded. "That's Phil and Sadie June's boy. Boy'll be a millionaire by time he's fifteen. Guarantee ya that. If not one by then, thirty won't catch him with much less than the Rockefellers. Pennies and nickels add up."

Seven nickels, twelve pennies, and two dimes later, there was no sense in going home. It was time for his regular job. Phillip made his way to Myers' Drugs and delivered more than his usual share of prescriptions before it began to get dark. He stared at the calendar and discovered it was his favorite day of the year, the first day of summer. Mrs. Johnson, her black moles dangling, called it the summer solstice. June 22nd. It was a day he liked to remember because few people knew that on this day something different went on in the heavens. The planets moved around until the earth's distance from the celestial equator was greater than any other time except for just before Christmas. Mrs. Johnson had taught him that a few years ago. Ever since, he'd labeled the day "summer Christmas." Not many people knew it. So you had to get your own presents, and that's what he aimed to do, find a present in the world meant especially for him. A new piece of knowledge, some kindness, like the coins clicking in his pocket. He kept the secret of the day to himself and was about to ponder what was going on in the heavens and what great present was still to come when Ol' Man Myers' throaty voice begged his attention. Phillip knew any sound at all coming from the man was an accomplishment, since the townsfolk said Myers had been smoking tobacco and chewing snuff one after the other, a sure sign of a "nicotine fool," since way before Phillip was born.

"Looka here, boy. 'Bout time for you to go. I ain't paying you to daydream." The old man grinned, good nature giving way to some of the brownest teeth Phillip had ever seen in a white man's mouth. "Take this bottle of pressure medicine to Mr. Tally on your way home." The pharmacist, his yellowed license above the register giving him the authority to grind powders, make all kinds of capsules, and measure out pills, put the container into a brown bag and wrote the price on the bag. Phillip stopped himself from shaking his head. Myers knew full well Mr. Tally could hardly pay a cent for anything upwards of a loaf of bread, and he really didn't expect the money. "If he pays you, li'l Phil, put it in your shoe till 'morrow. I trust you, boy. Now giddy-up on over to Tally's and make it home 'fore your ma be paying me a not-too-happy howdy do."

Phillip took the bag from the man's unsteady hand and left the store. He had no qualm with Tally, but he was sure glad he didn't live near him. His mother said, "Poor was one thing." It all but neutralized the South. "But poverty was another." He took her reminder to mean they were poor, but they did not live in poverty. "What you don't have in your pocket, make up for it in your mind" was what his father always said. Tally must not have ever heard any sayings to help him out because he was living in poverty, and although it would have been more justly said by someone at least two-score and one or more, Phillip knew full well Tally was dumb. The old man always came to the door half-dressed and complained all the time while he pulled two or three pennies out of his pocket for ninety-two cents' worth of medicine.

Phillip knocked on the door. The bell had been broken ever since he'd been calling on Tally. Phillip knocked harder. "I's a'comin'. Don't be rushin' me outta my skin." The voice, choked by coughs and spasms, came nearer to the door. Phillip got the package ready to push through the crack, but before he could thrust it in, Tally pulled the door wide open. His bloated torso and sagging breasts filled the door frame; a drool of something that could probably cause twelve diseases lay in a pool near the corner of his mouth. The man stepped forward as if he had some great wisdom to offer. When he was so close Phillip wanted to turn and run, Tally started to speak, choked, hawked, and spit over Phillip's shoulder. The phlegm landed on a patch of dirt that had once been a cover of withering grass. Phillip shuddered. His mother, Mrs. Andrews, and Mrs. Johnson would have fainted outright and required three graves.

"Boy, Ol' Myers got you working hard. I guess us niggers ain't got no rest in this place." The scent of a hog kill came from his mouth. He dug into his pocket with one hand and reached back to loose his pants from his bottom with the other. By mistake Phillip breathed in and the old stench of poverty streamed up to his nostrils. He hated the smell, and when he tried rather aimlessly to loose himself of it, tossing his head from side to side, it remained. He stuffed the few pennies into his best pants pocket, separate from his own coins, mumbled a thank you, and determined to take a shortcut through the field. "You's a smart nigger. So I'll tell you this," Tally said, leaning in as Phillip backed away. "Them there coins is all I'm giving Myers, take a coin or two off the top if you want to. Us niggers got to stick together. I gots mo', but the white man won't get my last. Humph. Take you a tip from Tally." The man's growl bridged the growing distance between the two. "Hey, heh, a tip from Tally."

Phillip only wanted the smell to be gone. He tried to brush it away with the back of his hand. The scent deepened and he realized that he'd touched Tally with that hand. He smelled his hand once more and discovered that if you got near it and stayed near it, poverty could seep into the layers of your own flesh.

Phillip let his hand air out by shaking it along his side and afforded himself a nice run. He took off, pacing his breathing so that he sucked in large gulps of the ocean-salted air. When he came to the field he thought again about this first day of summer and hoped it would bring something special. With all the commotion going on in the heavens, he wished for a sign, prayed for it. As he cut through the field away from the poverty-entrenched streets, his shoes got wet in the beginnings of the marsh. Moss hung languid from the trees. Phillip slowed and began to plod through the field. Oaks and poplars bred densely through the undeveloped land as his feet sank into damper ground. Something in the hesitant breath of summer's arid wind bid him caution but he was not afraid. Ignoring the warning, his thoughts turned to Tally. Some of his friends had started a refrain, "Old man Tally, lived in the alley, had a wife named Sally. Boom. Boom." It seemed like a long time ago when he'd joined in, but he could no longer recite the words once he'd made deliveries to the man. He felt sorry for Tally and wondered what made him so trifling. He thought the thing his parents often said, "With seven mouths to feed before we get to our own." Penny-pinching Tally had more mouths to feed than his own family. Phillip felt his foot sink softly and widened his trail to a drier path in the field. He didn't hate the old man, but he didn't understand him either and if there was one thing he took exception to, it was being called a nigger. A nigger was not a person, it was a thing. A thing not to be, at that. Not one teacher of his would ever let a student utter the word, not on the playground, the bathroom, or anyplace within hearing distance. "Look it up," Mrs. Johnson had challenged. "First *niggard*, then *nigger*." She pronounced both words with equal hate. "*Niggard*: stingy, a miser. A meanly, covetous, and stingy person.

"Now look at *nigger*." She'd trailed her finger down a few words in the requisite dictionary. "Negro, black, usually taken to be offensive. A member of any dark-skinned race." She took the glasses off her cocoa brown face, chocolate chip moles shaking with vengeance, gray eyes cold in the midday heat. "Now, you would have had to flunk Latin fifteen times to derive *nigger* and that meaning from *niggardly*, and it is, contrary to southern belief, a derivation. The white man made up *nigger* to make you feel bad and if you use it you will feel worse. You may not feel it at the precise moment you use the word, but over time you will feel meanly, covetous, and stingy. I do not teach niggers. If there is a nigger in the room, please walk out." As all of the class did whenever Mrs. Johnson went full throttle into one of her speeches, they listened and waited for her delivery of short spurts to change into one with regular inhalations. Phillip agreed with Mrs. Johnson. A nigger was something that made you see a reason for Black Only and White Only signs, if they read Niggers and Non-Niggers. You needed to keep a nigger out. A nigger was a lazy giving-up mind. Giving up right for wrong, giving up love for hate. Too stingy and mean to know the difference. A nigger didn't have anything to do with skin color: charcoal black, high yellow, ashy gray, or cracker white. The boy faced the word for what it was and decided no matter what happened in his life, even if he was destined to be a drugstore delivery boy all his days, neither white men and their offspring nor poor pitiful Negroes would turn him into a nigger.

He jumped high to hit the low branch of a gnarly oak tree, allowing a childish laugh to leave his throat. A song of previously unuttered words replaced it. "I ain't a nigger, won't be a nigger. No, not me a nigger." Then he took true license with his joy and used a word that was meant for grown-ups, and indiscriminate ones at that. "I ain't a nigger, won't be a nigger. No, not me a nigger. Fuck a nigger. I won't be that."

Out loud, the word no longer belonged to grown-ups. It was his. He wouldn't use it often but he could use it when he wanted even if he made it silent, a footnote to himself. *Fuck*. It felt like a tree to climb, a branch to hold on to. In an instant he was the thing the word was meant for. A grown-up. A man.

Reaching hard dry dirt, he looked down at his shoes, wet enough to make his mama mad. He looked up toward the road and found he was all alone in the field. Phillip quickened his pace, not afraid, smart. That's what they called him in school. Smart enough for extra work and helping the teacher with the slower ones. Smart enough to get away from the Tallys in this world as soon as he could.

He heard a car coming down the road. If it was a neighbor, he could hitch a ride. He walked faster to reach the road, but he didn't want to run. This was not the time for running. What if it was one of those church nosies? They'd see his shoes and tell his mama. He quelled a skip and remembered his neighbors wouldn't be out this way anyhow. Coming closer, he could tell the car was too new to belong to anyone from his neighborhood. A bare sketch of an old white man behind the wheel came into view. The car slowed. Its black finish shone in the sun against the marsh and the high trees on the other side of the road. Its driver was an old white man, at least sixty or better. Phillip squinted to see if it was anyone he knew from the drugstore, but he couldn't place the blurred face. He thought he saw the man reach for something on the seat beside him. The drying wetlands called him back, the sun in his eyes stopped him still.

The white man stuck something out the window. It was long with brown and silver that glimmered—the shining barrel of a rifle. The boy stood, his body wavering slightly like the tall grass. He lifted his eyelids over eyes that no longer cared about the sun, and they met the white man's cold blue stare. The boy called on God; I watched the request leave his heart. He could see his family, their faces, and the faces of people yet unmet. He looked at the man, straight into his blue eyes, then past them. He believed his Christ was confronting the man's devil and the two did war. *Same God of my mama and my daddy. Same God of Mrs. Andrews and Mrs. Johnson.* The thoughts left him and entered the battle until the man let loose a howl and his whole face broke into laughter. Phillip's vision remained steady. He traced each wrinkle and line in the weathered face as they became clear from yards away. The old man pulled the rifle back into the car and sped down the road. Dust leapt up behind the black car until it seemed an ashen white. Phillip took one cautious step, as if he were being followed.

"Fuck you, nigger!" he hissed through clenched teeth. As the words careened from his lips Phillip immediately felt calm and in control. Odd as it was, he felt sorry for the old white man captured by the devil. Only the owner of hell himself would bully gun a child. Man didn't know who he was. He agreed with his mama, daddy, and the deacons. Phillip Thomas would be something much more than an old white man out for a joyride with a gun. More than Tally fit for the alley. He'd keep going like his teachers told him and he'd take stock each year on the first day of summer, comparing it with the last such day. He'd drink out of any fountain he wanted and have money, too.

He was what Mrs. Andrews called "an enterprising young man," delivering papers in the morning and drugstore pharmaceuticals in the afternoon. On Saturday and on any midweek day when he had no more chores to do, he helped the people with their groceries at Dalby's. Three-fourths of his morning money he gave to his mother and three-fourths of his afternoon money he gave to his father. He kept the rest in a sock in the bottom corner of the chest of drawers in the room he shared with his three brothers. Out of the Saturday money he gave his Sunday school dues, put a dime in the church plate, and spent the rest. Sometimes he'd save up enough to buy doughnuts or ice cream for his sisters and brothers. Once, after a good Saturday, he bought a pocketknife from Lester's. The most he had done with it was to peel an apple. Whittling wasn't something he cared for and too often lately he guessed he'd have been better off with another doughnut. Once he bought a funny book, but it only had white men in it, fighting, jumping off buildings, and talking to girls, so he continued to save his money. He didn't need too much foolishness anyway. He was out to be something. His were big plans.

Nearing home, Phillip decided not to stop for a doughnut, even though the coins jingled in his pocket. His finger circled two nickels and a dime, then almost punctured a recently sewn seam where a hole had been. He wouldn't stop at the Krispy Kreme. He had control, if not against a pecan, he could resist a doughnut. Anyway, summer had started with a lot to think about. Today he'd be glad to see his mother putting food on the table, his father shining shoes, fixing a chair, or chiding his mother. And, if the truth be known, today, three sisters and three brothers weren't going to look like there was too much care given to them at all.

Phillip's thoughts moved forward and so did I, to years later, the day he met Jan. He was in his office, elbows leaning forward on his desk, swiveling in the faux leather chair and gazing at the calendar before him. It was June 22nd. He'd worked a full hour before nine that morning, had been out on a business call and back even though he hadn't closed a deal in eight days, was behind his goal for the month, and Felice wasn't due in until Friday.

He'd looked out the windows in his office, first to the skyscraper view of the city, a far piece from Myers' Drugs or Dalby's, and knew Mrs. Andrews would have been proud. Mrs. Johnson, moles as still as they could be with her head held high and straight, would have said, "Nothing less than I expected," but he didn't feel so grand or accomplished. He turned from the windows. Across the cubicles, he spotted someone new. The girl he'd seen at the elevator that morning was searching around her desk like a college freshman. Maybe he'd take the new office attraction out to lunch. Perhaps she could be a gift for the summer solstice, he'd thought, not realizing he'd still be waking up with her this fall.

I left Phillip, following his eyes, and drifted closer to Jan.

Salvation

 $\mathcal{I}$ am waiting for Jan to say something. Instead, waiters in short jackets, linen napkins over one arm, open bottles of wine chilling in silver buckets, recite the evening's specials, or periodically check on the satisfied and the insatiable. Clinking glasses, silverware against plates, and chatter pass between the patrons of Chez Paul's. Some people appear to be talking with dinner partners while others pretend to listen, and since most of them are so taken with themselves, nobody is saying much, so there is a lot of noise and little to hear. Jan is not the exception, either. In the dreams now, I remind her about the stories Charles told, full of lessons. I light plainly the way Ada speaks without uttering a useless word. Jan should know the stock she came from, and if not that, she could open her eyes. Sarah always speaks her mind, and even Don intoned what he thought was true. Jan had cleared her throat with Don but is only listening to Phillip, and I still haven't heard her voice.

". . . two hundred thousand dollars and they didn't think I was going to pull off the deal. Now they want a piece. Vultures."

Phillip was five minutes into another telling of some office coup. Jan loosened the snail from its shell with the seafood fork, the scent of garlic between them. She ate the escargot and Phillip reached for another piece of French bread, thinking the dinner was as nice as every other dinner. If it was paella, there was sangria; sushi, then sake; veal piccata, then red Lillet to start. Tonight a Cabernet Sauvignon had been ordered to go with the beef Wellington. After the escargots, they would have watercress and walnut salads, followed by the beef, artichoke hearts, and a julienne of zucchini and carrots, some too-rich dessert, then cognac.

The waiter removed the empty shells. The melted butter was speckled with garlic.

"So what's your take?" asked Phillip.

"You may still get full credit. Even if you only get half, you'll make budget." Jan missed the diversion of a plate in front of her. "That's what you always say counts the most. They'll accept the budget and you'll get another plan off your desk and onto the books."

Phillip squeezed her hand and moved his knee in and out.

She felt the movement of his knee. Compliments aroused him, and his knee moving in and out was a sign of that. Jan decided she was going home alone, and knew he wasn't going to take it well. If she wanted to see Ada, Jessie, and Charles this weekend she'd have to start out early in the morning. She watched Phillip and nodded her head, thinking maybe all he wanted was this— a dinner partner, agreeable conversation, and sex. She rubbed her forehead. She was getting tired of what seemed like dinner in exchange for sex.

"Are you okay?"

"I'm fine, Phillip, just tired." It wasn't a complete lie. He was gentle, slow, like all the women on the albums suggested. Still, Don had been a better lover. So it wasn't sex she stayed for and it wasn't all this food. She was going to have to run. Like Charles said, "Runnin' like you tryin' to get away from the police; what's the use of all that runnin'?" His reasoning made her smile.

The waiter cleaned the crumbs off the tablecloth with his crumber and placed the salads in front of them.

"Fresh pepper?"

Phillip nodded. "I have never missed budget. A few months may have been off, but I made up for it before the end of the year, and now the fourth quarter is coming."

Jan gestured when it was time to stop. Phillip seemed nervous and she wondered when he was going to admit how frightened he was instead of ordering more of the right wine, the "perfect beef Wellington," or "most tender veal piccata." She also wanted to know if he was willing to give up the woman in the black jacket. She wondered if he could stroke her arms like that and stop doing part of the same thing Don did, hiding the real story about himself. If he didn't tell it soon, she made up her mind to stop seeing him. She'd left Don, no reason to drag her feet. At least the child had gotten a taste of wielding her knife. I prayed for precision.

I approved of every thought, but earth folks had that one saying right: Man is not a mind reader. Jan was going to have to open her mouth and tell him what she thought and who she was. Instead, I watched her swallow her own words and retreat again. Her mind left Phillip sitting there, talking about a half-marathon she should enter. She didn't even say she didn't run for races or speed, and never needed to go any faster than she was going at the time. She omitted telling him something about herself and just wondered if Ada was having dinner alone, or with Uncle Albert. She imagined the kitchen, the lone lightbulb, a string hanging down from the fixture, Ada walking into the dark kitchen, pulling the string, opening the refrigerator, setting pots on the stove, lighting the pilot, and without one clove of garlic, making magic.

It was raining and a little after nine P.M. when Jan put the key in the door and smelled the star lilies. Phillip had sent them two days ago and they needed water. She cut their stems, put fresh water in the vase, and returned them to the top shelf of the étagère over the television. He'd pouted when she left and kept asking her if something was wrong. Jan walked over to the stereo and flipped through the albums. There was something wrong, but there was no place between them to discuss feelings she couldn't completely name. Isaac Hayes for a change. The phone rang. Jan picked it up, not looking forward to telling Phillip no twice.

"Hello."

No answer. Short breaths.

"Sarah?" Jan inquired.

"As always."

"What's that supposed to mean?" Jan asked.

"It means that I'm here like an old shoe, the girlfriend, while you're trying out all the new shoes, the boyfriends. And you probably gonna leave without buying anything."

"Thanks a lot."

"I'm in a mood."

"What's wrong?"

"Jonathan's asking the kinds of questions that make me think he wants to go live with his father."

"Sarah, you know how your mind works. You might be overreacting."

"Yep. How does 'Didn't the judge say when I get to be thirteen, I can choose to live with whichever parent I want' sound?"

Jan squeezed the receiver. "What are you going to do?"

"Come over to your place for coffee, try not to cry too loud on the bus, and leave here before David comes to pick Jonathan up and I kill them both."

Forty-five minutes later, Sarah stood at the door, her eyes red, her hair wet.

"Didn't you take an umbrella?"

"I forgot it."

Jan got a towel. Sarah stood at the window watching the dark sky.

"Jan?" Sarah turned, put her arms around Jan's neck and clung to her shoulders. "I'm not going to make it. I'm not fucking going to make it. You think I can handle everything. I could be cheated on, I could pick myself up, eat popcorn, and give that boy the real food when the support check was late, but I can't let him walk out of my life and live with that asshole and whatever woman he happens to have in the house at the time. That is my son.

"He's my fucking son."

We rocked. Sarah let out gasps of air, little hicks and moans that said everything we needed to know. After a while, Sarah leaned against the table and slid into the chair. Jan cut on the light near the sink and poured Sarah a cup of coffee, black.

"Will you cut the rest of the lights off?" Sarah said, reaching for the matches on the table near the candle.

"Sure." She did.

Sarah lit the candle. "I know I'm looking and acting like shit, before anybody tells me that I am."

"I'm the only one here, Sarah, and the only thing I'm going to tell you is that you're going to be fine."

They sat at the table staring out into the rain.

"November," Sarah said suddenly, sipping the coffee.

"What?"

"When I hung up the phone from you, David was there, ready to pick up Jonathan. Boy couldn't look at me when he kissed me good-bye, then David handed me this." Sarah pulled a crumpled piece of paper from her coat pocket. "We go back to court in November." She stuffed the paper back in her pocket.

Jan picked the towel up off the table, stood, and

began to dry Sarah's hair. They both stared out the window into more darkness.

"You're a good mother, Sarah. Jonathan loves you."

"He loves me, but he wants to be with a man, not a woman. If it didn't hurt so much I would agree, but it wasn't supposed to be this way. One man, one woman, children, till death do everybody the fuck part. If I knew this was going to happen, I would have stayed with the Negro."

"Do you really think you could have done that?"

"It couldn't have been any worse. Jonathan wouldn't have been pulled in two directions. The rest of it could have worked out. David was going through a phase, so was I. He could have put his dick back in his pants, let me grow up a little. I could have forgiven him. We screwed it up, that's all."

Jan put the towel around Sarah's shoulders, walked over to the stereo, and began to fuss with her albums. "Marlena Shaw, Sarah, Ella, Phoebe, Ricki Lee Jones, Carmen?"

"Ricki first, then mix it up."

"If he goes with David, what are you going to do?"

"I've heard women talk about it. Usually their kids leave for college or something. I guess I'll get used to it, after I go to the produce section and yell 'Fruits and vegetables can kiss my ass,' smoke a joint without sneaking on the back porch, bring a man over and screw in the kitchen, shit like that."

Sarah laughed a little and Jan tried to join her.

"You think you're the only one that likes to get some?" Sarah asked.

"I didn't say that."

"Jan, I'm not frigid. Trying to be so responsible made me afraid. Jonathan's father got enough for both of us." Sarah sipped the coffee. "And I wasn't afraid to screw. I just didn't want to get fucked."

* * *

The phone rang.

"Hello."

"Jan." Phillip was anxious. "Listen, our evening ended so quickly. Why don't you just tell me what's wrong?"

"Nothing's wrong." Jan wondered what he would say if she told him "My aunt has cancer; my father never loved my mother; my mother is fat and bitter; and my best friend's son wants to live with his father."

"If you want me to, I could come over. We could talk about it."

"No, that's okay. I'm fine."

Sarah motioned to Jan that she could leave. Jan mouthed no.

"Jan, are you seeing someone else?"

"What?"

"I mean, if you're busy and you can't talk, I can understand that." For all his understanding, Phillip sounded pissed.

"I am busy. But . . ." Jan looked at Sarah.

"Listen, don't explain. I'll see you later." Phillip hung up the phone.

Jan held the phone out. "Sarah, was I finished talking?"

"No, but why didn't you just tell him I was over?"

"He doesn't know who you are, Sarah."

"Girl, what's wrong with you? At least Don Juan knew I existed."

"It's not just you. Phillip doesn't know a lot about me."

"Why?"

"We haven't talked about friends, family, that kind of thing." Jan opened the refrigerator. "Are you hungry?"

"Then what do you see in him, and why are you spending so much time with him if he doesn't know anything about you?"

Jan closed the refrigerator door. "Sarah, there's something different about Phillip. He's like me. We're both just staying in the present right now."

"What's that supposed to mean?"

"He wants to go somewhere that's different from where he came and he's as lonely and as afraid as I am trying to get there."

"So, he told you all about himself, but he didn't listen to your story."

"No, he didn't tell me that. I can feel it. And I didn't offer my story. We haven't gotten that far yet."

"Jan, why do you think I'm sitting here?" Sarah poked her chest. "My life, my son, David. All of this stuff got messed up, not because I got a divorce; it was because of the reason why I got married in the first place."

"You were in love, Sarah. Some people still believe that's reason enough."

"Love, Jan. Hungry-ass puppy love. I learned to love David. That's why I stayed so long. But when I went after David, I didn't even love myself. I was running away from everything I didn't like about my life. I thought David was going to save me. And now I'm doing what I didn't want to do then, saving my damn self.

"If you're out there just playing another game, what you gonna do when it turns into your life and the man doesn't even know about your mother, your father, your aunt, me?" Sarah shook her head. "You are so young, Jan. But you've got to grow up sometime."

"Sarah, I am growing up. I'm sensing more. I'm not just saying all the right things. I'm thinking about it, choosing when and what I want to share. It's not just sex and it's not a game."

"Bullshit. You're afraid to tell him who you are and where you came from, you've made up his story in your mind, and he don't know nothing about you." Sarah clicked her tongue. "But y'all having big-time sex. That ain't playing?"

Jan took a breath and reminded herself that Sarah was angry about her own life, too. "He knows who I am right now and I know who he is right now."

"But it's all the other stuff that got you there that's important." Sarah lowered her voice. "When do you plan to talk to him? Show yourself? See if he likes who you really are?"

"Soon."

"Look, Jan, let's be honest, I'm having a shit day. Maybe I better head home. It's late. I needed to talk; I didn't mean to take stuff out on you."

"I know, me, too. You wanna spend the night? I want some company, too."

"I still meant what I said."

"I still want you to stay."

"Okay." Sarah rubbed the towel across her shoulders, then placed it on back of the chair. "Sure, I'll stay. You're better than a bus ride on a rainy night."

"Uhn, uhn, uhn."

Sarah put the towel on the table and peeled off her coat. Jan started to take the pillows off the sofa sleeper. Sarah got the comforter from beside the sofa arm.

"We pitiful. Two women spending Friday night together talking about Negroes. Wanna watch TV?"

"Put the thing on and turn the volume down," Sarah replied. "I got some more guts to spill."

Jan laughed and hit Sarah on the head with the pillow.

"You got any ice cream?"

"Yep." Jan turned the stereo off, cut the TV on, then walked over to the freezer and looked inside.

"Butter pecan? French vanilla?"

"Butter pecan. Since we talking about 'em, might as well eat the national Negro favorite."

Sarah stopped making the bed long enough to take the half-pint of ice cream from Jan and open it.

"Damn, you ate most of this."

"You didn't ask how much was left." Jan handed Sarah a spoon.

Sarah kicked off her shoes and propped the sofa pillows behind her.

"Are you falling in love with Phillip?"

"I don't know. Why?"

"Because when it's not sex and it's a feeling and you start to know things that you ain't been told, it sounds dangerous."

"Something pulls me to him. It's not like Don."

"Don was sex and discovery. I can tell this is different."

"I can say no to him easy."

"Don prepared you for that. Don was the one falling in love."

Jan stood her spoon in the ice cream. "Don, in love with me?"

"You couldn't see that?"

"No."

"Thank God. You might have felt sorry for the fool." Sarah bit into a pecan, then scooped her spoon over into Jan's ice cream. "He was trying to grab onto you, find some hope, pull himself out of the only life he knew. Boy would have took you down, though. I'm glad you got sidetracked on the sex."

"Excuse me. I was not sidetracked on the sex."

"Please. Don meant more as a sex object to you than you did to him. That's probably why he fell in love with you."

"I don't know if I agree with that."

"You can get all college on me if you want to, but that boy's nose was open. I saw it." Sarah put the ice cream down, put her index fingers on her cheeks, and pulled, stretching her nose.

"You're a real nut, Sarah." Jan tried not to laugh.

"Have you figured out why sex is so important to you?" Sarah asked.

"I don't think about it."

"Think about it."

Jan climbed back into bed. "Okay, I have always liked sex. From the first time I found out about it. Some boy when I was thirteen."

"Preemie."

"Yeah, I was. And don't act like I haven't mentioned that before. But now I think I know what made me like it."

"What?" Sarah scraped the rim of the carton.

"Sex told the truth. That was more than I could say for my mother and father at the time. If we were afraid about our lives, we touched each other with that fear. If we were comfortable with what happened in school, who did what, and feeling like what our parents thought didn't matter, the sex was like that." Jan ate a spoonful of the French vanilla. "After number one, they were all like that. We could lie to each other at the disco, but when we got in bed I could feel everything: how much they needed me, how alone they were, how much I wanted them." Jan wiped an unexpected tear. "When Don was angry with me and trying to act like he wasn't, I pushed myself against him as hard as he pushed himself in me. It didn't matter what we said or didn't say. When we made love, we spoke the truth."

"And Phillip?"

"He's a tough guy in the office, likes a formal dinner as well as he likes a casual one, but in bed he's been gentle."

"That helps."

"He's still kind of weird."

"How?"

"Afterward, he wants to stay in me all night."

Sarah rolled her eyes. "Damn, you get the winners."

"I know that sounds strange, but I think he literally wants to stay inside of me. After all that business over dinner and acting like he's got everything he always wanted, he wants to slow down, get safe, and stay there."

"You better write the *Essence* column." They laughed. "Girl, this ain't funny. You might be falling." Sarah scooped Jan's ice cream again.

"I don't know. I want to talk to him like I'm talking to you. But I can't make it all happen on my own. He's got to come to me."

"Wasn't he trying to get to you tonight on the phone?"

Jan remembered the conversation. "He kept asking me what was wrong."

"So he wanted to talk about it."

"I guess so."

"This is serious, Jan."

"If it is, this time I can handle it." Jan put her carton down and turned to Sarah. "I can get up in the middle of the night and go home. I can say no to dinner, and the boy makes dinner into a concert. But I meant it when I said soon. Chez Paul's is not enough. If he doesn't come to me, I can walk away." Jan took the cartons to the sink.

"Jessie and Charles' baby girl."

"Something else is happening." Jan climbed back onto the sofa sleeper. "I told you about that conversation with my mother."

Sarah nodded.

"It haunts me. My father didn't love my mother. My mother was so bitter and I can see how she just ate all her dreams. When I visit my aunt, I see Ada with only one breast. These are the people I know I care about, so if Phillip doesn't want to get real with me, I can walk away."

"I believe you. I knew you could do it."

Child had her hand on the handle of the knife. I knew she could do it too. If I wasn't holding on so tight, I would have danced on the table.

"I have to find out who I am, Sarah. When I was little Ada used to tell me that one day I was going to have to claim myself and get on the path to who I was meant to be."

Jan's voice was growing stronger.

"I love your aunt."

"My folks are going to visit Ada in the morning. I'll probably go over to their place tomorrow or Sunday, and visit Ada on the way home."

"You better go see your aunt."

"You're right. I need to see them all." Jan got up and blew the candle out. "I keep dreaming this dream."

"The same dream?" Sarah slid down farther underneath the covers.

"Yeah, not that often. But it's the same one. I had it a lot with Don, now Phillip. There are all these voices, women's voices. And then I'm running on the lake, then in a forest, and then there's a man. But I can't see his face. I never wanted him to be Don, but I think I want him to be Phillip and I want to live in this house with him. He rubs my back, makes me feel good. But I can't see him and I can't understand the voices."

"You will, Jan." Sarah was drifting.

"Are you going to sleep? As early as it is."

"Yeah, 'cause I feel better now." Sarah turned over. "When you go see your aunt, ask her what the dream means." Sarah stretched, then curled again. "It's nice to sleep with someone, mattress sinks, it's all warm."

Jan scooted to the end of the sofa sleeper and cut off the television.

"You're going to figure this thing out, Jan. And if you're okay, then I'm going to be all right, too."

"You've always been fine."

"I had to be. For me. For Jonathan. He thought I was mean, making him do right. He's getting too big for me to make him do shit."

"He loves you."

"You're lucky. You always had a father to love, and your aunt, and your mother. Maybe that's why you can love me, too."

"Sarah?" Jan stared into the darkness. "I didn't always love my mother." Jan listened to her own words and felt ashamed. "I'm not sure I love her now."

"Yes, you did and you do. Just like Jonathan doesn't think he loves me right now. You didn't love the pain, but you loved her." Sarah's voice drifted off again. She rubbed her feet together and pulled the covers around her shoulders. "You loved her like Jonathan still loves me."

"I'm going to make you breakfast in the morning."

"Good. Nobody ever makes me breakfast."

Passing Time

Sarah went to sleep before Jan did. I watched her sit in the dark, trying to imagine what Sarah had been through. We listened to the patter of rain as late night turned into early morning. Then Jan eased the covers back, walked quietly over to the vase on the étagère, and held a lily so close to her nose, it smudged her with orange pollen. Particles of fine powder sifted through the air and we thought of Phillip. Later, when Sarah and Jan slept with comfort, I touched their dreams, then traveled toward him.

When Phillip awakened, he sat in the middle of the bed, grateful for the weekend. Every other morning was a shower, a shave, and a briefcase. He walked into the bathroom, washed his face, and decided not to shave. It was Saturday, not Monday, and he needed an entire day off. He climbed the spiral staircase and looked at the loft. Near the top of the exposed brick wall in the southeast corner, white residue had formed on a few bricks. He made a mental note to bring up water damage in the next association meeting. The clock on the stove read 7:35, which meant it was 8:35 in Philadelphia. He could call Felice. When he picked up the phone, he dialed Jan's number instead.

"Hello." Jan's voice was sleepy, groggy. He assumed she was in bed next to someone else, quickly hung up the phone, and tried to assess the relationship in business terms. Jan was younger. He opened the freezer. Too young to outsmart him. He picked up a bottle of Stolichnaya that was next to the frozen waffles. The good stuff. He rationalized that an occasional stiff one in the morning didn't hurt, especially when there wasn't a damn thing he could do about the stiff one of his own. He smiled, uncapped the bottle, and turned it up. One swig, one more, capped. He took two waffles out.

He was going to have to find someone to take Jan's place when she was busy. She was playing his game. When they were together, he thought he had her full attention. The way she watched everything about him, even when he thought she was thinking about something else, he could tell she knew exactly what he'd said. Felice never did that. She was too concerned about the next time they would get together, if he would plan a party so she could meet the people in his latest city. In short, when was she going to get the status and, finally, the position of corporate wife.

Phillip put the waffles in the toaster and turned on the coffee pot. Jan Campbell. He guessed she made less than one-fifth of the money he did, had three-fifths of the education, one-third his savvy, but she had a way about her he both couldn't put his finger on and wanted to put his arms around. "Busy," he mocked her, and picked up the phone.

"Good morning."

"Phillip!" Felice practically squealed. "How's Chicago?"

"Come see."

"I'd love to."

"I'll pre-pay the tickets at the airport. Can you be here for dinner?"

"Ummm. Let's go for jazz at that place with all your friends, 'member?"

"Yeah, I'll call back with the flight number and time."

"I'll pack."

Phillip hung up the phone. The waffles were hot. He took some syrup out of the cabinet. The sun was coming in through the skylights. Last night's rain had led to a clear cloudless morning. Phillip sat at the table with his fork and knife, remembering Jan eating the escargot. He was sure she'd never had them before, but she pulled each snail out of its shell with a seafood fork as if she had been eating escargot for years. She tried everything, never gushed, and wasn't easily impressed, except when he touched her body. He saw all of her excitement then. Long erect nipples, thin torso, barely a mouthful of breast. If he spread his hands open, she could sit comfortably in them. While he held her up, pulled her next to his body, moved with her and watched her squirm, the veins in her neck stretched toward him. She almost forced him out with her convulsions. She let something go then, all the calm above her years, the adopted sophistication, the quick study. Vanished. Nothing but passion, stored up, let go. He smiled.

The waffle was crunchy, the syrup sweet, but it was cooling. Phillip dismissed the thoughts as best he could, decided to call the travel agent later, and unplugged the phone.

"Wake up," Jan said, bending over Sarah.

"God, Jan, it smells wonderful." Sarah twisted beneath the covers, then stretched.

"Coffee, pancakes from scratch, my aunt's recipe, eggs scrambled light, bacon strips, banana and strawberry slices," Jan announced, pulling up the shades.

"I slept in my clothes. I didn't go home. I'm irresponsible." Sarah pulled the covers back. "I didn't cry all night." Sarah jumped up and danced around the room, doing the bump with an imaginary partner. "Put on some Ricki Lee Jones." Sarah wailed:

Is he here? He's not in the drugstore.
Is he here? He don't come here no more.
Do, do do do do do do do!

"I'm sorry, but you just bastardized "Chuck E's in Love." Let me hurry up and get the album, before you make Ricki Lee choke on that joint she's smoking on the cover." Jan exaggerated rushing over to the bottom shelves of the étagère. Laughing, she pulled out the album. But Sarah was on to another set of lyrics.

Play that funky music white boy,
Lay down the boogie and play that funky
music till you die.

Jan stared at Sarah. "Girl, what's wrong with you?"

Sarah plopped into the swivel chair, exhausted. "I don't know and I don't care. But I will fight that Negro in court and keep custody of Jonathan even if I have to eat the judge."

"Why don't you just try eating my eggs before they get cold?"

Sarah went to the table, sat down, and placed her napkin in her lap.

The phone rang.

"Jan, are you busy?"

"Sort of, but I can talk for a little bit." Jan was thinking Phillip had nerve, since he'd sounded like he'd been two steps away from hanging up on her last night and was probably her silent caller this morning.

Sarah filled her mouth with eggs, reached for the orange juice, and said loudly, "I'm Jan's friend, Sarah. Hi, Phillip."

"Phillip, I guess you heard my friend."

"I did." He sounded relieved. "Tell her I said hello. Can we have dinner tonight?" Phillip asked.

"What time?"

"About six."

"Good, but I need another early night. I'm driving out to see my folks Sunday."

"No problem; I'll pick you up at five and make the reservations earlier."

"Phillip, I need my car. My parents, early night, remember?"

"Okay, then let's meet at The Bakery at five."

"See you at five then." Jan hung up the phone and eyed Sarah. "Now Phillip knows who you are. Are you satisfied?"

Sarah stood and bowed.

When they find each other, earth women weather time, becoming stronger as men come and go, holding on to each other when they can't stop shivering by themselves. They were well, and I felt the need to move toward Jessie and Charles, Ada, too. It had been some years since they'd sat together and they'd never learned how to tend to each other's wounds.

Breezes from Long Ago

Charles steered the copper-and-beige-toned Buick Electra 225 carefully past the two-flats. Some forty years ago the brownstones had appeared as citified mansions to him. His heels, worn down from walking back roads in the South, had met the concrete of Chicago's West Side with a near-dance through its streets.

Hands waved salutations from so many windows he'd believed they'd fanned their welcoming breeze into the South. In each flat, the family living upstairs was almost always related to the family downstairs. One person coming North, sending back for another. Jazz trailed through breaks in curtains, riding on the breeze until its melody melded into the gait of the people strutting below. Muddy Waters had brought his blues to these streets, Ella Fitzgerald had tisked her tasket on these sidewalks, do-woppers wopped and doed on stoops and breezeways that were filled with song.

Now Charles saw the familiar streets not as they had been, but as they are, and thought, so much had changed in one generation. "No-counts" decked the stoops of "half-assed" whitewashed porches. Papers, bottles, and discarded containers decorated hopscotched patches of grass. The music that lurched from radios with more bass than anything was barely recognizable, the lyrics, embarrassing.

Charles gripped the steering wheel tighter and his

movement caught Jessie's attention. He was barely driving twenty miles an hour, so Jessie assumed he was thinking about the same thing she was. They'd both seen the West Side's better days and avoided it these last years. It was no longer a place where brother, sister, and in-laws sat up late and talked of each day's foolishness, ate souse and crackers in lean times, and spread tables with plenty when the eagle flew and there was money to spare. Those days when she'd been the referee as Ada and Charles took turns lamenting and celebrating the days spent in the South had slipped into memory. All that talk had been replaced with more silence over the years, more distance being created than the few miles between Moleen and Chicago. Jan had become the bridge that linked a brother and a sister, a sister and a sister-in-law. Talk had been transferred into dollars folded in envelopes to buy Jan this, help out with that.

Jessie watched Charles turn down Keeler. He'd resented accepting Ada's money, but he'd accepted it when he had to. So she gave him credit for not being a complete fool. When the daughter Charles and Ada seemed to share, even if Jan came out of Jessie's womb and not Ada's, grew up and took off on her own, visits among the three of them were even less frequent. She couldn't remember the last time they'd driven this way. The streets were so different now.

Charles was trying to remember the last time he'd seen Ada. He knew Jan saw more of his sister than he did and, frankly, he reckoned he'd had enough of Ada. But ever since the news of Ada's cancer, the trip had been coming. Little brother to big sister, clocks ticking, death taking a seat all around them, people they both knew dying, leaving them somewhere next in line.

"Been a long time," Charles said in a breath.

"Time brings on a change," Jessie replied, and they leaned back into the silence.

Charles mused. K-Town. That's what they called it now, because of all the streets that started with K's; Kostner, Keeler, Kilpatrick, Kedzie. He'd seen it in the paper. Gangs were rumored to run the streets, taking kids' lunch money, selling pot. The rapscallions had to be the children of some of the same people he knew growing up, a bunch of snotty-nosed kids grown into hell-raisers. How could all that happen? He listened to Jessie's breaths, shorter now, like always when she was nervous. He cleared his throat but couldn't quite get the words out to tell her that this was not going to be a showdown, him in a huff with Ada over things that happened so many years ago they belonged in a museum. No, he was going to have his say, but calm-like.

Ada was dying and he had to see her, get a few things straight. Seem like he'd been straightening out his closet a lot lately. Got Jan told. 'Fessed up to Jessie. Now Ada. He watched the bums in the lot on the corner in his rearview mirror. They were eyeing the Deuce and a Quarter. He didn't put it past them to strip it down to four tires, a radio, and a battery.

Charles parked as close to Ada's flat as he could. His chest was full now, the way it brimmed up at night when the fluids almost met his throat, forcing him to cough and spit, breaking his rest. All that damn work at the steel mills, now he had to fight his own body. He suspected Ada felt the same way—all that praying, now cancer. He moved quickly to catch up with Jessie. The few brisk movements and the climbing of the steps caused him to break a sweat. He welcomed the breeze that enveloped him, a needed refreshment, and pulled his body up. He might not feel like a damn, but he could still look proud. He rang the bell and listened to Ada's steps coming down the stairs, almost the same steps. Full, determined, only slower.

"Charles, Jessie!" Ada's eyes welcomed them as much

as her voice. Her eyes always told on her. For all the fuss, the sternness, the I-know-it-all and listen-you-might-learn-something, she was pleased to see them both.

He thought he saw more of me resting in her than he'd ever noticed before, then remembered that I had never gotten old enough to have a head of silver hair. Ada's hair outshined a silver dollar. Here and there it appeared even more than silver, like Christmas tinsel, reflecting, twinkling. The two braids, once thick, now thin, were loose at the ends. He remembered my coal black eyes.

Ada was hugging Jessie. As Charles moved closer, he felt her arms around him, smelled the Ponds cold cream, Madam Walker hair oil, and aging flesh. Her hug was tight on him. The fake breast like a pillow against him, his knees grew soft as sponges. He hugged her back, less hard than he wanted to, then steadied himself and started up the stairs.

"Just keep going to the table, Charles." Ada prodded him gently in the back. "No use thinking I didn't fix you a proper country breakfast 'cause folks saying I got one foot in the grave. I made you a Mississippi Sunday breakfast, even if it is Saturday. And if Jessie will carry it in from the kitchen we'll eat. I may be out of strength, but the Lord power."

"I can bring everything in from the kitchen," Jessie offered from the top of the steps.

"Thank you, ma'am. Start us with some coffee and put the food on them platters I set out. Don't worry 'bout Albert either, he won't get here for another hour or two."

Charles pulled the last step, bypassed the dining room table, and made it to the sofa. He listened to the women and thought about Jessie always being in a kitchen. If not her own, somebody else's, and Ada was always giving orders. Jessie went to the kitchen saying something about how good the food smelled. He sat down on the sofa and Ada took the recliner across from him. He realized he hadn't smelled anything, too much concentration on just making it up the mountain of steps. Besides, he thought, he hadn't noticed much lately, almost had to be reminded that it was time to eat, time to sleep.

"What do you know good, Charles?" Ada asked. "Up early on a Saturday morning to see an old woman fallin' apart at the seams."

"Ada," he started. No sense in hedging, dive in while Jessie's deep in the kitchen, he encouraged himself. "Guess ain't neither one of us getting younger and I been having my piece all over the place lately. Done told my daughter to let them scragglies alone and get her own life straight."

Sunlight entered through the bay windows. I rested on the beam closest to Ada.

"Jan will be fine, Charles," Ada interrupted.

"I know. I ain't questioning how she's gonna be." He looked Ada square in the eyes. "She had both of us, didn't she?"

"Yes," Ada answered, noting the way Charles was careful not to spike his words. He didn't want a fight, she thanked God, but he definitely had something on his mind.

Jessie entered, already in an apron.

"I believe you slimming down, girl," Ada said to Jessie. Jessie filled the cups and smiled.

When Jessie left the room, Charles continued. "Ada, you done right by Jan. I ain't got no problem with that. But, as I was saying, I been having my say lately. Talked to Jan and done made peace with Jessie, and I guess I got a truth or two I been owing you."

I settled closer, near the piano. The red of my color showing enough for Ada to see.

"Guess it ain't no secret since Jan on her own we ain't had much to say."

Charles looked at Ada and thought of me. He thought Ada was as much me as she was herself now, and he was tired of running from both of us.

"You've bossed me all your life, but I guess bossin' is your way, like hating to be told a thing is mine." He looked at Ada sipping her coffee and noticed the left arm limp on her lap, swollen. It was on the same side as the pillow breast. "Still, we came up rough and you did the best you knew how." He cleared his throat. "Just want to say I ain't blaming you for nothing no more, you did your best by me, and you did right fine by Jan."

In the kitchen, Jessie almost dropped the platter of chicken. She eased it down on the table and busied herself putting the rolls into a cloth. That was as close to an apology as Jessie had ever heard from Charles. She shook her head and decided to stay in the kitchen a little longer, thinking time sure did bring on a change.

"Thank you," Ada said, knowing the words hadn't come easy. "I tried, Charles. I wasn't without my faults. It must've seemed like I treated Jan with more kindness than I did you when you were in my care. But back then, most days I felt too much hate. I hated those fields, the reason why you all had to pick cotton, the reason why I had to care for the children, and the reason why Mama died early and Paps lost his will to live." Ada took the little blue ball out of her duster pocket, placed it in her left hand, and began to squeeze. A new habit to go along with her thinking.

"Oh, I had things I hated, fears that stayed close enough to touch, but I never hated you or any of our kin. And when Jan was born, seemed like I saw Verga and you all over again. The way you two would get along and still disagree."

Charles remembered his favorite sister and laughed. Jessie, head down, feigning some preoccupation, entered and placed two platters on the table, one of crisp fried chicken, the other ham and red-eye gravy. "We can eat right after I heat the grits," Jessie said, knowing the grits were already on a low fire.

Charles leaned forward. "Ada, that's one thing I don't understand. Why didn't Verga come back? You know, I believe there's a God. I dropped on my knees and found him right there in the woods, but Verga was supposed to come back. If anybody could have come back, she would have."

"Maybe she did," Ada answered, more pleased with Charles' revelation that there was a God than the child-hood promise he'd made with Verga.

"If she did come back I would've known it. She ain't come back." Ada looked at Charles and considered him as the child she'd switched too many times, too many years ago.

"Charles, the dead don't just come back and walk around earth like they living. If they did, there'd be no reason for being dead. Now would there?"

Charles wasn't about to dignify Ada's sass with an answer and stopped himself from saying he knew to Sam Hill well the dead wasn't like the living. They'd been getting along fine, but her tone was starting to test him.

I made my voice known to Ada. *Slow to anger,* I told her, my spirit touching her flesh.

"Man is just living in a body, Charles, that's all that dies. It's the soul and the spirit that doesn't die."

"Verga dead, Ada. Or she'd have come back. I don't care what you say, soul, spirit, something."

"Maybe she did. I think the dead leave some of their spirits with us, not everything, but some."

Charles pushed his body down hard on the sofa, to keep from standing up. Verga would have known what to do with him. He gave Ada a hot glare. Jessie brought the grits in a covered dish, the rolls in a towel, then headed back to the kitchen.

"What was the thing you most enjoyed with Verga? What gift did she give you when she was living?" Ada felt my voice and I told her she was leading, teaching again, and must be careful not to torment. *Charles is edgy already, ready to stomp my toe. It's his nature, unavoidable.* Her spirit spoke to mine. I entreated her to go on.

"Verga calmed me down, that's what!" Charles snapped, and thought but did not add, *Especially after you'd rattled my nerves and sat yo' flat ass down on the last one.*

"So what calms you down now? What thing, outside of your body, calms you down?"

Charles thought until the words came. "A breeze, slow or fast, poor or enough to unhinge the windows. A good goddamn breeze."

Ada flinched and almost shouted to me. *I knew he was gonna do something, just waiting to stomp my toe, get me riled!*

Charles stewed. He hadn't meant to curse, especially using God's name with Ada, but he was all out of apologies for one day, fresh out.

I watched the two of them, amused. It took them a whole lifetime to learn to get along. I wondered what they'd accomplish with eternity.

Jessie entered with serving spoons. "Let's eat before it gets cold," she announced, remembering Carmen McRae's "Send in the Clowns." Here she was coming in after an upset had almost ruined the show. Time to be jolly, change the scene, remind them of the food, even if Charles' appetite was puzzling lately. She sunk a large spoon into the grits, uncovered the rolls, and sat one on each plate. "Everything's ready." Jessie looked at Ada and Charles, but saw something more.

Jessie realized the three of them were not alone. She looked at Ada, who was recovering from Charles' tongue lashing, and followed her stare. She could not see all of me, just knew that the piano had a glow about it, and tried to name it.

Auburn, like the time Mrs. Mont T dyed her hair to make her husband notice and he said she looked like a whore. Plum, like the fruit before it was ripe. Scarlet, like anger, something red. Red, like blood was all around that piano.

Jessie knew more than I'd thought. No wonder she'd had enough back to hold my son up in the world.

Charles took the expressway. As much as he wanted to get home faster, Jessie saw his movements were slow. His hands slid from his normal ten and two position until his wrists rested on his lap, maneuvering the car with little motion. The talk with Ada had come at a price. Jessie offered to drive and Charles took it as a kindness, knowing she hadn't driven on the highway in years.

"No, no. I ain't too tired, Jessie." He swallowed, pushed the fluid down, and breathed in slowly. "Been thinking, though, 'bout all that cleaning you been doing in your room." He pictured the open closet and books, some books were stacked almost window-high around the room. Boxes covered the bed. "We both tired, and if you want to, you can sleep in my room"—he coughed— "with me, tonight."

Jessie tried not to move. Only her eyes shot up and caught his.

"Just for tonight, you know. That's all."

She saw the pleading, remembered all that had happened on this day, felt the courage in his voice, and agreed.

"Thank you. That'll be okay, save me finishing up all that organizing tonight and I can get out in the garden before the rain."

Charles' hands tightened around the steering wheel and slid back up to ten and two. "I ain't thinking about touching you or nothing like that." He knew it would be enough to feel the way the mattress pressed down from her weight, feel the heat from her body, listen to her snore.

"It'll be okay, Charles." Jessie smiled. She knew Charles didn't have a working part to offer these days, or the inclination to try. They teased themselves with separate thoughts, Charles just wanting to get through the night without getting up to spit and cough. If he did that, he thought, preparing himself, she probably wouldn't come in again, make some excuse. Jessie sat there, sensing he'd want her to move back to his room.

Covenants Kept

Jan had promised herself an early night, and the evening did start with dinner at five. But by eight-thirty Jan was in Phillip's condominium, downstairs, on the level that was the master bedroom. The skylight was thirty feet above them. The king-size bed and an end table completed the room's furnishings. Music came from speakers on the wall; a door across from the bed led into both a bath suite with a Jacuzzi and a set of walk-in closets.

Invisible, but in earth form, I sat on the curve near the top of the spiral staircase. The Stan Getz quartet worked "One Note Samba" on the stereo system, but below me, it was Phillip's voice that sang.

"Jan." His hand ran the course of her body, pressing so tightly the tips of his fingers hurt. The phone began to ring. It had rung when they first got there and he ignored it, so Jan did the same.

Now, Phillip turned her over and entered her again. Working his hands up and down her back with less intensity, he kissed the back of her neck, behind her earlobes. Jan traded the phone's ringing for other sounds, remembering the way his voice cracked when he thought she was busy. She closed her eyes. After a short pause, the phone began to ring again. It had to be the same person. Jan thought, if Phillip was being pursued he could have disconnected the phone. It made her think

of Don, and the thoughts of men who cheat led her to
the fantasy of Don's mouth, not on her neck, but against
the left side of the magic he had found. She took Phillip's
hand and placed it there, moved it until she came.

Above me the skylight darkened, no clouds, just time
passing and something else that rumbled. I felt the earth
shatter in a place I couldn't see. Fissures spread outward
but I could not see them. Below me, Phillip bit against
Jan's neck, his face rough against her smooth one. The
short, unshaved hairs caused her skin to tingle. He
turned her around, wiped her with the sheet, placed one
hand on each side of her opening, and placed his mouth
where thoughts of Don had been. His chin moved back
and forth, the stubby hairs and brisk movement prickled
her into a place where she didn't care that the phone
began to ring again, didn't realize until he was on top of
her, faster and holding her shoulders down, that he was
coming too, that they were collapsing, that the phone
had stopped ringing and he was whispering her name
again. She only knew she liked the way it bounced from
his mouth, to the pillow, to her ears. Jan heard herself
answer "Yes." But Phillip just kept repeating her name.

Earth people do what they have a mind to. They make
plans, break them, try to cleave before they jump
brooms first and mourn after. I have seen them make
love and offer hate at the same time. I wanted Jan to find
her voice, use her knife, and ask for the love she's
wanted ever since her early days, when she saw men and
women make fools of themselves and each other. The
child was smarter than what she had seen, I felt her
power, she had to feel it, too. But I felt something more
and it caused my spirit to shift.

The earth had begun to quiver and it would not stop.
Jan was peaceful now. I kept my eyes on her and joined

Phillip as he wrapped his arms around her, but the earth continued to move.

Jan woke up. It was after one A.M. and Phillip was asleep. She pulled on her clothes and left. At the apartment, she didn't bother to cut on the lights or pull out the sofa sleeper, just felt against the wall until she found a blanket and her pillow. When she fell asleep, the voices returned, Sarah, Ada, Jessie, and me. She couldn't place my voice, but she heard it, knew that in some way it was a missing part of herself. She thought it comforting, more like light than sound. Everything was so rich. Jan was coming closer to us. I knew the child had enough spirit to see in our realm. She picked up another voice fast and sharp like wind. The colors brightened; she was running on the lakefront, getting closer to the house, listening to the voices. We told her when she reached the man to tell him to turn around, so she could see. Still the earth had not stopped trembling, so I left my voice with the others and moved toward Ada to see if she knew why the earth quivered.

Ada knelt by the bed to pray and I could tell she did not feel the tremors or become unsteady near the cracks. I heard her apologize for Charles taking the Father's name in vain. She asked that Jan come to the end of herself and find Christ. She thanked God for my guidance and then began the long line of requests for others. But the earth kept calling me and so I went toward Charles.

Moleen had met the night's quietness. From overhead only the fish house blazed with lights and music. Homes that neglected to turn off the television set, or left a bathroom or porch light on, appeared like faint lanterns dotting a path to Fifth and Stanton. Outside, a street lamp filtered shadows into the bedroom where Charles lay in bed next to Jessie.

He felt Jessie's warmth and heard her breathing. It was peaceful. He touched her hair and felt the fluid in his lungs rise. He was tired, so he swallowed and it rose again. The curtain lifted against the breeze entering the room, lulling him gently until he felt his childhood return. Instead of the thick mucus, he tasted the times when he'd sat on a southern porch, rocking in the sun, talking with Verga, the sister who understood him, who cared for him after I had died.

The fluid rose higher but he smelled the fields and the climbing bush of roses near the house, then saw the sway of a porch swing. He tried to rouse himself, it was time to go to the bathroom, but he was content and still the fluid rose. He wouldn't turn the lamp on, just go quietly without coughing and spit, but the desire ebbed into a more pleasant thought and drifted far away. He lifted his arm and felt the comfort of the night instead of the telltale tingles, then allowed his childhood to lay it back down again. The curtain ballooned into the room and the space where he had breathed filled so that the place where he had felt the pain of love could stop.

Sunrise on a Black Mourning

I hastened to Jan and found her on the lakefront. The sun had yet to rise and she had barely slept two hours, but her spirit had moved her to place firm feet against the sand, pummeling the ground with a faster pace than usual. Streaks of perspiration traveled down her arms and I saw that she was also running from the dream's dense forest that meandered into a clearing; its garden path that led to the back door of a quaint country house and the man whose soul she felt but whose face she had not seen. Now, she thought, Sarah was right. Ada could tell her what the dream meant, and she'd ask her. She wanted to get to the man in the dream, tell him to turn around so she could look at his face.

Jan had heard our voices! Our spirits had spoken to her across our time and she was able to hear. Sweat collected in the bends of her arms, she slowed, walked, glad she'd thrown her duffel bag in the car on the way to the lake. She wouldn't go back to the apartment where parts of the dream still stood. Just go straight out to my parents', shower there, she told herself, getting in the car. I could not tell her that the earth cracked and combed a fine-toothed tear into each layer of my spirit and would soon reach hers.

I could not tell her that before I knew I had begun to keen, without sounds, the ancestral screams joined so many others until they reached the wailing women and returned to God. I have seen my blood children pass from this world into one that rejoices, but Jan would know the depth of mourning that never stops. Later, we would tell her that only in time does it emit a fainter cry.

Sunday morning had dropped its sanctifying blanket over Moleen. It was so early that Jan imagined the church women had yet to pull on their best stockings, search for a hat that wouldn't, although it most likely would, clash with the print of their dresses, or begin the hunt for the right purse and shoes that would champion style even if they stole three hours of consolation from their weary feet.

Jan felt the bumps and vibrations from the railroad tracks and was temporarily distracted. She wondered if her car could stand too many more rocky rides, then, realizing that she was years away from a new car, returned to the images of the town women on Sunday mornings.

In her mind's eye they were draping themselves with house robes, hair pinned, scarved, or in curlers. Ovens were being lit and stuffed with pot or pork roasts, chickens, or hens. Potatoes, turnips, carrots, onions, the colorful and colorless root vegetables fresh from their gardens were being tossed into their roasting pans. Jan imagined stove tops: bacon, sausages, and ham pieces frying; red-eye gravy and grits bubbling; eggs scrambling with melting cheese. There was something about the food she missed. Jan was trying to decide if she wanted to eat a Sunday morning Moleen meal, smell it, or simply see it when she turned off Stanton onto Fifth where the quiet of the morning broke.

A well of grumbling and murmurs rose. An ambulance, lights flashing without sound, stood in front of her house, its back doors open. Neighbors were gathered, robed, pajamaed, all disheveled and standing still like the air. Deacon Yancy had his head bowed so low until he looked neckless, headless even. His wife displayed three tiers leading to her stockinged legs and slippered feet; a red robe with yellow flowers, a lavender dress with hints of sky blue, and a slip hanging, trimmed in white lace.

Jan drove through the stop sign and stopped the car in the middle of the street. She watched one of her hands turn the ignition off, the other opened the door. She looked toward the house and saw Mrs. Mont T standing beside her mother, near the flower box. The marigolds flashed yellow eyes as the two women rocked from side to side, swaying slow like the willow. People began walking toward her. Their arms rose into the air, graceful and slow, a flock of birds, turning. Their hands waved as if signaling a silent migration. Men and women going South for the winter. Their lips moved, but the only sound Jan heard was a loud grunt. At the front door a paramedic moaned as he walked backward. Jan lifted her head and it sprang up light and high like the birds. She put the car in park and got out. The will to run fought with her legs.

"Mama!" Jan yelled. Jessie looked up and Jan followed her gaze to the front door. A white sheet completely covered the mound that was Charles' body. Her ankles gave way. Jan's knees felt grass still wet with dew. Her body rocked forward until her lips touched the blades, parting to take in the moisture and pulling her closer to the dirt.

Jessie watched Jan fall and all her love caught up and sent across the lawn could not stand the child. Charles had died and a piece of Jan went with him. Jessie held her arms out toward Jan but could not move. Charles' body passed between them and Jessie felt Mrs. Mont T's cold fingertips, then the firmness of her hands pulling her own arms back down to her sides. The paramedics were heaving, groaning under the dead weight of Charles' body.

"Good-bye," Jessie managed the salutation in her mind, only part of it slipping through her lips. Her throat dried and for the time it took for her to swallow, she closed her eyes and remembered old movies: *Pinky, Cabin in the Sky, Stormy Weather*. The music, the jazz of Louis Armstrong, the songs of Joe Williams, Ella Fitzgerald, Billie Holiday, and Dinah Washington. When the movies and the music were over you could leave the theater, turn off the TV, or remove the record from the stereo, and fold the clothes, season the meat, or stand by the window. Mrs. Mont T's fingertips pressed her back again, old but sure hands. Charles' body was in the ambulance. On the grass, her neighbors and one of the paramedics framed Jan's body. Not dead but dormant, the limbs of her child were sprawled, withered across the grass like perennials in late fall. "Jan," she whispered from the parched throat. Mrs. Mont T steadied her as she moved toward her daughter.

"Should have called her before daybreak, but didn't want to wake my girl with that kind of news. Unh, unh, unh." Jessie sighed.

"Did right, Jessie. Done it right," Mrs. Mont T sang.

"Girl always did think her Daddy was some kinda something, coulda shot the president and stole from Jesus."

"She'll be fine. 'Member how that girl used to eat head cheese and souse from up Minnie Ellie's and Joe Riley's store when she was'n' tall enough to peep the countertop?"

"Uhm," Jessie moaned, and thought, *What that got to do with it, Mrs. Mont T?* but left the thought hanging in the air.

"Chil' takin' all that hot and spice gon' be all right in the world. She be okay, Jessie," Mrs. Mont T answered.

Jan heard the voices first but was afraid to open her eyes. It would not be a dream this time. The white of the sheet and the shape of her father's body pressed against her eyelids. He must have died while she was clinging to Phillip. If she had only visited her parents a day earlier. A day late, a dollar short. She remembered the saying and tasted the salt in her mouth.

Jan felt Jessie's hands wipe the tears from her face, but she didn't want to open her eyes.

"It's okay, Jan," Jessie whispered, wiping more tears.

Jan heard Mrs. Mont T's house slippers shift across the floor. When the door had been shut she said, "I'm sorry, Mama," and opened her eyes. A wave of sight, sound, touch, smell, and taste flooded her body. The room, its brightness, her mother's face, their breathing, the way her mother's hand felt against her cheeks, made her close her eyelids again. She smelled the odors of sweat, food, and fear. The taste of salt left from tears forced her up and pressed her down at the same time. What about Jessie? Who was going to sit by her bed and wipe her tears? Jan tried to get up again.

"Jan, it's okay," Jessie repeated. "Ain't nobody to be sorry when death comes. Days always been numbered like the lilies and birds. Numbered. God's got order."

Jan felt the closeness of her mother's body and wondered how long Jessie would live and how she would manage without Charles.

"Mama." Her voice tumbled into the room. "Mama!"

Sun coursed through the skylight. Phillip slept with the memory of Jan's body curved around his back, lean, smooth, smothering. Sometime later he drifted into the lazy phases of a dream, believing he could get up at will and open his eyes. The belief was so strong and the dream so beyond unconsciousness that he knew he could touch the forest of verdant greens. A flower garden appeared. It had been tended with such care that the majestic purples, deep to faint blues, yellows, cardinal reds, and a luminous white seemed to hold a love. The colors hypnotized him and threatened to make him stay among their blooms forever.

Impatiens, geraniums, begonias, and zinnias grew around his ankles, then began to disappear. With the stirring of a wind, blades of grass covered the spaces where the flowers had been, and leaves fell and began to turn brown on top of the grass. A huge willow bent toward him, the arms of its branches brushing against his face. The willow wrapped its arms around him and he tore away, only to feel his mouth fill with fluid. He recognized the bitter taste as his bottom lip jutted forward and he spat the brown juices of snuff in front of him. The liquid spread in front of him; meeting the air, it turned into a concrete path. Phillip broke free of the willow limbs and ran. Moss fell around him. Words whispered about his ears, growing louder until their screech pierced the forest, and formed the curl of a snake around him. Then their laughter joined the woods in pushing Phillip out until he stood alone, birthed into a clearing. He stepped backward, his hands reaching forward.

Now, his eyes opened and he saw his outstretched arms reaching for Jan in the space beside him. Sometime in the night, she had left. Sun poured down from the skylight. The day had begun hours ago, but Jan was gone.

Jessie stood by the kitchen sink. It was too dark to see the willow.

"You might as well stay the night."

"I am." Jan put a bowl wrapped in foil into the refrigerator. "I called Sarah and told her to call the station in the morning."

"How's that chil' and her chil'?"

"Fine, Mama." Jan stood beside Jessie.

Jessie turned from the window. "Let's cut out the lights and go in my room. If we leave a light on, somebody might stop by."

Jan followed her mother and put on a nightgown that dwarfed her with its size but enchanted her with its smell and warmth. Jessie came back from the bathroom in a long muu-muu and sat down on the bed. Books were spread around the floor, piles stacked near the windows. She moved two boxes off the bed. When she stretched out, Jan thought about sleeping next to Sarah.

"Well, where should I start?" Jessie asked, comforted by the dark.

"Start?"

"Jan, you've been circling me ever since you got the life back in you. In between each visitor, you've been asking enough questions to kill a cat."

"Mama." Jan steadied her voice. "It's just that I need to know some things, like why you married him in the first place and did you ever love each other."

Jan grasped a vision of herself, Phillip's hands and Don's lips. "Why do people go through all this living and dying together?"

Jessie settled Jan against her breasts and began to speak.

"People try to find another person to fix the part that's broken in themselves. I guess we forget the person we after is broken, too. But every bruise don't show and just 'cause you find what you think is a means to an end don't mean you ain't gonna find yourself at another starting line."

They rested awhile.

"When you grab hold to another person, at first you see what you wanna see. Then you can't help but to see what you got, but only the part they let you see. Later, you find the part they tried to hide from you. Meantime, you got a pain of your own that ain't fixed. Then one day you stumble upon the part of that person they've been hiding from themselves, God, and everybody. By then you so locked in you can't get away. You have children, a house, a place you like to be without all the things you like in it. So you may think you got the energy to change it, change them, make it work. Only thing is, by then your pain is so deep and heavy you used to it. I didn't love him at the beginning, Jan, I only loved him at the end."

Jan returned from the melody of her mother's voice and the rhythm of the heartbeat beneath her breast. "I don't want to do that, Mama. That may be what happened to you, but somewhere it's got to work out."

"It can happen and it'll happen to you. Your daddy used to say you weren't gonna live like us."

"He did?"

"Uh-huh, and I believed it, too. Believe it now. At first I thought your being yellow help put a chip on your shoulder, but you never liked being yellow. Then you got to where you didn't even think about it. Your being different is bigger than that, deeper than skin."

"Mama," Jan said, remembering the church women of her youth. "People have said that chip-on-my-shoulder thing all my life."

"That's because people saw what you couldn't, that your life was meant to be something more than where and who you came from, that you had enough gumption to get where you needed to go. You see a part of that, Jan, but you going to have to believe the part you can't see to get there."

"A chip on your shoulder means you think you're better than everybody else."

"Humph. I think it just means you take stock in yourself, and what's wrong with that?" Jessie grunted. "People can twist a saying and a meaning however they want to. But if you gon' live in this life, you better think you're better than a lot of what you see. That's what your daddy meant. You got to learn to see in this world and see beyond it, and you learned how to do that a long time ago. Now your change, your time, is coming."

Jan breathed until her heart felt every word and it opened her mouth. "Mama, that's what I've been feeling. My time."

"Then don't miss it. Everybody gets a time or two when God calls your name and offers you a change, lets you know he knows what you've been through. It can come in the middle of so much stuff you think if anything more happened, you wouldn't know what to do, and more comes."

"Like now."

"I don't know everything going on in your life, but losing your father is losing a lot for you. I heard what he told you, what you been wanting to hear, you finally heard it, now what you gonna do?"

"He told me what? What are you talking about?"

"The last time y'all talked. I was downstairs getting clothes out the dryer, his bedroom vent was right by my ear, and he told you that he loved you ever since you struggled out of me. Remember?"

Jan pushed in closer. "I remember." Now she heard the love in Charles' voice, felt the power of it, and accepted the gift.

"It's not whether Charles and me was in love. You made our mistakes so important, you forgot to love yourself and take what we could give you."

Jan pulled in closer to Jessie, breathing with her, feeling everything a mother had to offer and all a father could leave behind. "I understand it, Mama."

"Then you know love when you see it, and you got to make a choice to eat from that same pot or go hungry until you can taste it, not settle, not make do. Everybody got to walk through their own hell, Jan, but you always get to choose whether or not you gonna sit down and have dinner with the devil."

Lights from a car passing cast shadows of Jan and Jessie against the wall. They saw themselves wrapped tightly around each other.

"My time came to me at least twice. At first, I made the wrong decision and the second time I tried to right that wrong." Jessie stroked Jan's hair. "And now I think I did.

" 'Member I told you about my aunt Nell?" Jan nodded against Jessie's chest.

"She was hard as packed dirt in summer after a dry spring. Had the kind of hands that you could see scratching but never hugging anybody.

"Aunt Nell didn't like Robert, the man I was supposed to marry. She wanted me to marry and move out of her house sooner than later and didn't have the patience to wait for Robert, but I should have. Back then some folks thought going off to the military meant you were hincty, thought yourself better, and it also meant a wait. I caught the fire of Aunt Nell's anger and thought Robert should hurry up, too. I started to go out then and when you were waiting for a man from the service, going out wasn't a thing to do."

My daughter-in-law was doing well, steadying herself and preparing to tell what earth folks call the whole truth and nothing but the truth. She was talking with her mouth and praying in her mind, encouraging herself not to swallow the parts of the story that could make Jan see.

"Aunt Nell watched me leaving with my friend Lila. At first we did go out together, but later on Aunt Nell and Uncle Billy were just watching me change into a party dress. I was on my way to what I thought was a means to the end I wanted. Nell suspected something because when I came back home she would wait up and make me pee in a bucket. Whenever I asked her why, she said, 'Your pee is my business, long as you staying here.' Well, I hated that, her making me pee like that, and it seemed like I couldn't get a letter from Robert fast enough."

Jan imagined Jessie, young, the girl in the pictures, even younger.

"At first, he wrote all about our plans to have a house and children and even travel, but then the letters stopped coming. That must have been when Aunt Nell started tearing up Robert's letters and I thought he'd stopped writing. I was beginning to give up on Robert and the house and babies I wanted all my life. That's when your father came along, and so did another man, old Mr. Otis. Mr. Otis worked on things around the house and he'd noticed that I was going out.

"When I caught Mr. Otis eyeing me, I listened to what he had to say and I did what he told me to. He made it all seem so simple, grinning out of them bubbling lips of his.

"'First, I'll give you two hundred dollars.' Well, that was more money than I'd ever seen. 'You go downtown to State Street and buy a party dress that sets off your shoulders and clings close and tight to your waist.' That's what he told me. 'Buy the finest silk stockings, and a flower for your hair, and high-stepping shoes. Come to the Signal by ten Friday night. I'll be there setting me up a game before nine. I'll be playing cards with some men who'll think they're as happy to see you walk through the door as I am. You just sit on a stool in the middle of the bar and turn facing the card table when I tip my hat, then turn away when you got the men's minds wrapped around that pretty smile. One of my friends, Louie, will walk up to you and buy you a drink.'

"When I looked at him like he was crazy, he said, 'It'll be Coke.' Then he gave me more instructions. 'Laugh fancy and toss your head back when Louie talks to you. Twist a little on the bar stool, cross and uncross your legs. Rub one leg with the other like your ankles itch, then part them slowly, shut them tight, and part them again.'

"When Mr. Otis told me that, the pink of his lips bubbled against his black face and I could tell by his eyes that what he wanted me to do was against all I'd been taught. But then he made the pot more sweet. 'I'll be dealing my deck while you tease with those pretty legs and we'll both be fat in the wallet by midnight. That's two hundred dollars for you to dress from head to toe and another hundred dollars for your pocket and my promise no one will touch you.'

"He kept his promise and I started stepping through the wrong door. I needed a way out of that house I was living in, and since it didn't seem like Robert was going to be my ticket I made money through a con game. I traveled to bars all over the city and saved my money for a house."

Jan listened and tried to see this side of her mother; flirting, cunning.

"Of course, I had a job, taking care of the handicapped kids. But I was only making the kind of money that forced you to decide whether to be clothed or eat. You couldn't do both, and education cost more money than I could have and get a house too, so I gave up on that dream. I didn't want to have a baby without a man, so I saw your father. I figured if push came to shove I could marry him. Right around this time, the Jews I was working for offered to send me away to study for school for the first time. Then and there I could have gotten away, learned more about caring for handicapped children, and Robert may have gone with me. At least I could have told him about it. Even if he didn't understand, I could have given him the chance. He understood so much because he'd traveled the world. But your father was around with promises of a home and a family, and I had a little money, so I took what I thought was the easiest way out."

For all the times that Jan had heard parts of Jessie's story, she settled into its hearing, its telling, the way it had lived in the house with them. Now it was leaving.

Jessie stopped and remembered Charles as a young man, then older. She saw the moment, hours ago, when she realized that his body no longer had breath in it, and forced herself to speak.

"I thought your daddy was a good way out of a bad place. So I grabbed hold of him. Your father got in cahoots with Nell. I missed Robert and my education because I didn't have the patience to wait or go hungry until it was time to eat the meal prepared for me. That was the first time."

"I thought you said Daddy made you miss your opportunity to study teaching the handicapped," Jan murmured, trying to piece together the stories told by Charles and Jessie. It was all still a disconnected patchwork quilt.

"Well, that was the second time I got offered the opportunity to study." Jessie stroked the child's hair. "Jan, I was mad at myself. I blamed your father for a lot, and it's true he didn't want me to go, but that was later. When my first opportunity came I was the one who decided not to go. It's easy to blame men, but I guess it's still like Dinah sings."

"So when Daddy stopped you, was that the second time God called you?" Jan asked, yawning as much as she tried to stop herself.

"I would tell you, but you ain't foolin' me. You're sleepy enough to miss most of my story, and since it's your story too, I'll save it for daylight and bright eyes." Jessie lifted Jan off of her chest and Jan settled in the covers beside her. "You've got a big job ahead of you to-morrow."

Jan tried to sink into the covers more deeply.

When Jessie had called Ada to tell her about Charles, Uncle Albert told them Ada was in the hospital. Jan was going to have to go and tell Ada about her father in the morning. Jan pushed backward and snuggled into Jessie once more. The only man that loved her ever since she was on the planet and wanted nothing more than for her to be who she needed to be was gone. Jessie was here and Ada might be slipping away. She kept her eyes closed. It was one thing to see the darkness behind her eyelids, but to open your eyes and find only darkness felt too much like death.

Death came and went and still didn't have the final word. I could have told her that and believed someday I would. For now, Jan needed rest. It would be daylight soon. Hours later we would go, both of us, to talk, cry, hum, and sing, with Ada.

Meant to Be

Jan sat by Ada's bed.

"I know." Ada opened her eyes, broke the silence, and patted the bed beside her. "Come on."

Jan sat on the bed, studying Ada's face. "How could you know?"

"I saw your father leave before daybreak yesterday morning." Ada wrapped her fingers around Jan's palm. "The body is a house, Jan. We are more than flesh and I can see beyond this flesh. Our spirits are not confined to these bodies, Jan."

Jan lay down next to Ada and sunk her head into the one breast left.

"Are you sick, Ada?"

"We're all sick, Jan. I just have cancer."

"Why are you back in here, Mama Ada?" Jan peeped past the white curtains. The sun shone through the window. "You just got out, you were home yesterday. What's wrong?"

"What you really want to know is am I about to die. And I don't know the answer to that. These folks calling themselves doctors have me in here because they can't figure out a whole bunch of things I know the answers to, like why I've been through months of chemotherapy and didn't lose my hair. If they asked me, I'd tell them."

"What would you say?"

"The truth." Jan felt the laughter in Ada's breast, before she heard its sound.

"What's so funny? What's the truth?"

"That I'm old, ornery, and not about to give up one strand of my hair unless the Lord say I have to. I inherited my black, earned my silver, and I'll let it go to the ground when I'm good and ready to follow it."

Jan and Ada laughed until they both became quiet with thoughts of Charles.

"You'll miss him, Jan."

"It hurts when I sleep, Mama Ada. I know that I am going to have to laugh, smile, play my music, and brush my teeth, but something else is staying with me now, paining me like it will never leave."

"It will hurt for all this lifetime. When you do something that he always did or pass by a place that you two would go to together, remember the way he thought of certain things, and when you see him in yourself or in your mother, it will hurt."

"Then what am I supposed to do?"

"Let him grow in you and you will grow because of him. He will be bigger in his death than he was in his life, and that is how you will know death is not the end of everything. Just the end of this part of life. Then it will hurt less and someday become a comfort."

They were silent again and Ada began to hum. Jan remembered the song, "Lead Me, Guide Me Along the Way."

"There's so much in a song, it's strange." Jan felt pulled all the way back to Sundays in Moleen, summers at Ada's. "That's why I like my music."

"It's bigger than your music, Jan." Ada looked out the window. "You always thought the thing you trusted came from the music, the instruments first, then the singers, but that's not all of it. Whenever you talked about the music, you mentioned sitting by the window or being out on the lakefront. I think I know what it is for you now. Look out the window and tell me what you see."

Jan raised up on her elbow and followed her aunt's gaze. "I don't see what you saw. Daddy's spirit going into the sky. I don't see that." Jan lowered her voice. Her insides ached. She couldn't be Ada and didn't even want to try. It was too much to see things no one else could see.

"I'm not talking about your father's spirit. Just tell me what you see." Buildings and trees, cars on the expressway, birds, and even a plane flew by.

"I see the sky." Jan remembered summer afternoons spent gazing at the sky with Charles. "The sky."

"That's where you find God, Jan, in the blue of the sky. Can you remember touching God in your young days, when you mumbled a prayer that time you called me, said you had prayed away an evil spirit and asked God for a chip on your shoulder?"

Jan remembered. It was the day she found out her mother and father were not in love. "Yes."

"You were in meditation and prayer and you found your peace in God through the sky."

"When I hear the music, or run, or sit by the window, or when I sat on the porch all those summers." Jan was talking more to herself than Ada. "I always spoke to the sky."

"And God used His blue to touch Himself in you. For your father it was the wind, clear, calming, and strong. For my mother it was the sun, and a red fire burned inside her. Some people thought it was anger, but I knew it was love. When she left this world she told me that Indians didn't need the words we had. They knew about the sun, the wind, and the sky and they trusted it enough to know there was a God.

"Before she died she sat up in her bed. It pointed east

and she blessed the people around her. The first person she blessed was your father."

Jan remembered Ada's skin was darker now than when she was younger, she imagined I looked the same way. She thought of me as Hannah, the mean mother her father always talked about, wiping pee on babies' faces to keep them soft, handing out chores.

"So it is not the music, it's the sky."

Ada began to sing, softly. Jan remembered the song "When I Get to Heaven Gonna Shout." One cried tears of joy, the other of sadness. I wiped them both.

In the car, Jan drove past the hospital, toward the lake. She wanted to call Phillip, Raye, and Sarah, but she could only think of Charles. What would he be doing right now? Would he be with his mother? Would they be better together now? Would they get along? She thought of me, forming the picture she had held since childhood—brown and red skin dancing into swirls of cinnamon chocolate, black hair shining in the sun.

The sun's reflection shone in the lake. She reached over and rolled the other window down. Breezes swept from one window through the car and out the other. She thought about calling Phillip again. But those thoughts only fluttered about until she was left with memories of Charles. Tears dripped over the edges of her eyelids. She wondered what blessing I had given Charles and realized his last talk had been a blessing for her.

Jan exited Lake Shore Drive near North Avenue, found a park, got out, and began a brisk walk. She had known love, not the way she wanted it, but the way it had been. Charles had said, "loved you ever since you struggled out of your mama." She had listened when Charles told her, but didn't hear it until Jessie reminded her. She was loved. She could find the feeling again and return to it, accepting nothing less than its roots. She

walked alone, unnoticed by the people around the
beach. Stopping at a large oak tree, she stood against it
and slid downward until she sat with her back supported by the tree. She hugged her knees to her chest,
and when her body stopped shaking and the tears came
less frequently, she looked across the water and upward
to the sky.

"In the summer," she began, "when I sit on a porch,
or anywhere doing anything, and watch the heat come
from the sky and feel the wind, I'll remember my father.
The heat will remind me to look for myself, trusting no
one for my welfare but the God in me. In the cool of late
spring, when the rain comes down slow but steadily, I'll
remember that my mother says it's 'good growing
weather.' And I'll grow with the rain, the sun, the death
and the life. I'll grow because you loved me and love because you loved me. I believe in the same God and
Christ that you, Jessie, and Ada do. Your plate is my
plate. And when it's time to eat, I will look for the meal
prepared for me."

Jan couldn't think of anything more to say. It was only
Charles' body in the ground, she told herself. She would
keep the part of his spirit he had given to her and she
would nurture it and let it grow.

Jan stood and walked back to her car.

In the apartment, she showered, then closed the shades
and found the album Sarah had given her. As the sounds
of rain fell around her, she climbed onto the sofa sleeper
and pulled the covers over her head. "Patience." She said
the name out loud and not long after, began to dream.

Colors came quickly. In a rush of wind that stirred the
lake, Jan saw herself traveling on the color green as she
moved from this time into a time she could not remember. Moss hung on palmetto trees, red dirt surrounded
the trunks of huge oaks, and she walked through the for-

est. Housing projects faded in the distance and her feet stepped in between the rows of cotton and collards. Yellow eyes of marigolds laced a path. Sweet william and purple cabbages mingled with geraniums and the big black eyes of sunflowers. Then the cottage appeared. She didn't hurry this time, but took determined steps. Once inside, the man appeared, back first as always. This time she watched herself walk toward him. She hadn't picked any vegetables and she didn't stop near the stove or the sink.

"Tell me," she began, and placed her arm on his shoulder, turning him around. When she looked in his face, she found her own. She stared back at herself and one smiled a welcome to the other.

Epilogue

$\mathcal{T}$he child had found her voice, dipped in the moisture of dew and pulled back from the dirt. She had picked up her knife and was using the lamp I held. There was a lot for her to see. The child-turned-woman had learned to pray the earnest prayers again, to step outside of herself and bless others, to remember she had a well of power in her heart. I could roam freely now, and so I went to see Charles. My spirit led several others across the gold-paved streets. Professor Jack, tall and stately, with all three of the spirits that had been his wives on earth, flowed close behind. Our white robes traveled midair, caught in the wind of our movement. In the numinous hue of green and in the blue of skies, Verga and Charles swung on the white porch, their pigments mingled, entwining with each other.

In the distance, child spirits, having spent little time on earth, danced in a circle, polishing the gold beneath their feet from the light of earnest prayers. Moses, in his earth form, walked near, creating even more merriment by doing the two miracles that those who read Exodus 4 knew to be his favorites. First, holding his staff out ahead of him, he dropped it, and it changed into the only serpent allowed in heaven. Next, the miracle he loved even more. He stuck one large brown hand inside his robe and pulled it out, displaying the hand's whiteness, then putting it back in and out, he held it up, restored to its natural color. The young child spirits especially liked this and one left the porch and called to the prophet. Moses saw the spirits ahead dancing, swaying, and rocking while others flew. Some donned earth feet and ran to the porch.

Moses quickened his step, staff clicking, as he approached the porch.

"Who hails?" he asked.

"My daughter," Charles answered, and the others took on their earth forms. He and Verga stood and dosi-doed each other as partners. Moses shook his head, amazed at the strange formations spirits picked up from their earth days, but understanding the joy one has when another reaches the promised land.

"Below," Verga shouted. The gold under their feet became clear and they saw a young woman walking amid the frenetic earth bustle of Michigan Avenue. But I could see what they could not, and instantly my heart placed me back on the child's shoulders, to remove almost invisible lint from her hair. Sitting about her shoulders, comfortably shifting until I was in the place that had come to mean home, I waved and prepared her to receive the coming news with joy. Moving aside, a luminous glow appeared underneath the skin of her bare shoulders. In heaven the spirits joined hands and each color filtered into one another, Charles' blue, Verga's green, Professor Jack's brown.

Moses dropped his staff and the serpent grew long, ankling between and around their legs. Together again and some for the first time, they began to emit the thought things that would travel across precious lengths of time earthward until they reached their destination, the same as it had been done years ago.

*   *   *

In her beginning, the spirits of the ancestors joined.
From particles less than dust, they began to build. Some
were as old as the antiquity of time and the place of
Eden, some as young as their recent journey to the
youthful hills of Mississippi. Each brought all they had
to offer the earth child.

In regal splendor the spirits loosed the gifts excavated
from their souls while on earth—each trait packaged as a
mere hint of color. With a flourish of rays and pigment,
the faint colors emboldened as they met more of their
kind, satisfying each hue, until blue in all its depth re-
curred and mingled with a bright warm yellow. Fall's
shades of rust, dry earth, and aging leaves combined with
gray tones that led to a black darker than any earthly
night. Purples, feisty and strong, stirred frenetically with
an angry red. And lastly, as if as an afterthought, the
white of clouds that move in slow confidence about the
earth provided the frame around the chip as it formed
the smallest sliver of matter. Now complete, it heeded the
call from earth.

As the chip began its descent from Heaven, anger, passion, peace, and the bounty of lessons each spirit had
learned from its earth life traveled through eternal miles.
Manifested within this tiny chip, the spirits marveled at
the many forms they had witnessed—a voice more im-
passioned than the nightingale's, feet fashioned after the
gazelle, a beat added to a fragile heart. Each spirit found
comfort in being summoned as a chip, for they never
minded the way in which they came, their own enchant-
ment was simply to be summoned at all.

Finally, reaching the earth's outer atmosphere, then
softening into a texture thin enough to permeate flesh
without notice, the chip reached its destination. Its pow-
erful yet supple substance melted into the shoulder of
kindred flesh, penetrating the still forming bones, the
marrow for which their blood had long ago laid pur-

pose. They were the privileged ones; unlike many of the
yearning spirits they had left behind, their mission was
being fulfilled. A girl-child had requested their presence
and now they could wed their eternal wisdom with her
fading innocence, become bone of her bone and flesh of
her flesh. In an ageless, inevitable vow, they would assist
as she became the woman she was Meant to Be.

Acknowledgments

$\mathcal{F}$or me God has finally become first in my life, not a close second, not a foul-weather friend or part of my B game. I thank the Holy Spirit and Christ for setting the table, making the bed I lie in, and proving to me that I can do all things through Christ, who strengthens me. On earth, behind this good woman is a man who grew with me and never wavered in commitment. Hal, with consistency you talk away negative emotions and continue to grow beyond former heights. But mostly, I love the way you call my name out at least once a day in prayer. I'm proud to have one of your ribs and our two babies. For Christine, I have never doubted your gifts or good success; I thank God for my part in your journey. You are the girl I always wanted. Lee, when I questioned you and wondered if this work would be received as too raw and you said don't call it raw, call it real, I saw once more your growth in wisdom and understanding. These are the blessings of a Proverb woman (check out Proverbs 31:10–31). I thank my mother, Willie Coburn, for shepherding me when I thought I was the one tending the sheep, and my father, Charlie (see, I named a character after you and continued the family tradition of storytelling) Coburn, for being there always, telling stories that lasted longer than his life, and teaching me that such should be no surprise. Love and encouragement come from and go out to a sister, Joyce Ringo Hayes, for giving me Erica, a niece to call me auntie, and for being an editor with loving eyes and a healing hand of friendship. Thanks to Aunt Ida, Flora, and Virginia, for all you gave in life and death, and to Uncle Jessie, thanks for being one of the two men who knew me all my life and only wanted for me what was best.

Too many people have done too many things to remember them all or give them the breadth they deserve. So forgive me when I don't remember all of you. To the first writing group, Mary C. Lewis and Dawn Turner Trice, more debt than you know. To the little girl who changed Anna's name to her own, Hannah, your near-death experience changed my life and the name of my character, literally and figuratively. More writers exchanged great work and we all grew because of it: Muzette Hill, Anita August, Herb Jackson (my brother), Steve Brouchard, and the OBAC Writers' Workshop. Two wonderful stays with women writers from The Cottages at Hedgebrook leave me indebted to Nancy Nordoff and the staff at Hedgebrook. They have found a way to freely give the gift of their own words back to women. May you freely receive. *Obsidian II: Black Literature in Review* was kind enough to publish the then first chapter of this book in its literary magazine Spring-Summer 1994 edition; thank you for keeping a girl going toward the mark. I was also nurtured by an encouraging instructor, author Jonis Agee.

Thanks to the women in my life who pray without ceasing and called this book into being, Barbara Murff, Erica Reynolds, Kathy Riley, and Christy Howard-Steele. If that wasn't enough, I found a training ground in ministry through the capable oil-laden hands of Berniece Parham, who continues to lead the New Faith Baptist Church Prayer Ministry to high places of service. Within that group I find both peace and a place to sow my seeds. Prayer partners Robert and Marzella White, I appreciate our Wednesday mornings. For me New Faith held this writer in its pews with vision and under the teaching spirit of Pastor Frank Thomas. I owe more than tithes and time to the black church with all its good and all its bad. No matter the city, it has always offered worship and opportunities for friendship. Now God goes off sometimes and gives you what some people call Grace and the old folks say, "some exstree." I received some extra from two friends that serve up support like the Creator does sunrises, Sarah Pearl Carrol and Trudy Newman.

Once all is written and done the story must reach out into the world to find its wings. Victoria Sanders is a wing builder, a critically acclaimed architect and an un-matched champion of flight. My editor, Melody Guy, charted the course with enthusiasm that dispels fear and attentive insight that takes me from countdown to a des-tination we've yet to see. Sybil Pincus and the editorial production staff worked diligently with tender hands, bright minds, and constant effort. Casey Hampton and Dan Rembert know very well that looks matter. Brian McClendon started the buzz, and L. Peggy Hicks amassed a ground crew and knew that the way you take off has a whole lot to do with the way you land. And to you as readers, for lifting *Meant to Be* off the shelf, I can only say make it real. Love your families beyond any faults, give women a pass and a prayer, and one day you'll find yourself understanding why turning the other cheek is worth the lesson of finding out that your spirit is so strong it can take the sting out of any slaps this world has to offer. To the brothers, no matter your past, learn to see yourself as trees (for further instructions, see Mark 8:22–25). Some say that man was seeing himself in the spirit before his sight was given a second touch of holy water.

In my youth I had the good fortune to read wonderful

stories that I did not initially have the good sense to own.
Toni Morrison told it anyway and keeps telling it so well
that black folks can find no hiding place. Thanks, from
The Bluest Eye to *Paradise*. Facts ladled in creative insight leap from the pages of all her works, so it's no wonder that Dr. Maya Angelou speaks life and her presence
truly shows us how to live the walk. Ancestor Zora
Neale Hurston validated the many lives we live. James
Baldwin and Richard Wright made sure that the truth
be known in fiction and in fact. Many writers of the
Diaspora, Cyprian Ekwensi, Edwidge Danticat, and
J. Nozipo Maraire among them, enrich the work of our
culture. While strong, clear, honest voices such as those
of Amy Tan and Shauna Singh Baldwin make sure we
break down the stereotypes that could continue to separate us from being our brothers' keepers, reading the
works of these writers and having conversations with
some of them helped me understand that you must write
the story as you see it. When I began *Meant to Be,* Chris-
tian fiction did not exist for African-American readers.
And while I don't believe I fit neatly into this category, I
do appreciate the work and the willingness of many
African-Americans who take their faith to that next
level, using fiction to write the testimonies on how we
got over. You know Grandma and Ma Dear were praying. I am glad to see the work of Victoria Christopher
Murray and Stephanie Sanford, and on the front line of
this movement, African-American bookstore owners are
making the difference. Support them. I have WBEZ,
Chicago public radio, to thank for making it possible for
me to interview a myriad of authors. With special shouts
out to Teshima Walker, Tish Valva, Claude Cunning-
ham, Dorse Kelly, Jody Becker, and Torey Malatia.

I began to write *Meant to Be* in 1984. Among its chal-
lenges was waiting for the world to be more accepting of
interpretations of faith expressed through the novel.

When I began this work, I did not begin it with such spiritual intentions, it simply grew as I grew. May God bless you that far before you reach the end of your journey, you become enveloped in the spirit of all that you are meant to be.